Given The Brave

Nicholas Hoover

Thanks to my wife, Glory, and our children, Memphis, Atticus, and Reverend, for being my partners in adventure. Thanks also to my mom for guiding me to the light and to my dad for displaying great patience in raising three troublemaking boys.

CONTENTS

THE UNWELCOME GUEST

HE CAME with the first breath of winter to the Gallant camp. Youthful was his countenance, yet his eyes held the wisdom of millennia unremembered by man.

"Leave this place," The Seer said to the chief. "A terrible cold is coming, one that most cannot endure. Winter south near the sea. Your home will wait here for you."

"The Afon Valley has secured my people through hard winters before," the chief said, seemingly without considering the Seer's words. "We do not fear the cold, and we will not abandon our home by virtue of a stranger's foresight."

"Stranger?" The Seer said indignantly. "Such a brand does not belong to me. I believe you know that. Did I not usher the Gallant to this valley?" His eyes contacted the little girl Given's and lingered for a moment. "My heart for your people has not changed; I wish for their safety still." Refocused on the chief, he continued loud enough for only a few to hear, "But if not for your people alone, for the sake of that which you've been entrusted, you must leave."

The chief ignored the Seer's quiet caution, raising his voice in retaliation. "Never will we leave." The words echoed from the far riverbank. He wanted the gathered tribesmen to hear, to share his confidence. "There is no difference between protecting our inheritance and staying in the land that supplies our needs. No, we will not depart from this land, but you must." He waved his hands at the Seer as though shooing a dog. "Leave...leave us be!"

The chief said it, but the words were not in the hearts of his people. Still, they obeyed; still, they remained.

CHAPTER 1. BETTER THINGS AHEAD

"*HERE YOU* go Gritsy," Given whispered as she guided her babe to breast. The ensuing bite caused her to wince, but the pain eased as he suckled. She smiled at him, soul full of love.

Grit nursed until content while Given finished roasting a couple of fish over a bed of coals. She placed them, already on wooden dowels, in front of Bledig, her small doggish master, who was sitting on a mat inside his cabin. His eyes, cold amber, examined the meal hungrily and wandered up to Given. She was eyeing the meat with similar ferocity.

"Hungry are ya wench?" Bledig said flatly. "There'll be scraps-enough after I've had mine." He growled a few curses in her direction before redirecting his attention to the meat.

Given stared at the dirt floor. "Yes, sorry master. Thank you."

Almost bypassing his mouth altogether, Bledig shoveled down the fish with one hand. In the other he clutched his prized possession, a red stone he'd *found* when Given was too swollen from pregnancy to accompany him trapping. She often wondered why it captivated Bledig so. Things of beauty meant little to her in her destitution, as her sole focus was survival.

She waited hopefully as he ate. Perhaps his appetite would be less than usual—maybe she'd get to eat this time. But when he'd finished, nothing but the heads remained. After picking them clean, she returned the skulls to the same river the fish had been pulled from. Her vision blurred as she stared at the lumbering waters, and for a moment, her mind, like the skulls in the river, was overcome. All she could think was escape. Remaining with her tortuous master was no longer an option, and though the thought of ending his life had meandered through her mind on more than one occasion, she could never carry through.

***

Shadows thickened over the cabin as Given hummed Grit a lullaby. Usually a tyrant at bedtime, the boy rejected not slumber on that night. The devoted mother breathed a thankful sigh and fingered the sleeping babe's hair. "Be with him and guide him in all things good," she whispered in prayer. "May he protect the helpless and speak for the speechless." Many more *unusual* prayers were cast toward the heavens in thought. Her creator heard.

After rolling out her master's sleeping mat, she placed her own beside and lay on her back with eyes sealed. Her insides twisted. Bledig would be in soon from his evening saunter, his lust, like his hunger, Given would be required to satisfy. Tonight would be the last time, she thought.

Dull moonlight snaked through the trees' canopy and lit the room just enough to form shadows. Bledig's appeared in the doorway, but she didn't open her eyes to see. She knew he was there by the rasp in his breath.

"Looks like the little mutt went down easy tonight." He raked the threshold with his nails and found his place beside his wench; for after all their time together, after years of servitude and birth of child, that was all she was to him. And though she had to swallow the sickness that climbed her throat, she fulfilled her *duty*—one final time.

His deed left her filthy inside and out, but he fell into slumber without care. He was satisfied. Given rose to cleanse herself. She flung her tattered clothing over the branch of a willow and slid from the shallow bank into the cool waters of the River Afon. Bumps sprouted over her skin as the water rose past her thighs to

3

her belly button, and a single tear, filled with disgust and regret, slid from her cheek into the infinite flow. It was another prayer whispered to the heavens. She inhaled deeply and held for a moment. When she released, she was ready.

From the river she sprang, no longer focused on the past but what needed to be done. Beneath the thicket near the coal pit, she unearthed a clay pot with enough smoked fish to last her a couple days. She wrapped the jerky in cloth and laid it outside the cabin. She would take no water, weapons or tools. Water could be found, weapons and tools constructed in time. She had a costlier load to carry.

She peeked inside the cabin. Grit was in the shadow, a thumb tucked in his mouth. He'd outgrown swaddling, but cherished the long blanket that covered him. On the other side of the room, her master twitched and jerked with his back toward the door. Given's own heartbeat was all she could hear. *Could Bledig hear it too?* No, it was a silly thought. He rolled. Eyes shone from beneath half-closed lids. They seemed to create a light all their own. Given froze. *He must see me,* she thought. *Running will have to wait.* But even as she pondered her next move, Bledig began to thrash: grunting, moaning, contorting. She watched for a minute or more as it continued and realized that he was dreaming—caught in a nightmare. Perhaps it wasn't the best time yet. The nightmare could jolt him awake at any moment. Would there ever be a better time? Her son was not yet a year old and already Bledig was making plans to sell him. She had to get away, now.

She crept to Grit and lifted him from his mat. He whimpered and twitched, but she rocked him quickly back to peace. She made for the door and her freedom, but a cry, the howl of a snared coyote, froze her. Fear she was caught crawled over her. Standing as a mouse cornered, her eyes were wide, heart throbbing. Seconds passed like hours as she awaited her beating, but none came. Bledig was still writhing on his mat, the bonds of his nightmare he could not break. Given's were loosened however, and after snatching the jerky outside the cabin, she found the westerly path alongside the river and fled into the sultry gloom.

Sweat streamed into her eyes, but she had no free hand to wipe away the sting. Her erratic breathing could not be controlled. Fear wouldn't allow it. Pebbles and twigs jabbed her calloused feet through her moccasins, but nothing would slow her for miles—leagues. Grit was content, cradled against his mother's breast as she ran for their lives.

When fatigue finally overcame adrenalin, she stopped, gasping. She looked around. The river, her lifelong companion, was nowhere in sight. Behind was a path worn by her alone, dimly lit by the white crescent. A jamboree of frogs and crickets filled her ears as she strapped Grit to her back with his swaddling. He was awake now but not wide. A little more walking and he'd fall back to sleep. A little more walking and Given would need rest as well.

After a few more miles her worn body got its wish, and she lay with Grit in a patch of switchgrass to sleep. In the blackness she dreamt she was struggling in Coyote Lake, near the mouth of the Afon river where Bledig's cabin sat. The water tugged her body and choked her cries as she battled. With muscles worn from the fight and lungs full of burning liquid, she began to sink. But a man, faceless yet familiar, ripped her from harm and into his boat and embrace. She knew him, though too many seasons had passed to figure how. Still, she recalled his voice, remembered its warmth.

**

For days she traveled with none to assail her except exhaustion and hunger. On the sixth eve of her flight, when the last scrap had been swallowed and the candle of hope flickered dim, she staggered upon a village of tiny houses scattered among hills and trees.

Clutching her babe, she crept the outskirts as quietly as she could and surveyed for company. Nothing stirred. She spotted a well and was on her way to drink when a delicate voice called, "Go no further."

Startled, Given turned toward the stranger and viewed the unexpected: a tall lady with white cloth draping her curves, raven hair splashing over her shoulders in waves. In the flicker of a candle, the woman was surely the fairest Given had seen.

The stranger stepped closer, lifting her candle toward Given. "Who are you? What are you doing here?"

"My name is Given." She held Grit tighter and retreated a couple of steps. "I've been lost for days with no sign, or direction, or help. I am in need of food and drink." It occurred to her that she was helpless, fully at the mercy of the stranger. She felt like a beggar groveling before the king. "And refuge…I need a place to stay. Please madam, I mean no trouble."

The woman's brow lowered, whether in concern or contemplation, Given could not decide. "If you speak the truth, I may be able to help." She motioned toward the cloth that concealed Grit. "What is this?"

Given's hand trembled as she uncovered her son's head just enough for the fair lady to peek. The stranger's expression gave no indication of surprise, though having a young mother traipsing through her village at night was surely uncommon.

"Where are you going with such a costly load?"

"I don't know." Given stood silent for a moment, contemplating how much she should divulge. "I only knew I had to flee. My wish above all things is to not be found. Please don't ask too much of me."

"Don't be anxious. I'm only making sure you're not a threat. We do our part to remain safe, but rumors of new wiles keep me especially wary at night." Her stare became more severe, almost severing.

Given wouldn't have been able to lie if, indeed, she were up to no good. "Believe me madam. I've no part in anything bad, I just need a meal and a place to rest—a fresh start."

The woman seemed to ponder Given's words, her situation. Her cutting gaze softened, a half-smile replaced the scowl. "Without doubt, I can see you are no threat, but there is no room for carelessness." She moved a finger from side to side. "Some who live here are refugees like you. They stay because the law in Bardorf is different: there's no master or slave, and except for the rent, each answers to himself. The houses and land are lorded by Eurig. He lives there." She pointed toward the north. "Those who've taken up here pay him for use of a house and the well."

"What kind of man is Eurig?" asked Given, loosening her grip on Grit to let him sway a bit.

"All-in-all, he's not a bad one, though a bit greedy. He's shrewd in deals and keeps no account unbalanced, not much on understanding late payments, but he'll barter if you have not gold to pay. Stern in dealings with outsiders yet kind to his heirs and tenants who pay." Cupping her hand beside her mouth and lowering her voice she continued, "He's a rarity: only has one woman. A man of such means with only one—who's heard of such a thing? One is burdensome enough, he says." She smiled at her

7

latest statement and stiffened. "Though with him around, you can be at ease for your safety. There's not much mystery about him, only a bear in size and manner, who could attack if roused."

Given shuddered to think of a bear-sized man. Her master was not large. Still, she could not resist him when he was provoked. Blue, black, and red she had often been painted by his wicked little fists. For speaking out of place or offering suggestions she was thrashed; for not gathering enough food, she was slapped and clawed and kicked; and for being pregnant, held down and punched about her eyes till swelling and blood blinded her. What could this bear-man do if provoked?

"Rouse him, how do I keep from that?"

"Simply pay what is owed and mind your business. You'll be fine." The stranger swept her hand through the air. "Now follow, we'll fetch you drink and meat. No guest is to starve on my watch."

She took a narrow path past several houses as Given and son trailed close behind.

"What's your name?" asked Given.

"Depends on who's calling. My name is Aderyn, Birdie in the common tongue. Most know me as such."

Given thought this was a fitting name, for the woman's loose white raiment contrasting her dark features and how she appeared to glide above the path reminded her of the most beautiful birds swooping over Coyote Lake.

"If a bird, you are the fairest of their kind. Aderyn suits your beauty."

Aderyn didn't speak for the remaining steps to the well. She did however wear a warm smile, for long had it been since such amiable words were spoken to her.

When they arrived at the well, Aderyn gripped a wooden bucket and bade Given to stay. "Your burden is greater," she said, motioning toward Grit. "I'll fetch the water."

Given peered over the edge to see a twist of stairs that lined the wall, descending steeply to a pool of water. As was the custom, Aderyn entered barefoot. She drifted with a candle in one hand and a bucket in the other into the darkened pit. From the top, Given could see her stoop to fill her bucket and slowly ascend.

Aderyn placed the pail in front of Given, who at first stooped with babe in arms, but realized the difficulty. She would need to free her hands to have a proper drink.

Guessing the dilemma Aderyn said, "It looks like you have three choices now: you could lay the babe in the dust or have me scoop water into your mouth—*or*—you could let me have a hold." She put down her candle and held out her long slender arms.

Given hesitated. *No one but me has ever held Grit, but no other have I needed. And if she wanted, this woman would have taken him from me. I wouldn't put up much fight as worn as I am.* She stood and handed her son over, still wondering if she could trust the stranger.

"I'm in your debt."

"I'll consider it paid in full if next time you fetch the water, and I hold the baby." Aderyn peeled back the cloth to reveal the sleeping boy and kissed his forehead. "Sweeter than honey and more precious than gold. What's his name?"

"Grit," A proud smile sprang upon Given's cheeks. "I named him for the fight he put up at birth. I labored for four days as he held on with all his strength, and when I finally pushed him free, I swear he gripped the cord with both hands and tried to climb back up."

"A fitting name for such a tiny fighter." Aderyn caught Given's gaze. "I'd say, you have a mighty share of grit yourself after winning that battle."

"Yes, perhaps," said Given, a little embarrassed. For a moment fear abandoned her as overwhelming thirst beckoned her to her knees. She scooped water into her mouth with both hands until the rough hewn wooden pale gnawed her knuckles.

When she'd finished, Aderyn extended a hand to help her to her feet. "Come let's get you filled."

The new friends traced the dirt path, Aderyn toting Grit and Given the candle. Aderyn invited Given into her home and handed Grit over. Two mats along with a dome shaped basket were placed at the center of the one-room house. Aderyn removed the lid to reveal a bounty of cured meat.

"Have as much as suits you."

Given objected not and made quick work of the jerky as Grit began to stir in her lap. After Given had her fill, Aderyn returned the basket to the shelf and sat on the other mat. Grit was now wide eyed and beginning to fuss. His mother wasn't the only hungry one.

"Pardon," said Given. "It's meal time for Grit too, though I don't look forward to it. His bite is unbearable."

Aderyn gave her a moment to guide Grit to his dinner and sat back to examine her guest. "You are so young," she said, as though she had just discovered the fact in the candlelight. "How old are you?"

"Not yet Nineteen."

Aderyn tried to hide a questioning look, but Given noticed anyway.

"You want to know more."

"Only what you wish to tell."

It didn't take much prodding to get Given to want to talk. A listening ear was impossible to come by at the cabin near Coyote Lake. For the next hour, Given rambled as with a dear friend.

She told of her tribe, the Gallants, of her childhood, and her mother, "Mot was short and strong—like me I guess. Women in the tribe would say that we looked so alike I must have been formed from her spit. I was always proud of those comments. She was beautiful... and she loved to sing." Looking down, she hummed a short melody. "Perhaps it was imagined, but to me her songs contained magic. I wish I could remember all of them, but many were lost on a little girl."

The joyful light in her eyes extinguished as she began to recount the day a seer came to her village to warn of a terrible winter, but the chief, her father, ignored the warning. "It turned out to be a bad winter, the worst I've seen. We were starving, freezing. The traders came for me, but Mot fought them. Her crumpled body in the snow is the last memory I have of her. I still wonder if she survived the fight.

"My master and another carried me through the woods. I remember them boasting about their findings and the small price they'd paid for goods and for me in my tribe's desperation. My master's words still linger, 'Two beaver hides and a basket of fish for the chief's daughter. If we had a few more fish, we could've taken her mother too.'" She shut her eyes for a few seconds, rubbing Grit's blanket between her thumb and forefinger. "Selfishness makes me wish they had had a few more fish. My master took me alone to his cabin...I was only eleven years old.

"I dare not burden you with the filth he put me through, but I am thankful for the life born out of the evil." She kissed Grit. "Beauty from ashes he is...and a breathing miracle. He survived the womb though my master tried his hardest to beat him to death." A tear streaked her cheek. "My baby before was not as fortunate, but Grit —Grit would not be denied life." She looked proudly at her son. "I may not be worth much, but you are right: he's more precious than gold."

She paused, surprised she had told a stranger her life's story in their first meeting, and a tad embarrassed said, "My apologies for stealing your air. It's not often I get to talk to an attentive adult. I'm used to my master's responses, snorts and rude gestures. But now that you know me, what about you? What brought you here?"

"A mighty tall tale that is," said Aderyn with a tone and look that made Given guess it wasn't a story her new friend preferred to tell. "Better save it for a time when you've caught your sleep and I don't have to work."

"What kind of duties do you have at midnight?" asked Given. "I'll help whatever it may be."

"Answers you'll soon have and help you may give—or perhaps not." Aderyn smiled, seemingly amused by the offer. "But tonight you and Grit must rest."

She pulled a large fur from a weathered crate, instructed Given on how to barricade the door, and with a lit candle and the fur glided back through the door toward the village edge.

"Don't expect me until first light," were Aderyn's last words as she flew out to fulfill her neglected duties.

Given barred the batten door and prepped a pile of straw with a mat on top. There she and Grit bedded. Her exhaustion allowed no time for reflection. Moments after her back hit the mat she was asleep. It was a deep ebony sleep, only interrupted once by a short dream she had had several times before of being drawn out of the water by an unrecognizable figure.

CHAPTER 2. ART OF NEGOTIATION

THE NEXT morning came in a blink. Given was startled awake by a rhythmic tapping at the door. Aderyn's voice followed, "Given, it's morning, time to wake."

"Be there straight away," said Given.

She left Grit sleeping on the mat and stumbled to the door, trying to get her legs under her. After unbarring she swung the door wide. Aderyn, standing in the morning sunlight, looked heavenly. Beams lit her clothes and glistened in her dark hair.

"Good morning friend," she said. "Sleep well?"

"Don't remember a bit of it," replied Given sleepily. "I'm sorry if you needed in sooner. Heavens, it must be the third hour."

"Indeed it is, but no matter. You needed your rest, and I needed to work. My patrons don't care the time of day I complete my duties, only that they get their gold's worth." She held up a basket full of food and a bit of gold. Peaking around Given with eyes bright she lowered her voice to a whisper. "How's little Grit?"

"He must've been as worn as his mother," said Given. "Didn't stir at all last night." Given bowed slightly. "Once again, I'm indebted to you. Who knows what today will bring, but I give you the highest thanks for saving us last night."

"Think nothing of it, but if you'd like to stay in Bardorf, we need to see Eurig. Let's have a bite. Afterwards, we'll be off to find him."

The thought of visiting Eurig caused Given's insides to knot. She hadn't had a single positive experience with a man since she was sold into slavery—or many before for that matter—and here she

13

was needing to talk to a bear-sized one. What's more is she knew of no way to pay for a rental.

"A—alright," said Given. "What should I tell him?"

"Well, the truth would be as fine a way to start as any," Aderyn placed her hand on Given's shoulder. "But don't worry. He already knows some of your story. I saw him as I was coming home." She looked at Given's worn clothes and smiled, "We'd better get you something more presentable to wear before we set out." She pulled a rolled up garment from a basket, and tossed it to Given. "I think this will do."

Given unrolled the gift, eyeing it with delight. It was a deerskin tunic—much like she'd worn as a child. She stroked the hide and ran her fingers across the seams. "It's been a while since I've worn anything but ragged cloth…Your kindness has no end?"

Aderyn smiled acceptingly. "I'll step out so you can slip it on."

When she returned moments later, Given was standing in the light beaming through the doorway.

"It fits like skin," said Aderyn excitedly. "Your beauty would be coveted by any princess—and desired by any prince. Now that you're in good order, we'd better eat and be off."

Given could sense the sincerity in Aderyn's voice, and though she didn't yet feel like a princess, for the first time in years, she felt she might be more than Bledig's wench.

As she'd done the night before, Aderyn set the mats on the floor at the house's center. She gave Given a broiled fish from the basket she had been toting and kept one for herself. Nothing remained but the bones and scales when the two finished eating. After waking and feeding Grit, the three were off to meet Eurig.

With only about a score of scattered houses in the little village, he wasn't difficult to find raising another house on the southern border. Given could see two young men hauling bricks to two older fellows, one mixing mud, the other on his knees spreading it with his hand and laying a brick row. All, even from a distance, looked nerve wrenchingly giant and seemed to grow with every step she took. Sick with fear, Given stopped.

Aderyn turned to see Given's colorless face. "Oh my! What's the matter sweetie?" She stretched her arm around Given and spoke as a mother to her child, "I know the pain men have brought upon you and say that I too have had to overcome many of the same feelings, but Eurig has been nothing but fair since my arrival. He's a man of business and nothing more."

"Ss-sorry," said Given, mortified. "I don't think I can do this."

"Unless you've found greener pastures elsewhere, you don't have much of a choice. For Grit's sake, come; I'll introduce you."

Given gave into Aderyn's persistence and they finished the trek shoulder to shoulder. As the two passed the brick toters, Given could see they were both men in figure, but their faces were smooth and boyish. *They're not too far from my age,* she thought, bowing her head to the two young men.

They stopped their work to gawk at the two ladies invading their workspace. One let out a slow whistle that started high and ended low.

"BACK TO WORK!" bellowed the brick layer, bringing the two dazed young men to reality.

"That would be Eurig," whispered Aderyn, nudging Given.
Given grimaced.

"Hello, Eurig," said Aderyn with a bow. "This is the friend I told you about." She slipped her hand onto Given's shoulder.

Given said nothing, her head already bowed. Aderyn squeezed her shoulder. "Talk to the man."

Before Given could speak, the man mixing mud said, "Looks like Birdie's brought you a couple of strays." He had a hungry look about him, like he could devour his own children if times grew hard enough.

"Mind your work Gar and leave us be," said Aderyn, flicking her hand. "We're none of your concern."

"Indeed they're not," Eurig said, rising to his full height.

Given looked up and took a step back. A grizzly now stood where the man had knelt. Black hair shined on his goliath arms and barrel chest. He flung the mud from his massive hands, wiped the right across his weathered brown tunic, and extended it palm up toward the terrified young lady. "I'm Eurig, pleasure to meet you."

"G—Given's m—my name." She placed her hand on the giant's palm. "Good to meet you too."

Eurig closed his thumb over her hand and gave it a gentle shake. "What brings you to my village?" he asked, as if he didn't already know.

"To be plain sir, my son and I need a place to stay. We've little hope of finding a home elsewhere." She glanced at Gar who'd busied himself mixing mud, but guessed he was eavesdropping. Something familiar about him perpetuated her discomfort. His presence conjured memories of her master.

Eurig looked concerned. Any decent businessman could differentiate good business from a charity case, and this situation stank of charity.

"We have a vacant house next to Birdie's," said Eurig. "But how do you intend to pay? Have you some undisclosed fortune?"

"No sir, I have nothing—only the clothes I wear and a hope for a better life. Though I am no stranger to labor, I can cook and wash and even build if need be."

16

"Useful as those services may be, we have no need to hire them out. People here gather and prepare their own food and wash for themselves…and though we are a growing village, we have plenty of builders for now. Besides, what contribution could such a tiny lass make compared to these strong lads." Eurig swept his hand through the air indicating his sons.

Given's insides sank, but she was not overcome. After some troubled thought, an idea illuminated her countenance and she said, "I can trap! though I need time to gather the tools."

"Oh?" Eurig's brows raised, and a smirk flashed through his wooly black beard. "You have much experience in the wild?"

"Surely, my whole life has been spent in the wilderness. I was born to the Gallant Tribe of the Afon Valley where fishing and trapping was our survival. From youth we are trained in the ways of our ancestors."

"Funny, a girl with all that *heritage* would wander in so much need to our humble village," Gar said. "Look at her Eurig, she'd be no better in the woods than a seaman in the desert." He turned toward Aderyn. "Hey Birdie, why don't you teach her how lonely women earn their keep? Judging from her child, I'd say she'd slip right into your line of work."

Aderyn gave no sign of agitation and didn't utter a word; instead, she whistled a low tone. Given looked at her in confusion, but before any question could be asked the answer plunged past Gar, grazing his tall pointed head, and landed gently as breath on Aderyn's outstretched arm. To Given's astonishment and Grit's delight, a brown and red hawk with speckled underbelly perched proudly upon their friend's limb. With her fingers Aderyn combed the bird's feathers. She lifted her arm high and whispered, "Off you go my friend, happy hunting." The bird stretched out its wings, pushed off, and after a few powerful thrusts, soared out of sight.

"Will that be all Gar?" Aderyn said with a sneer. "I'm sure Freckles won't mind a second visit."

Gar glared at Aderyn as he removed his cupped hand from atop his pointy bald head. "Go easy Birdie. I'm just trying to keep my friend from going broke on these…refugees. As for you, laugh while it's still day." He held up a bit of gold and smiled. "I know you'll be moaning tonight!"

"It'll take more than you've got to buy my moans," Aderyn said.

Eurig's sons, who were eavesdropping, attempted to suppress their laughter but cracked. Both sputtered loudly.

"Alright! I've had enough of this game for today," bellowed Eurig. "Let's leave these lads to their business so we can talk some of our own…in private." Leading the ladies past his sons, Eurig strode toward the western edge of his village where the well sat.

Along the way, Given calmed Grit. He seemed upset by the confrontation with Gar, and even more so because Freckles had flown away. It was summer's middle, and being an early winter baby, Grit had become well aware of his surroundings and even voiced his preferences regularly; and though he could not walk yet, his crawl was fast and efficient—almost like he was crafted with four legs instead of two.

When they were out of Gar's earshot, Eurig started, "Don't let Gar disturb you. He's never been fond of outsiders—or many insiders for that matter." He glanced at Aderyn. "But he's good in a pinch and has been like a third hand since before my lads were big enough to help. He's never failed to bear his own burden, and his concerns are just." Looking uneasily at Given he asked, "And how are you aiming to care for your lad *and* matters of rent? I've known good trappers—excellent trappers—but never one nursing a child." Pausing as if deep in thought he sighed and said, "I want to help, but ends are ends. I can't rob my children's bread and give it to others. Now, maybe you can trap strapped with babe and all, and maybe you can't, but Gar did present another, possibly better, option, even if his presentation lacked tact. Has Birdie mentioned how she makes a living?"

"Well—a—no," said Given, questioning Aderyn with her eyes.

"NO!...No. That shouldn't be the first option," squawked Aderyn. "I have chosen that course because I have no other option, but Given has some skill that I lack. Let her attempt another path, and if she falters, I'll show her my way."

"And if she fails her rent, even for a time, who's to shoulder the weight?" said Eurig with a look that suggested he was not the answer to his own question.

"You know that I'm good for many seasons' rent," said Aderyn. "And I vow to pay any she may lack when the fee is due. Have we not all been in need of help and hope. Even you, I wager, have been in a squeeze that only a neighbor could help loose you from."

Eurig chuckled. "I'd take your bet knowing this body has never been in such a press that I couldn't deliver myself from; but your word is golden to me Birdie. If you are willing to help, that's your business, while collecting the rent is mine." He turned to Given with a smile, "Looks like there's no vacancy in Bardorf. Come, I'll show you to your new home."

Given smiled; a wrinkle of thought formed on her brow, and her lips straightened. "I'd love to come, but I think we missed an important point...How much is the rent?"

Aderyn turned, surprised by her friend's question, but Eurig laughed and said, "A lass after my own heart. Even in her plight, she's concerned about the ends. Yes, well I've known Birdie a long time, and since she's swearing for you, you'll get her rate. It'll be one sep of gold per season. If you lack gold, payment in kind must be made. How's that sound?"

Given looked down and moved her mouth silently while tabulating in her head. A soul warming smile shone on her face as she said, "Deal!"

CHAPTER 3. SHADOWS OF DOUBT

IT TOOK no time for Aderyn's new neighbors to settle in, for they possessed nothing but the rags they wore. Given collected some straw and fallen leaves on the village outskirts with a happy Grit strapped to her back. With those and a borrowed mat, she made a pallet for sleeping. She also rented a large stone water jar from Eurig, borrowed some items for cooking and storing food from Aderyn, and set out to find materials for tool making.

Not far from the village, she discovered a dry creek bed where she collected a large hammer stone and enough quartz to form a couple of knives. With the knives she cut bundles of grass, which she knotted, twisted, and weaved into rope. Later, she stripped the inner bark from a slippery elm, and with a strong slender branch fashioned a bow-drill for fire starting. Convinced that she wouldn't need to travel far from the village to find good trapping ground, Given left with a light pack with only the tools and rope she had made, a skin of water, and some dried fruit—and of course Grit went along as well.

As she set out her thoughts focused on the difficult tasks before her. For one less knowledgeable they would be impossible, but Given possessed more cunning than most and had been tutored in the crafts of the wild her entire life. Even as Bledig's slave, her skill grew, for he rarely trusted her to be alone and would take her trapping and fishing whenever and wherever he went. While most would have been losing nerve traipsing deeper into the wilderness, Given's confidence grew. It was her home, her sanctuary, and with proper tools in hand, it would provide all she needed for a new life.

Not wanting to chance a run-in with Bledig, the two explorers trekked mostly west but a little north, which was the opposite direction of his cabin. She wished to find some body of water, either standing or running. In truth, she feebly hoped to rediscover the mighty Afon River and with it her family, not realizing that the river had snapped sharply north when she had fled only a couple leagues to the west of the Bledig's cabin. Indeed, the Afon's icy headwaters were snowmelt from the Wooly Mountains, which were the southern boundary of the Mammoth Steppe, fifty leagues north of Bardorf.

But even though the Afon was out of Given's reach at present, its tributaries were plentiful and meandered about the fields and forests awaiting discovery west of her new home. After slicing her way through rough terrain for about two miles, she came to a great emerald meadow divided by a monstrous row of water loving trees crowded alongside a little river. Her heart quickened. She whispered to Grit who was struggling to free himself, "Even nature has become our ally, my love. A fountainhead is provided." A tear slid down her cheek. She knew that more than chance had ushered them to their new home—and with a major water source not even a league beyond. "Blessed Day! Blessed Day!" she sang as she freed Grit from his bonds, held him high, and whirled around. They crossed the meadow to view the little river.

At first sight of the calmly flowing waters, Grit launched himself forward, but Given snagged him out of the air before he went crashing over the riverbank. "Not without me," she said. "Let's have a closer look." She slid down toward the water with Grit in her arms, plunged her bare feet in the lazy flow, and dunked an ecstatic Grit up to his bellybutton, letting him splash about. "I suppose a little dip now won't hurt. I need to find a good river stone anyway."

The water was clean and shallow and cool. Beautiful green and red striped fish gleamed from below. "Rhun Gill!" Given said. "Mot's favorite fish...She could be a little downstream and not even know we're here."

"Oh, how I wish to see my mother again. You would be her treasure Gritsy. She'd never let you go."

Grit flailed excitedly.

Holding him in one arm, Given sloshed about a dozen steps to the middle of the stream where the water met her kneecap. As if beholding the wonders of creation for the first time, she threw her free hand into the wind and thanked the heavens for such wonderful things. Spying the perfect stone—which she hoped to shape into an axehead—she descended quickly from heaven back to earth. "Time for work," she said to Grit. He gave an understanding look.

Taking the river stone to shore, Given began to mold it. She chipped it with her hammer stone, flipped and chipped some more, rotated and chipped, slowly sculpting her most needed tool until finally the axehead was complete. Beautiful it was not—dull gray and asymmetrical—but it was sharp, plenty to hew saplings at any rate, which was its main purpose.

The two paused for a bite of dried fruit, which didn't satisfy Grit one bit; but Given was weaning him early so she could work with less interruption and to avoid the pain that his pointy teeth conjured. After their meager supper, Given felt content with the day's discoveries and decided it was time to return to the village. There was enough day left for working, but plenty of chores waited for her right around her new home.

The late afternoon sun warmed them from behind as they scrambled back across the meadow to the forest edge. Slowly, the explorers crossed into the dense wood, searching for the path that had brought them there; but before they were surrounded completely by massive red oaks and sugar maples, Given turned back toward the river to have one last look at its beauty for the day. To her shock, a man stood in the shade on the near bank, a strong, tall figure in waist cloth and nothing else. He was staring in her direction but at first made no advance. A chill ran from her soles to her head, freezing her for a moment.

It's Gar, Given thought, but the man was really too far and shadowed to know for sure. *How long has he been watching us?*

The two stared across the meadow into each other's eyes—or so it seemed—for about a minute. The stranger moved slowly from the shadows into the field. Given thought his bearing oddly noble, resembling Gar less and less as he drew ever nearer. Now his face, though still fuzzy, could be made out.

Definitely not Gar, she thought, but the thought didn't ease her one bit. *Something's not right with this one.*

As he came closer, she could see his body was upright and strong as if wrought with bronze, but his flesh was warped and his face— his face resembled a monster more than a man. It was scarred— hideously deformed—and on his head grew but a few scattered strands of hair that shone golden in the sunlight. Given wanted to run but couldn't loosen her captive, gaping eyes.

At length Grit came to the rescue by tugging her hair, thawing her enough. "You're right son," she said. "Better get along while we can." But with a baby and tools to tote there was no way she could outrun a man—not without a half mile head start at any rate. It didn't stop her from trying. She tightened Grit in his papoose, gripped her axehead in case she was run down and away she flew. Under limbs and over stone, through the bushes and up the gradually climbing terrain she sprinted. The forest flowed past her like rushing water, and she made no wrong turn or move. She arrived at the village winded but still energized by fright.

Aderyn was coming out of the well with a pail full of water when Given burst into sight. With a screech, Aderyn dropped the pail and flung her hands into the air. When she realized who it was, she asked, "What's going on? Are you okay?"

"We were scouting and about to come back," Given said, panting. "I saw a man—thought it was Gar, but as he came closer it appeared to be something much worse. We didn't stay to find out whom—or what— it was, but I want no part of him."

"Where were you?" asked Aderyn.

"Not two leagues west there was a meadow with a river dividing it. I saw him across the way when I entered the tree line on our way back here."

"Sounds like Wether's Field," said Aderyn. "The little river is Ewe's Delight. Sheep are pastured at Wether's now and again. Did you see any?"

"Not one, only—that thing," Given shuddered.

"Hmm," Aderyn's brow wrinkled. "He probably wasn't a shepherd then. Can you describe what he looked like?"

"Outside of being horribly scarred over his body and face, he seemed tall, but I was too focused on his deformity to notice much else."

"You are sure of what you saw?" said Aderyn, with a look more of interest than alarm. "It wasn't just fear fooling your eyes?"

"He was no further from me than the well," Given pointed. "I doubt not what I saw."

A hint of sadness displayed in Aderyn's eyes, and she breathed deeply. "Well, I wouldn't worry." Her voice seemed diminished. "I doubt he meant harm. Could he not have run you down if he wished?" She shook her head. "No, I'm certain he meant no harm…whoever he was." Regaining her poise she said, "As for Gar, he may fish that river sometimes, and you might even bump into him on occasion. Don't be too concerned with him though, he's a whole lot of growl but not much tooth."

"Begging your pardon," Given said. "I've plenty reason to concern myself with Gar—and that thing—and any man I see." The fright had worn some, but now she was on the edge of crying. Never had she feared the wild beasts; wolves and bears she could outwit. But beasts that skulked about on two legs searching for some ill opportunity, taking what they shouldn't and stealing innocence; those kind terrified her. Truly, man was her greatest worry. She had no trust for him and didn't see how she ever could.

Given glared into the woods. There was no hint of a pursuer.

Aderyn slid closer and put her arm over her friend's shoulder. "I know you've been through the worst of it. I'll help however I can, but you've got to do something for me first—breathe."

Given exhaled. She hadn't realized she was holding her breath. Having Aderyn close was a comfort—not what she was accustomed to. For the past eight years, when Bledig's agitation swelled, no one was there to protect or comfort her; and however badly Given wanted to escape his abuse, she could never gather the courage to run. Now running was all she could think to do.

"I'm sorry," said Given. "I couldn't take a chance. All I know of man are his shackles and abuse. Neither Grit nor I will be another's possession again if I have to run for the rest of my life."

Both women were silent for a time. Aderyn gave Given's shoulder a reassuring squeeze as they stared into the trees. At length she said, "You know sweetie, every person on this Earth desires freedom. From the king in his palace to the harlot trying to make ends, not one wishes for a cage. But that's life's curiosity: most, without even realizing, are caged—the king by his duty and desire for riches, the harlot by her stomach. As for you, you've liberated your body, but your mind is still locked up. Fear has become your master, and he's the cruelest of such, riding you everywhere you go. When you're in the field, he's there. When you're washing, he lingers still. Even when you're dreaming, he steals in. Running? Yes you could try that, and never look back—just keep running—but he would always be riding along."

"What else could there be for me?" asked Given.

"Much more than you could even hope," said Aderyn with a smile. "You've got a friend now who'll help you along the way. I'm no stranger to the inside of a cage, but I was set free and I can help free you now. More than chance has brought you here. It's time to stop running and stand your ground."

Given peered into Aderyn's eyes. Goodness blazed in them. Her dark brown irises flashed in fiery compassion, and as Given gazed deeper, her fears began to burn away. She hadn't trusted anyone since being stripped away from her mother, but she found herself feeling wholly secure around this woman she'd met only the night before—this peculiar yet caring *bird lady*.

"I know you wonder about me," said Aderyn. "You've told me all about you, I guess it's time you knew a little more about me. Why don't we fetch some food for you both, and I'll help you with your chores. We can talk while we work."

"I do have questions, but you don't have to help—"

27

"Yes I do," said Aderyn before Given could fully object to the charity. "Serving others is what we've all been called to."

Given made no further objections. They marched to the other side of the village to Aderyn's where Grit and Given ate some much needed meat. Even at only nine months, Grit had most of his teeth and could easily chew substantial pieces. This made weaning him easier, but it—coupled with his crawling—also caused Given to wonder. The little she could remember of infants told her that Grit wasn't an average child.

With fuller bellies, they set out in search of a good hardwood to fashion an axe handle. Aderyn discovered a freshly felled maple about two hand lengths across at the stump that had already been rough cut into bolts—probably by Eurig's company for cooking fire.

"They won't mind if we borrow a piece," said Aderyn. "You'll save them a little splitting."

Using stone wedges, Given split into billets the best bolt, which had no knots, branches or twists. She etched a handle pattern on the top of her choice billet and began to skillfully chip away the wood with her axehead and knives.

The green wood flaked off easily, but Given took her time hewing, carefully shaping it. The finished tool was fitting to her grip and strong enough to withstand many hard blows. At Aderyn's suggestion, it was cut to the length of Given's forearm so the axe could be easily wielded for protection. With the handle now complete, Given needed only to bind the axehead, and she would be able to begin chopping saplings for her fish trap. For the binding she used deer hide and sinew—courtesy of Aderyn.

The work that followed was strenuous, but having a friend there lightened the load. Aderyn bent the young trees, and Given swung

28

the axe while a naked Grit scribbled in the dirt with a stick and showered himself with sand. And even though Given desired to ask Aderyn many questions, she decided to wait until the brunt of the work was completed. After the two had finished felling the trees, they retreated to the well for a much-earned swallow, then back to sharpen the ends of the hewn saplings—each lady with a knife.

CHAPTER 4. FREE BIRD

SHADOWS STRETCHED ever closer as the tired and dirty laborers sat cross-legged near the bundle of tiny trees and whittled. The late evening sun, casting the village in dull orange, was still warming them—though not for long.

"So, how long have you lived here?" asked Given, trying to lead with less invasive questions.

"It'll be two years this fall," said Aderyn. "My home is west, more than a hundred leagues beyond the Rebel Mountains. There, a peak called Eyrie shoots up among the Bighorn Mountains like a tree in a garden. Atop its eastern cliffs, I could see for miles, and as the crow perches warily in the tree above the garden, so I too sat watching. I told you I had been caged before. Like you, I say never again. No fear of pain do I possess, and I even welcome death. But captivity, I despise even its mention." Aderyn's eyes glazed, and she gazed into nothingness as if her mind's eye was searching for some hidden memory. She winced.

"No need to go down that road," said Given.

"It's not pleasant, but that road is where we need to go, for it is the painful path which reveals our purpose for being here."

"I don't understand," Given said, shaking her head. "What do you mean, *our* purpose?"

"It will take some time to explain," said Aderyn. "Like I told you last night, mine is a very tall story. Have you heard the name Solas?"

"Never," replied Given.

"But you've seen him," said Aderyn, pointing a finger at her friend.

"Forgive me, but I don't believe I have," said Given with a searching look.

"Yes, you've seen him and even know him, though not by name. You've been aware of him since you were young, wanting to obey his call, the prophecy your chief ignored."

"The Seer!" said Given. "But how do you know his name?"

"I've known him a long time. In fact he sent me here. Solas is my Lord and yours.

The Shepherd of men
Earth's garden he tends
Giver of good things
Brokenness he mends
Second of two Sons
Now the only one

"Men have inhabited Earth for thousands of years and animals tens of thousands, but Solas's story begins long before.

"It was the first Age, the Age of Hortus, the Garden Age. The Earth was pure, untouched by beast, undefiled by man. Two brothers, sons of the Creator, tended all the planet. The eldest Derog, who was wrought from the finest fabrics of earth, was endowed with a mind to maintain order. His immaculate gardens were always well organized with each type of plant outlined and bordered. Nothing grew wild or out of his control, and all had a season and a purpose.

"Solas, the second born, was formed from lightning and fire and gifted with a heart for creativity. His gardens were not well

31

maintained: they grew wild and free. Plants jumbled and meshed. Mosses and vines clung to trees. Bushes grew in meadows, flowers in forests. Though his gardens lacked the order of Derog's, they were no less beautiful. The great forests of the West were Solas's plantings, and the life that now exists in the coldest reaches of Earth was ushered there by his warmth and light.

"Despite their differences, the brothers loved one another, and each cherished the gardens. They walked thousands of miles side-by-side, planting, tending, laughing at failures, and rejoicing in successes. Yet as millennia passed, they grew ever lonely still. They asked their father to make something new.

"For Derog animals were created, so that he had dominion over all that swam, crawled, creeped, and flew. Realizing quickly that the task of shepherding all the beasts would be impossible even for one with his power, Derog implored his Father's help. The Creator listened to his son, and thus from fragments of Derog's own body he formed the Deroheed, which were guides for each kind of beast. Like Derog, the Deroheed were gifted with the ability to commune with and even control the animals, protecting them, ushering them to food and leading great migrations. With the guides under Derog's command, every creature knew its place and purpose. Everything was orderly and controlled. Derog cherished the creatures and the Deroheed, regretting only that his Father hadn't created them sooner.

"As Derog's beasts spread throughout the Earth, Solas patiently waited for his Father's gift to him. He enjoyed animals and hoped for something similar, but when his gift finally came, they were much unlike beasts, walking about on two legs and needing cloth and shelter to survive. They would have been nearly helpless except for their ability to reason. Despite their weaknesses, Solas loved them and cared for them like a mother would an only child. And like a child there was much to love about them. They had the capacity to show compassion and to work together and solve problems. With all their good, came flaws, and for better or worse people, the prize of all creation, were granted freewill by Solas. No external power would there be to control their thoughts and actions. Solas would only advise them, allowing them to make their own decisions.

"Derog couldn't fathom this gift of choice his younger brother had granted. His desire above all things was for order and control. At first he accepted them for what they were, but as years passed he grew ever impatient with them. They crossed his borders, captured his beasts for food and clothing, and inhabited his lands. Some were more reckless, destroying his gardens and killing his animals for sport. As time passed people thrived and spread throughout much of the Earth, all the while Derog's impatience transformed into resentment, his resentment into hatred. And in his stewing hatred, he finally snapped, resolving to regain control of Earth at any cost.

"Not convinced that the Deroheed and animals at his command would be enough to accomplish this task, Derog began interbreeding Guides with other Guides and humans with Guides. The breeding went on for decades as the plan worked to Derog's delight. He was able to control the offspring almost as well as the Guides themselves.

"In the foothills of the Rebel Mountains Derog began his assault on the solitary and helpless. Farmers, trappers, and small tribes were the first victims. Men were slaughtered, women and children devoured. Legions of his mind-controlled hoard burned through the countryside. Nearly all the way to the Eastern Sea they blazed until they came to Auber Civitas, the greatest settlement of man. It's high outer wall ran north to south, connecting the cliffs of the Sawtooth Heights, a jagged range that stretches hundreds of leagues up and down the coast.

"Derog's army smashed against the wall like a hammer on a tree, doing nothing more than bruising it. Even by great mammoths from the North, the stones could not be shifted. With each attempt to breach, scores of animals and Deroheed were pierced with arrows from above. Men proved stronger than Derog had guessed, and as days passed, his brother's return drew nearer.

"Derog's last hope was to go over the wall rather than through. For this purpose huge ladders of wood were constructed. The final assault began in the evening. The setting sun was at the attackers back and in the eyes of the defense. Arrows rained as the brunt of Derog's forces broke against the wall. The ladders were raised with great cats of prey on them, and scores of birds swarmed from above. The defense of the city faltered. Derog wasted no time. His army flooded through the city's gate as he brought up the rear. As the onslaught continued, the ground began to quake and black clouds whirled above. All gazed in awe—except Derog. Knowing his fight had come, he readied himself. A blinding pillar of blue flame crashed. The blast consumed Derog's guards and launched those surrounding to the earth. Before Derog stood Solas in unapproachable fire. The struggle did not last long. With blasts of lightning Solas ripped his brother apart, leaving the gems and precious metals from which Derog was formed heaped on the ground.

"There would be no way to replace the lost lives or repair the damage to the hearts and minds of the people and Guides. Solas too was altered. He mourned Derog's death bitterly and swore to never again use his power to kill or destroy. The relics, once Derog's body, were preserved, for though it seemed they no longer had the power to control Guides or beasts, the lives of the Deroheed and their offspring were bound to that from which they were wrought.

"Solas divided the relics among the kings and chiefs of men and ordered their safety. They were to be a reminder of the evils birthed from lust for power and a sign of freedom for all. To the king of the Hidden City in the west, an emerald, one of Derog's eyes, was given; to the Gogledd tribe of the North the other was sent. Auber Civitas was entrusted with Derog's diamond mind. Your tribe was endowed with a great ruby, Derog's heart, or the *Shepherd's Heart,* as it is often called.

Solas buried the skeleton made of bones and precious metals deep at the roots of the Rebel Mountains' highest peak and named the mountain after his brother. Even after the evils Derog had committed in life, Solas wished to honor him in death.

"Thus the Age of Shepherds ended. Solas, bound by his word, would never harm man or beast again, and all control was dispersed. The Deroheed and people would be free to choose their own path. Guides still looked out for their beasts, but the animals already knew their purpose and followed it. Men rebuilt their villages and cities. The Deroheed's offspring continued to produce, and I would guess that men and women all around contain their seed—maybe even someone you love." Aderyn glanced at Grit.

Given didn't like the suggestion and shook her head in disbelief. "That *is* a tall story, Aderyn—too tall for me. And even if all were true, what does it have to do with me?"

"Time will reveal your role in this tale. I know a little and can only guess a little more, but my story is true. I believe you've made the connections and know it—but allow me to erase your doubts."

Aderyn closed her eyes and didn't speak, as though in deep concentration. When Given started to question, Aderyn held up her hand and mouthed, "Wait." Minutes went by before Aderyn moved. Her eyes opened and she motioned toward the trees. "Look," she said with a smile.

Given was taken aback by what she could make out through the twilight. The trees were now filled with all kinds of birds. Hawks were perched high and owls low, with crows lined up on the ground. There were jays and cardinals, birds with fat yellow bellies and common looking brown ones. All were glaring toward Aderyn as though awaiting orders.

"Fly!" she said.

Seemingly with one mind, the birds lifted off and disappeared into the shadows of the forest.

"What does this mean?" Given whispered. She looked at Aderyn in astonishment. "I've never seen such a thing in all my life. How did that happen?"

"Well sweetie, I am one of Derog's daughters—formed from his body—the Bird Guide." She scooped a handful of sand and sprinkled it into the breeze. "I have control over all that flies with feathers, but like I told you there's not much need. The birds know their purpose and follow it. But humans—they're a little different, and the fight is still alive."

"So—you were there?" asked Given. "When Derog tried to destroy men?"

Aderyn looked down. "Yes, I'm sorry to say. They were the worst of times." Pain raked her face and she clenched her eyes.

Given grasped her friend's hand. "You've said plenty, no need for more."

"No, the story needs to be told. I told you I understand your fear and your pain, the hopelessness of slavery and the disgust of rape. Those were my cages too. Though I had no control of my body in those dark days, I was still aware. My memory is haunted by the faces of the slain—both men and women. There were children too —children. After murdering parents—I—I tried to resist—I tried to regain control." She sobbed.

After wiping the tears from her cheeks she continued, "I was ravaged for my wings. Derog saw potential in having a force from above, but for all the times the Deroheed and men raped me trying to produce Derog's army, I was pregnant only twice. I had a son and a daughter—but neither have I seen since the siege began. Not a day passes that I don't assault the heavens with prayers for them, wondering if they are living." Aderyn looked at Grit. "Cherish him."

"Sorry I doubted," said Given. "And I'm sorry you had to go through such horrors. I would wish them on no one." Given held her friend close for a while and tried to digest all that had been revealed.

At length, Given broke the silence, hoping to lighten the mood a bit. "It seems ridiculous now, but before you told me your story, I was beginning to believe you were a prostitute."

Aderyn laughed. "People often believe what's easiest without trying to find the truth. It makes harlotry an easy guise." With a victorious look she concluded, "But there's more to a bird than just wings and tail feathers."

"That's no lie," said Given. "Can I ask you something?"

"Anything sweetie."

"You said Derog wanted you for your wings. What wings?

"You've heard stories of Skinwalkers I suppose?" said Aderyn.

Given nodded. "Mot used to scare me with them; said they were witches disguised as animals."

"Well, there's some truth behind those legends," Aderyn said. "Beings that can take both the form of an animal and a human fits the description of the Deroheed pretty well. They've—*we've*— been called witches ever since the massacre. Only once since have I changed form, and that out of absolute necessity. I don't know if I ever will again."

Already awestruck that her friend could control birds' minds, Given was blown away by this new revelation. "What's it like…to fly?"

Aderyn gazed into twilight's gloom and whispered, "Freedom."

Aderyn laughed. "People often believe what's easiest without trying to find the truth. Eurig and his sons believe that I'm a harlot." With a victorious look she concluded, "But there's more to a bird than just wings and tail feathers."

"That's no lie," said Given with a smile. "Can I ask you something?"

"Anything sweetie."

"You said Derog wanted you for your wings. What wings?

"You've heard stories of Skinwalkers I suppose?" said Aderyn.

Given nodded. "Mot used to scare me with them. Said they were witches disguised as animals."

"Well, there's some truth behind those legends," Aderyn said. "Beings that can take both the form of an animal and a human fits the description of the Deroheed pretty well. They've—*we've*— been called witches ever since the massacre. Only once since have

I changed form, and that out of absolute necessity. I don't know if I ever will again."

Already awestruck that her friend could control birds' minds, Given was blown away by this new revelation. "What's it like…to fly?"

Aderyn gazed into twilight's gloom and whispered, "Freedom."

CHAPTER 5. POLISHED BY FRICTION

NIGHT FELL, day rose, and Given was out at dawn sharpening the remaining saplings. Her sleep had been deep and dreamless, and she felt energized. Grit was still snoozing in their new home, and Aderyn was out of sight—it's difficult tracking a free bird.

Once her chores were finished, Given fed Grit and strapped him to her back. She had separated the saplings into two bundles and bound them. The bundles weren't light, but she'd fixed rope handles that made carrying them easier. For her the heavy part was not the labor; it was overcoming the fear.

Loaded like a donkey, she stood at the forest edge. Thoughts of Gar blocked her path for a moment, and memories of the monster in Wether's Field chained her legs. She closed her eyes searching for comfort and courage. Both came quickly with a vision of Aderyn's eyes blazing and her words, "You've got a friend now." Given had never had a friend. Knowing she did now was somehow all she needed to carry on. The chains of fear loosened, at least for the moment, and into the forest she trekked. The path she wore the day before was easy enough to follow, and she made it back to Wether's in no time.

The meadow was every bit as lovely on the second day as the first, but she wasn't about to rush out into the emerald beauty like yesterday. Her wary eyes gazed all about the field and up the tree-line with no danger to snag them. Neither sheep nor shepherd, Gar nor monster could be seen. Given and Grit were alone. She packed her load to Ewe's Delight, sliding down to the water as she had the day before. She relieved herself of all her burdens and began poking the sharpened saplings deep into the riverbed, forming a kind of fish funnel that curled around like a snail shell near the bank. Her hope was that fish swimming downstream would go in but wouldn't be able to navigate out. Her biggest sapling she kept as a "gate" to shut the fish in when harvest time came.

While his mother worked, Grit played in the wet sand on the river's edge. Given kept her vision split between her labors and Grit—and the possibility of dangerous visitors. Thankfully, Grit only made one play for the water. He was much more interested in the mud and throwing rocks into the river than tossing himself in.

After completing the weir, Given only needed to make a couple more tools to harvest the fish. She cut down a bushy sapling that was about her height, left it by the water's edge, and set out with Grit in search of a straight young hardwood to fashion a spear shaft from. This she found back across the meadow not too deep into the forest. She hacked it down and fastened to it a bone spearhead she had borrowed from Aderyn.

The sun had not yet peaked and Given, satisfied with her progress, sat down with Grit for a meal. Under the shade of a giant oak, dried fruits and fish were once again on the menu. Grit's fuss for something more didn't sway his mother. She was steadfast as an oak herself. "In a couple of days you'll forget all about these," said Given with her hands over her chest.

No sooner did the words escape her mouth than a reply came from an unexpected source, "Now how could he forget something so—tasty?"

Given knew the voice that went with the vile form she jolted to gaze upon. It was Gar towering a few feet behind her in the forest. *Why didn't I hear him coming?* She thought as she grasped her spear and stood with it poking into Gar's middle, the tip nearly tearing into his tunic.

"Not a step closer!" said Given.

Gar retreated a couple paces, looking down at her. "Came all the way out here to lend a hand to my new neighbor, and what do I get for my troubles?...Gutted. Lower your weapon battle ax. I'm not gonna hurt ya." He smirked.

Except for his egg-shaped head, Gar wasn't bad to look upon. He was tall and brawny with strong masculine facial features and a dark complexion. But his presence twisted Given's insides in knots until she was ill. He was a villain; she could feel it. More than that, she suspected she'd seen him before. In some terrible memory he was there, but she couldn't place him. She couldn't lower the spear, at least not with him near.

"What's this game of yours?" said Given. "You call me a stray in the village, but you're my friend the next day. I've been in the pit long enough to recognize a snake." Given jabbed the spear through the air toward Gar. "Now leave or I'll split your skin."

"Whoa, don't be getting riled over yesterday," said Gar. "I was only trying to help all parties, especially my friend Eurig." He examined Given for a moment. "You see, it's hard to believe you'll be able to pay the rent out here working like you are. Even without the youngin, it'd be past rough, but with him, nye impossible. And there's that old turkey buzzard living around these parts. I've never seen him, but I hear the tales from the shepherds." His lip curled in disgust. "Mean looking fella they say—like seeing death walk. I wouldn't want to be out here all lonesome like you are." Throwing his hands up in surrender he said, "But if you're gonna poke a stick at me for trying to help, guess I'll be minding my own affairs."

Given felt the knot loosen as Gar turned and walked back toward the path. When he was a safe distance away, he turned and said, "I

42

could get you started. The money'd roll in with you working, so young and tasty." He clicked his tongue. "I could bring 'em in and make sure they pay—and you're kept safe. All I'd want in return is a bit of the gold and a little *appreciation* now and again." He jabbed his finger toward her as if to make his point stronger. "You know it's how Birdie's making it. Half of Bardorf's been with 'er, and when the sheep are grazing this field, you can bet the shepherds get serviced too. She'd probably cut you in—except you'd steal her customers." He raised his eyebrows. "I could show you how easy it'd be...here and now."

Given's blood boiled and her face flamed. Fear fled the intense heat of her anger. "BE GONE FILTH!" she said, lifting her spear. "Never would I lower myself into your hole. I didn't cut the head off one snake only to become entangled by another!" She felt strangely calm and in control.

Seeing her resolve—and the spear pointing his way—Gar decided not to risk injury forcing the issue. "Have it your way," he said before turning away. "You'll come around soon enough—that is if the old buzzard don't get to ya first." He slowly vanished into the undergrowth.

With Gar out of sight, Given's insides settled a bit, but his words pricked her mind. She had seen the terrifying "old buzzard" and hoped that maybe he was only a wanderer passing through yesterday, but Gar's story told otherwise. It mattered not. Her options were limited: either stay at Wether's and risk an encounter with a possible evil or sell her body to a definite one.

She gathered her tools and Grit and headed back to work at Ewe's Delight. Under a willow in a dense patch of love grass she laid her groggy son. Stroking his back and head, she sang her mother's favorite song:

43

After bitter winter the south breeze comes
So nothing can keep you from my love
And after tempest anger, smiles the sun
So nothing can keep you from my love
Nothing can keep you from my love

She left Grit sleeping, and holding the bushy sapling she'd cut earlier, crept back into the river a couple hundred feet upstream. Side-to-side, she began to slap the water with the sapling as she walked downstream, hoping to drive fish into her trap.

The plan worked well, and before long her weir was full of glimmering red and green Rhun Gill. She thrusted the *gate* deep into the riverbed trapping them inside.

Now came harvest time. She held her spear above the water and started to jab downward into her prey, but a lingering thought restrained her. In all of her years setting lines and traps with Bledig, not once had she speared a fish. Gallant law forbade women from taking a fish's life. Given's mother had used tribal lore to explain why. She told of a girl named Nataurie who lived long ago, a member of a peace loving tribe that settled the Afon River Valley. One tragic evening before dusk, a nomadic tribe with a warlord for a chief destroyed their village. Nataurie watched in horror from the river's edge as her family was slaughtered and the village burned. After the massacre, the enemy approached the river for a drink, and she was spotted among the reeds. Knowing that her only hope for survival was to get to the far bank, she dove into the deep and was snatched by the torrent. But before she was swept away, she cried out to the Creator: "My life is yours if only you help me swim now!" At that moment a deep magic from the river entered the girl, transforming her into a great red and green fish. She would spend the rest of days in the rivers, helping the great migratory fish find their way. Never would she approach a man near the shore or on a raft, but missing her mother dearly she longed for communication with women and girls—to hear their delicate voices was enough to warm her in the icy waters.

Given believed the tale as a child, and not wanting to harm the girl, she never speared. Doubts about the story's truth did grow as she aged but meeting Birdie, the Deroheed—a Skin Walker in the flesh—erased most uncertainty.

"I don't know," she said. "If any of you were once a girl, show yourself."

The fish just swam away trying to stay as far from Given as possible in the tight pen.

After eying them for a minute she said, "N—Nataurie, are you here?" She felt silly talking to fish but in some small measure expected a reply—which never came.

"Okay, I guess none of you are her!"

With those words, Given threw down her spike into the largest one. It flipped and wiggled as she drew it slowly out of the water. She took it to shore where she swiftly ended its suffering and stashed it in her tote where it stayed until dinner. Her feelings tussled, she was both relieved and happy that her trap had worked but sickened that she had taken a life—and broken tribal law doing it.

"Please forgive me," she said to the other fish still splashing in the weir. "I don't like killing, but I do as I must."

Given took her catch to flat sandy ground, collected some seasoned wood, kindling, and tree-down and put her bow drill to work. While bearing down on the spindle, she forced the bow

45

back-and-forth for what felt like hours, until finally, when the burn in her arms approached torturous, an ember sparked in the dust. Scooping it up with a green leaf, she carefully shifted it to the tinder. The tiny orange glow sank into the middle and smoke twisted up. Given blew softly until the down ignited. From small pieces to large she piled on kindling until the fire blazed, but only needing the coals for cooking, she let it die.

She cooked the fish whole, all the while Grit continued to nap. Wanting to wake him to celebrate the first catch, she lay beside him in the grass and ran her hand down his face. "Time for supper, my little Gritsy. Mot's got a surprise." He gave no response, so she tickled him. He squirmed and giggled and opened his eyes. They were yellow like his father's but without the bizarre glow—or so Given thought. Mother and babe stared at one another, both smiling.

"Hello baby, Mot loves you."

Grit mumbled a reply, and though his words were unintelligible, Given knew he was saying I love you too.

She removed the fish from the coal bed and placed it on a large smooth stone. After it cooled, she gave Grit a bite. He couldn't voice his opinion, but his face told all: it was scrumptious. Given thought it the best meal of her life. Being free made everything more enjoyable, and for the moment, it was enough to wash the fear of Gar and the "Old Turkey Buzzard" from her mind. Not even memories of Bledig interrupted their dinner. It was only her and Grit feasting to their heart's delight.

They ate their fill, and Given saved the entrails. She would use some to lure more fish into her weir. The rest she used as bait in deadfall traps.

The sun had made it over the big hill in the sky and was rolling downward, and Given wanted to get back to the village. After harvesting the remaining fish, she gathered her tools and Grit and headed for the path home. Stopping about the same place she had the day before, she turned once more to gaze upon the beauty she was leaving behind. Although she half-expected to see the monster from yesterday, she was certainly not disappointed to find the field empty.

"No need to fear what's not there," she said.

Grit rocked in agreement.

Going home was much easier than coming to Wether's, not only because she had exchanged her two heavy bundles of saplings for six fish and a few scraps, but she had also traded the heavy emotional bundle of doubt for some confidence. Her fear was leagues from being vanquished, but success fishing and handling Gar proved that she could make it. It would be beyond tough, but this new life of freedom for her and Grit would be possible. Her gleaming smile lit the forest shadows as she went. It was difficult to believe that she, only days before, was bound in grotesque servitude; but harder still to grasp was that this same girl, having escaped the monstrosities of slavery, would soon return willingly to the darkness.

CHAPTER 6. A MASK REMOVED

WHILE GIVEN sank her roots deeper into the fertile soil she had discovered around Bardorf, many leagues to the east in the grand stronghold of Auber Civitas, a young prince of twenty years grew increasingly unsettled. As the eldest son of Magnus, king of the Civitians, Dane had grown up with his two brothers, York and Lief, in privilege. He lacked nothing except his father's affection, and still the love his mother, Astrid, bestowed upon him more than made up for Magnus's neglect.

Unfortunately, Astrid was the object of Dane's growing disconcertment. She was ill and had been for a while. When the conventional medicine of the Civitians failed to bring about healing, the king enlisted foreigners, wizards and witch doctors, to cure his wife. Although, it wasn't out of love that he sought to save her; rather, he was concerned with losing his most valued possession. Astrid's beauty was a magnificent gem in Magnus's crown, one precious enough to war over, and having defeated many suitors for her hand, he would have been damned to the fiery pit before giving her up without a fight. But a cure was not to be found, and Astrid's condition waxed ever worse.

Of all the involved parties, Astrid was the most content with her situation. She looked forward to swapping her life, with its misery, for a new one—even if the afterlife was a mystery. The difficult thing for her would be leaving her children, her reason for living. Before Astrid breathed her last, she called in each son, one-by-one, to encourage them and say goodbye. The last she called upon was Dane.

As he moped into her vaulted chamber, his tall muscular frame sagged under the pressure of immense sorrow. With his head low he approached Astrid's bedside and grasped her hand. She opened her eyes, and at the sight of Dane, lit the dreary chamber with a smile. Even on the edge of death, her beauty could not be equaled. Her gaze was enough to rob a man of his breath. Dane tried in vain to match her smile.

"You don't have to be strong for me," Astrid whispered. "I see your pain."

Dane knelt and kissed his mother's chill hand. "Does it have to be so? The reaper could earn his wage for anyone. Why you?"

"Eternity calls us all in time beloved," said Astrid. "He beckons me now." She lifted Dane's head, and for the moment her own solemnity was enough to conceal her extreme physical pain. "I know seeing me pass will be hard for you, but your heart will mend. The story of my life on Earth has come to its close, my body ablaze with a fire no medicine can quench. It's time—time to be rid of this torture." She swallowed hard as though choking down sand. "Before I pass, I wanted to talk to you three...For you, my eldest, my rock, I have much concern. I believe my dreams have revealed danger in your future." Turning her eyes toward the ceiling, she continued, "Two nights ago I dreamt of a garden with a beautiful tree full of ripened fruit. So loaded was the tree that its branches scraped the earth. The gardener began to pick the fruit and put it into his basket, but he stopped when he spotted a golden piece among all the ripened red fruit. For a while his gaze was fixed upon it as though he was at a loss for what to do with it. At length he plucked it as well, but he didn't place it in his basket with the rest; instead, he cast it into the darkened forest." Astrid paused in contemplation.

49

"Why does such a dream concern you?" asked Dane

"It's difficult to explain how I know, but this dream is about your future…Perhaps you'll see too. I believe the tree bearing fruit is this kingdom and the fruit its people…the gardener is Magnus and —."

"You think I'm the golden fruit!" interrupted Dane. "But what could it mean?"

"I can't say for certain what will happen, but my heart tells me that you should beware of Magnus; he's not who you think he is. His past evils I have sworn not to speak of, but know this: his recent dabbling in wizardry is nothing new. He's brought these conjurers in to find a cure for me, but I wonder what else they have brought with them. The forbidden crafts have always interested him." Shaking her head, "now I'm afraid he's gone deeper than before."

"Yes," said Dane. "Now that you've said it, I have noticed… oddities in him. He's never liked me near as it is, but even less of late as he breaks bread with witches and other strange men. He seems to be hiding something in the King's Hall as well, most times going there alone but on occasion with his new council, Baird. An ill looking man he is, with a temper as nasty as his appearance. I once overheard Father and him speak of purifying the savage tribes to our west. Father breaking Civitas's isolation is beyond understanding. Soldiers have been sent out to foreign lands, not only to search for your cure, but rumors tell they hunt for something more—something to do with the Minister of the Wild—"

"The Minister of the Wild?" Astrid gasped. "These are strange tidings indeed. Magnus would obsess over myths of the Minister when you were young. Carrying Civitas's relic—a huge diamond—

everywhere he went, he believed it was a piece of the Minister's own body. Eventually he grew weary of chasing the legend and concealed the diamond. Perhaps his past passion has been rekindled."

Astrid glared contemplatively for a moment and continued: "There's no way to know what evil Magnus is conjuring. I believe treacherous roads lie before you, but be encouraged. In my dream brilliant light pierced the forest's gloom where the golden fruit was thrown. Even in the pit of despair, there is hope."

She closed her eyes, and still clutching Dane's hand began to recite:

> *Sun shaded by cloud*
> *Ready to shine but for this shroud*
> *Tis darkness without*
> *But within this light*
> *Yearns to radiate the suffering night*

"Those verses were spoken to me by a dear friend when I was around your age." Astrid struggled with what she should say next. Gazing into nothingness, she continued, "Tragedy came and he was sent away. I've not seen him since...before he went, he tried to encourage me as I have you. He also gave me this." Astrid opened her hand up, revealing a diamond pendant hooked on a silver chain. It was an unusual piece for a queen to possess. Its edges were uncut with one side fragmented as though it had been broken off something larger. Still, it was beautiful, and though it was raw and rough, when light passed through it, the surroundings danced in vibrant colors as though it had been expertly cut. "It is called

Ingeborg's Star, and I want you to take it...to remind you to burn brightly when the world around you has gone black."

Dane, who'd never seen the *Star* before, hesitated. "I dare not. It must be a comfort to you."

But Astrid forced it into his hand. "It'll be no good to the dead," she said. "What's more, as eldest it is your inheritance, so keep it safe."

With eyes closed Astrid drew her son's hand to her lips one last time and said nothing more. Dane caressed his beloved mother to sleep and left her chamber. She never woke from that sleep, drifting peacefully into eternity.

***

Wails could be heard throughout the kingdom as news of her death spread, and for more than a week, the Civitians donned mourning cloth. The people had loved their queen. Yes, she was beautiful, but even her beauty was dwarfed by her kind heart and joyful spirit. She wore justice as a robe. Good deeds were her scepter.

Surely the pain of the three princes surpassed that of all the other mourners combined, but Dane was having the worst of it. His pain couldn't be flushed out with tears or the void filled with food or other fancies. He would have gladly exchanged his life for Astrid's.

Locked in his chamber for seven days, he ate nothing and spoke only to Leif, whom Dane cherished above all—except for Queen Astrid herself. Leif, a rather small fellow for his age, was beside himself, crying uncontrollably at times. All Dane could do was hold the bronzed skin boy and run his fingers through the boy's curls. Both said little, for even the kindest of words are without worth in times of great anguish.

When he wasn't consoling Leif, Dane passed the time trying to conjure happy memories of his mother, but often found himself contemplating their final meeting. *Maybe there is something in her dream,* he thought. *What is Father planning? Why all the secrecy? Why am I—his eldest—so subject to scorn?* He would soon discover the answers; rather, to say his answers would soon find him would be more true.

On the eighth day of his fast, there was rapping at his door. He expected Leif but knew it wasn't him. Leif always used the secret knock Dane had taught him. Remaining quiet, he hoped the visitor would go away but to no avail. From the hall the familiar voice of the king's esquire called, "Prince Dane, the king sends his condolences but says time for mourning has passed. He desires your presence in the throne room."

Dane, still quiet, sat wondering what his father could want with him. *Has he finally come to tell me his purposes—why all the secrecy? Maybe there are important matters of the kingdom to discuss.* He had never been summoned to the throne room, but the death of the queen was no small matter. *Perhaps her duties are being reassigned,* he thought. No matter the reason, Magnus was right. The time for mourning had passed. There was a kingdom to govern, and with the queen, the heart of the Civitians gone, Dane needed to help fill the void she'd left.

"Thank you Seamus, I'll be there straight away."

"Very well, he'll be expecting you," said Seamus dully.

Dane removed his sackcloth, and in honor of Astrid, who was as fine a weaver as anyone in Auber Civitas, donned the royal blue linen tunic she had woven for his birthday. He oiled his face and hair and tried to pin his shoulders back, but the hole in his stomach created by days of not eating caused him to slump over a bit.

Lastly, he slipped Astrid's pendant over his sunny waves of hair and tucked the diamond under his tunic.

When he flung his chamber door open the aroma of roasted mutton teased and his mouth watered. After seven days of fasting perhaps even the scent of roasted rat would have evoked the same response. He made the short walk down the simple timber and stone crafted passage toward the palace's center where the throne room was. Even with little ornamentation the lofty ceilings lent a sense of grandeur.

As Dane passed through the double arched entry to the throne room, he could see the throne elevated in the middle, but no one sat upon it. Except for a solitary soul standing beside the throne, the room was devoid of life—not what Dane had expected. He approached the tall bronze skinned man and knelt at his feet. It was King Magnus of course, but dressed peculiarly in a tunic of green —the color of common folk. Tucked in the crook of his right arm was a circlet of gold. Dane recognized it as the King's circlet, but it had been altered since he had last seen it. An enormous diamond was now inlaid in the exact middle of the crown's front. It was an odd addition, for the Civitians—especially the King—liked things simple and orderly. This giant uncut diamond seemed out of place in his kingdom.

"Stand boy," said Magnus. "There's no need to display false respect." He looked at Dane with disdain—as was his custom. "I've grieved your mother's loss—as have you I suppose—but grief's bitter hour must end." He touched the arm of his throne. "Sit."

Dane was surprised by the order. As a child he was never allowed to even come near the throne, though York and Leif would often sit on it and command their imaginary servants.

Hesitantly, Dane did as he was told. Once perched on his loft, he began to feel both physical and emotional discomfort—not at all what he'd expected for his first time on the seat of power. The high back timber chair was straight and hard, and he couldn't get past the fact that he was doing something that for so long he had been forbidden to do.

Magnus walked behind him, keeping one hand on the throne. "Our people expect you to inherit the kingdom," he said. "As did your mother…but know it shall not be. It will go instead to York—my true eldest."

Dane turned and looked into Magnus's dark, deep set eyes. "What is your meaning Father?"

"Father?" Magnus scoffed. "A peculiar word—father. It would suggest that I begat you, or maybe that I at least have a care for you." He waved his hand through the air as if to dismiss the thought. "No, *I* am not your father. It's a secret I swore by oath to your mother not to tell, but now that she has passed, the truth must reign." Leaning forward, he lowered his voice, "You are a bastard, the product of the most grotesque happening. I regret to tell…you are the son of none other than a rapist. He ravaged your mother before she was queen." He paused to watch the poison of his words sink deeply into Dane. "You've known I do not desire your presence. I loathe it in fact. You are but a herald bringing news of that terrible day—ever reminding me of your mother's pain. My stomach churns when you're near."

Dane clenched his fists. His insides were a vortex of anger and affliction. "I can't believe a word of it!" He shouted.

Magnus turned his back, "It is unfortunate, but nonetheless true." Dane couldn't detect the king's smirk, the satisfied look in his eyes. "But there's more to loath about you than who your father is,

55

and how you came to be." He turned toward Dane with a scowl and raised his voice. "Your heart is covetous. Your eyes hunger for the crown. Like your real father, you can't keep them off what isn't yours." He knelt before Dane. "You would enjoy it, you as the king bestowed with majesty and arrayed in fine cloth, me the lowly commoner dressed as such."

If Magnus had persisted he may have ended up dead where he stood, for Dane's rage had built and the volcano was about to blow. But before he could thrust out of his seat in attack, Magnus stood and slipped the crown onto the prince's head.

Dane's vision whirled under a power he could neither control nor explain. His body numbed and his fists loosened. After the spinning had stopped, the throne room and the king seemed to blur as Dane's mind focused on distant things. He could sense an army, but not of men, rather of beasts. It was strange: he felt he could control them but had no eyes to lead. To him they were but a silhouette, and to them he was a blind guide.

His thoughts were interrupted as he was suddenly brought back to the throne room by Magnus's laughter. "Hope you've enjoyed it, boy. A minute as king is more than you deserve, but before Astrid died she had me swear to crown you. I dare not break an oath." He tore the crown from Dane's head.

For the moment Dane forgot his anger. "What devilry is this? The things I saw make no sense."

"How ignorant you are, ignoring what was spoken to you as a boy by the raconteurs: '*Take his Mind and control, With his Eyes you will see, Mend his Body, make them whole. Give his Heart set them free.*' These lines are more than rhymes for children. There is a truth in them, power to be gained. The great heirloom of Auber Civitas, the gift of Solas, you know nothing of." Pointing to the huge stone in the middle of his crown he said, "It is the Mind—the Minister of the Wild's Diamond Mind. Part of Derog still lives in it...Alas, you shall never know it again."

He struck Dane on the face with his open hand. It was enough. The volcano finally erupted. Dane leapt on Magnus, and with blow after blow, released the pent up fury from all the years of neglect and verbal degradation. Even with Dane weakened by hunger, Magnus would have been no match, but it mattered not. Dane had been nothing more than a pawn in Magnus's wicked hand. Seamus, who was lurking out of sight, alerted the Royal guards that he heard Magnus's cries and saw Dane attacking him. There was no need for trial. One does not attempt to kill the king and retain his right to live—whether prince or vassal—albeit the king's decree to exile Dane still baffled many. A king banishing his heir was unheard of.

Until his sentence could be carried out, Dane was locked in his chamber with guards posted. By the king's order, no one was allowed to visit, and food was withheld; but even without having eaten for nine days, Dane had no desire for meat. His simmering anger and whirling confusion were plenty to distract from his empty stomach. Thoughts that Astrid, his beloved mother, had lied to him his entire life pricked his mind, but deep within he knew Magnus was the liar, and the yeast of hatred and revenge began to work through. "If only I could escape and get to Magnus's chamber," he whispered. "I'd tear his wicked head from his body." His malice had grown too thick to even recall his mother's encouragement. He could see no light in his forest, only dense blackness.

When he had resolved to forfeit his life to end Magnus's, a tap came at his door. At first Dane was too absorbed in his brooding to take notice, but after the second and even third time the caller repeated the same rhythmic tatter, Dane realized who it must be.

He stood in the place where he had been curled tightly on the floor and gave heed. The fourth bout of tapping began, but Dane interrupted. "Is it you brother?"

"Can I come in?" came Leif's small voice. "Erlend said I could but for only a moment." Erlend was the captain overseeing Dane's imprisonment. He knew the three princes well and was especially fond of Leif.

"Yes, Come in," Dane muttered.

Erlend cracked the door just wide enough for tiny Leif to slide through. Although Dane was ashamed and angry about his imprisonment and future exile, at the sight of his brother he broke down with joyful tears of relief. Of all the things and people that had been torn from Dane, losing Leif was the worst. He feared never seeing him again. He lifted Leif from the floor in embrace, and the brothers wept.

"They said you attacked father...and now you have to go away," Leif sniffled.

"It's true," said Dane heavily. "I hit him many times and have been banished from our people because of it."

"Why? I don't understand," said Leif.

"There is much that I don't understand about what happened. Your father said things that are difficult for me to believe." Gripping his chest he said, "He told me that he wasn't my father... that mother...that mother had lied to me my entire life. He told of his disdain for me, and when he struck me...I...I struck back." Dane's countenance changed in an instant from contemplative to malicious. Revenge filled his vision, and for a moment Leif was blurred.

58

"Dane?" Leif shook his brother. "Are you alright?"

"Not at all," Dane said after regaining his awareness. He snugged Leif against his side and kissed his head. "Except for you I have no one…and soon you will be taken as well. Nothing have I known outside of Auber Civitas, yet I wonder not how I will survive. My heart has been pierced and my mind seeks only revenge. Please forgive me brother, for I cannot help but hate the man you call father."

Leif made no reply and the two sat in half embrace, neither wanting to lose his brother, but only Dane knew at that moment that it would soon be so—that the only place he would see Leif again would be his memory.

Both wept once more when Erlend came to separate them. Having watched the boys grow and loving them both, Erlend wept too. Even the hardest of souls would have struggled to withhold tears in that chamber. Erlend lifted Leif and carried him out, leaving Dane like a melted candle on the cold stone floor. And though Dane desired to take Leif and run, he dared not challenge Erlend. He was perhaps the only man in the Kingdom for whom Dane was no match.

The next knock Dane heard on his chamber door was not the secret knock of a loved one, rather the heart rending pound of a stone fist. At midnight the executioners of his sentence had come to strip him away from all the things that once were his. He no longer had a place in his palace or even his city. Where home would be now no one could know, but it wasn't with the Civitians.

"The time is here," a distraught Erlend said from the doorway.

Dane fixed his eyes on the floor and offered no reply. The volcano had erupted; the aftermath was cold and hard. He had nothing to say to anyone as they led him from his chamber past

Leif's and out of the keep through the kitchen. *I have become a thing of scorn,* thought Dane, *not fit enough to be escorted through the front entrance*—though really Erlend was trying to keep the peace by evicting Dane in secret.

The entourage plodded west down Hemlock Path toward the Silver Gate. Seeing the market stands forced memories of Astrid into Dane's hardened psyche. As a child he cherished coming to the open market with his mother for food and supplies. Astrid liked to hand pick her own fish and vegetables and mingle with the commoners, but her true motive for coming to the market was to survey the condition of her people, something Dane didn't realize until he was a man. Those with needs found them met with Astrid around. She would give to those who had little and pay extra for the goods of farmers and fishermen who'd fallen on hard times. The memories and thoughts of this good lady brought some solace to the suffering Dane. He touched the diamond pendant that still hung beneath his tunic to honor her.

His reminiscence was short lived though, for his eyes snagged on a newcomer to the night's journey. A cloaked figure strode alongside the group about thirty paces out. Though the moon cast a menacing veil over the person's face, Dane recognized Magnus by his gate.

He's taken all I love and now he even steals in on my memories, thought Dane. "Probably here to finally wash his hands of me," he muttered inaudibly. Turning toward the figure, he said, "Come to make sure the job is done…to see that your thorn is properly removed?"

The cloaked man made no indication that he could even hear Dane's words, but kept pace with the entourage.

Dane tightened his fists and nasty thoughts of revenge slithered in. He calculated whether he could get to the man before the guards could reach him but knew the answer. He was surrounded by spearmen with points facing him and so might get a step or two towards vengeance, but they would be his final steps. Better to live and have an honest go at it later, Dane decided. Though much of him desired to end it then and let things lie as they might—even if he ended in the dirt.

They walked on through the night toward the heavily armored yet lightly guarded wall that had separated Auber Civitas from the *uncivilized* world for generations. Erlend's orders were to release Dane through the Silver Gate, the smaller of only two gates on the great span of Harbor Wall. The Silver Gate was the only one still in use, for the King's Gate, primarily used to traffic goods into the kingdom, hadn't been needed since the Civitians had become self-sustaining.

The final paces were agonizing. Memories of Astrid, Leif and York, holidays and festivals, of good food and drink, and of young love mocked him. Normally happy memories came only to taunt in his worst condition, to show him what he would never have again. And the person who had stolen his entire life from him was only a few leaps away. *I'll go through this gate tonight, but somehow I'll make it back to you*, Dane thought toward Magnus.

Two guards flung the gates wide for the entourage as they neared. Dane was escorted a good distance from the wall where Erlend retired the spearmen. He remained.

"There are no words." Erlend swallowed hard. "This is wine at her bitterest."

He unsheathed the dagger belted around his waist and offered it to Dane. "You needn't go naked into the wilderness."

Dane accepted the gift and embraced the giver. Not another word was spoken as the two parted, Dane heading north toward the Afon River and Erlend returning to civilization. Dane didn't look back as he trudged across the Golden Highway, the main road that ran into and out of Auber Civitas via the King's Gate, to the river. His life was to his rear—at least what he knew as life. Dense forest that he had only seen from atop the wall bordered the Afon before him. The woods were deep and dark and nasty, a place where few men would enter at night by his own accord. The menacing appearance mattered not to Dane, for he had no intention of entering. He hoped only to infiltrate the wall through the arched portal the river flowed through.

He began to breathe out thoughts to the night. "Well Father, for your sake may the royal guards be awake and ready at their post, but for mine, may they be fast sleeping. I'm coming with a gut full of hate and a dagger of recompense."

He jabbed his weapon into the darkness and turned toward the wall, but the wry voice of Seamus sliced through the night halting him.

"Your vengeful thoughts betray you Dane. Did you not think the king would see your banishment carried through?"

Dane turned toward the voice and strained his eyes to see the tall thin figure that belonged to the king's attendant.

"Indeed I did," said Dane, "but now I see he has sent an esquire to do a knight's job and am uncertain."

Dane readied his dagger and stepped toward Seamus, who didn't move. Another step…and another, and still Seamus remained planted. As Dane drew nearer he could see the reason for Seamus's steadfastness. He wasn't alone. Concealed in the shadows of a willow stood the cloaked man who'd escorted Dane's company

62

from the kingdom, and beside him was another, an archer with an arrow drawn.

"Alas, you have assured my sentence will be carried out," said Dane.

"Yes, we must be sure that even the splinters from the thorn are removed," came Magnus's reply.

For a while neither side stirred nor spoke as they waited on the other. At length Dane broke in, "Permit me one favor before you have me killed Father…let me see my executioner. I want to look at him—to know what kind of man would shoot another blindly in the night."

"As you wish," said Magnus as he motioned to the bowman.

The bowman crept forward—as did Dane—confirming what Dane had already suspected. It was Magnus's foreign coconspirator Baird with his bow drawn. But this interested Dane less than Magnus knew, for the estranged son had truly hoped to inch a little closer to his target before he was shot; and now he was indeed close enough. Dane wasted no time flinging the dagger, but it seemingly missed its mark as it sailed over Baird's head. Baird reacted all but simultaneously, releasing his arrow as the dagger left Dane's fingers. Dane was hit. His upper breast where the shoulder meets the chest was pierced. The arrow bit deeply. He howled in agony as pain pulled him to his knees. His executioner drew another arrow and nocked it, but before he could take aim, a horrifying screech came from behind.

A mortified Seamus had discovered Dane's true target, Magnus, slumped on the ground with a dagger buried to the hilt in his gut. Magnus clutched the handle and moaned. The son had found revenge after all.

"Make haste, Baird!" Seamus said. "We must take him to the castle!"

Baird turned to give aid, and the two servants of iniquity hustled their evil king back to the castle, leaving Dane outside of the wall, bent and bloody, and in much pain.

If death had found him that summer's night, Dane would have died content knowing he had at least deeply wounded Magnus. But his life would eventually serve a far higher purpose than that of his own petty desire for retribution.

Baird turned to give aid, and the two servants of iniquity hustled their evil king back to the castle, leaving Dane outside of the wall, bent and bloody, and in much pain.

If death had found him that summer's night, Dane would have died content knowing he had at least wounded Magnus. But his life would eventually serve a far higher purpose than that of his own petty desire for retribution.

CHAPTER 7. CALLED AND CHOSEN

GIVEN HADN'T seen Aderyn in a couple of weeks, and though that concerned her, she had managed to get along without her friend's help. Building two more fish weir upstream from the first, she hoped to take advantage of Ewe's before the late summer sun could lap up the shallow river's last puddle of water.

Her apprehension about taking fish lives had lessened a bit, but it still bothered her. Though she tried, Given couldn't convince herself that her mother's stories about Nataurie were only legend. *How awful it would be to kill the shepherd of the rivers.* Even worse was the thought that if she did happen to spear Nataurie, she would probably be eating her too.

As far as growth was concerned, Grit was outpacing the weeds, and to his mother's amazement, he was now faster than her—when he was on all-fours. Given would never have admitted it, but Grit was looking more akin to Bledig every minute. *As long as he doesn't start to act like him we'll be okay*, she concluded.

Eurig's two overgrown bear cubs, Torben and Orson, had become smitten with Given. Whenever their father would unchain them from their daily labors, they would offer their services to her. At first, Given felt fearfully reluctant to allow their help, but the two behemoths were politely persistent, and Given soon realized that they were both harmless. Besides, she did need their help with some of the more physically taxing chores like felling trees. And she couldn't help thinking the eldest, Orson, was handsome.

Many things were going well for the young mother, but best of all was the absence of Gar. Given had neither seen him in the wilderness nor in the village since their last encounter at Wether's Field.

It was morning, and she was up early fetching water from the well and hauling it to the stone jar outside her house. She liked to keep it filled for times when going all the way to the well would be inconvenient. Seeing Eurig and his boys on the road, she stopped.

"I much appreciate your help with the firewood," she said to Torben and Orson. "I'm going to Ewe's today to clear fish from my traps. To show my thanks I was hoping to convince you two to come share the catch for dinner."

"You bet we will!" blurted Torben.

"Yes Miss Given," said the more reserved Orson. "That is, if it's alright with Papa." He glanced at his father, hopeful.

Eurig looked at his two sons, then at Given. "If you're willing to empty your coffers for these lads, I can't argue. Their mother'll be glad to have a break from cooking for once."

"Thank you," said Given with a smile. "They've earned every bit of what I can cook for them." Her eyes met Orson's, "I'll be expecting you two before dusk."

***

Given poured her last pale of water into the jar and went to rouse Grit, who to his mother's surprise, was already awake and pilfering through last night's leftovers.

"What do we have here? Not even a year old and already helping yourself to breakfast." She sighed and lifted the squirmy boy. "There's no end to your orneriness. Now, let me fix you a proper meal before we get off to check the traps."

After their usual feast of fish, Given tightened Grit in his papoose and slung a tote over her shoulder. "Today is going to be a good day, Gritsy. It'll be our biggest catch yet."

As the two headed down their usual path toward Wether's Field, Given could see Torben and Orson sawing a tree with their massive crosscut saw. *I surely do appreciate you two,* she thought. *I'll fix you the best meal you've ever tasted.*

It was a hot day, even the trees seemed to sweat, but as Given and Grit pushed deeper into the woods, the shadows and breeze cooled them. The earth was thirsty, and much of the undergrowth had withered, making the already trampled path even easier to navigate. Given checked her deadfall traps along the way. The first one—empty. The second was empty as well. A rat, a suitable meal for most occasions, had met its end in the third trap Given checked. She scooped it into her tote and reset the trap with fish scraps for bait. Wind swept through the trees causing the leaves to rattle and clap as if applauding Given's catch.

Grit started to squirm and moan as the two trudged closer to their destination. He liked his papoose less with every trip the two made to Wether's. Given had already compromised once by letting his arms loose to swing freely, something she now thought a terrible idea, for when the wind blew her hair far enough for Grit to reach, he would grasp it and give a hardy tug.

"Perhaps it's time to loosen your bonds even further," said Given reluctantly. "But if I do, you have to *follow* closely."

She unraveled the cloth that held Grit tight against her back and let him slide to the ground. "There you go. Now be good, or I'll have you tied back up quick as a blink."

Grit whirled around on all fours like a dog chasing his tail. He wore nothing but a cloth to cover his most sensitive areas, but even that he constantly tried to remove, preferring to go through life as naked as he entered it. Given slapped his hand when he would try to undress. It took several attempts for Grit to get the point.

Given trekked on with Grit crawling speedily behind. He had no problem keeping up, and kept passing his mother by and slowing down right in front of her. "Not much for setting a pace," she said as she lifted Grit by the hips and set him down behind her. Grit wasted no time darting back in front again—and again. But the last time he didn't slow down; instead, he dashed forward and slipped off the path into the undergrowth.

"Get back here, right now!" said Given, perturbed. Grit didn't obey, slinking even further from the path.

"I should've known better," Given said as she gave chase. Though she couldn't see Grit through the brush, she followed his rustlings. *What does he think he's doing?* "Grit, you come back now! You're in trouble…I'm going to wrap you so tight you won't be able to move. You're going to be in your papoose until you're five."

Fear overtook her as the rustlings grew fainter and stopped. "Grit, come back sweetie! Come back!" Only the wind whispered in response. She darted forward through the brush calling frantically for Grit. *I've lost my son. What kind of mother…*

Before she could finish the thought, she broke through the last tangle of fallen limbs and weeds and stumbled into an open meadow. A tiny figure sitting under a patch of black jacks in the field's center immediately caught her eye.

"There you are Gritsy," her voice cracked as the tension of panic loosened. She ran to Grit and drew him into her bosom. "Never do that to me again. I thought I had lost you."

Grit didn't hear a word his mother said. He was fixated on something, rather someone, that Given hadn't noticed in all the excitement. A man was sitting in the shadow of the oaks and catalpas not even a stone's throw away, his bowed head covered by a giant catalpa leaf.

"Da," Grit mumbled, pointing toward the stranger.

"Oh my! We needn't disturb him." Given's eyes were wide. "Let's be back to our duties." Clutching Grit, she turned back toward the direction they'd come.

"No hurry," said the stranger with his face still covered. "It's not every day I have visitors. One can get lonely on his travels."

Given didn't much care how lonely the stranger was. She didn't want to be his company and preferred to get back to her traps so she could cook something delicious for Torben and Orson.

"My apologies sir, I must be getting along to my chores. We've only wandered here by mistake." She sounded small and without confidence as though she was speaking to Bledig.

"I understand your dilemma, but I insist on your staying."

At his word, Given was completely frozen mid-step. It wasn't a frightful freeze—though she was terrified. As though by bewitchment, she simply could not move either leg.

"What on Earth have you done to me? What do you want?"

The stranger stood. The leaf slid from his face to the ground. He wasn't a large man—but a man nonetheless. His dusty gray tunic was a peculiarity in a neck of the woods that saw folks mostly in animal skins. His curly mahogany hair was wind blown yet tidy.

"Do not fear, daughter. I am not here to harm you, but it is difficult to speak while you are running."

Given looked closer. "Who are you? Your voice, it sounds familiar."

"Yes, you know me. I will free you for a closer look…if you agree not to run."

"It seems I have no choice."

The stranger made no movement with hand, foot, eye, or mouth, but Given's legs unlocked. With a look of confusion, she stepped closer to the man. *Familiar,* she thought, *but from where do I know him?*

When Given was close enough to get a good look, she was taken aback. A harmonious blend of strength and beauty was the man's countenance. His olive complexion gleamed; his eyes were a mountain stream washing away apprehension. Given gaped, and goosebumps sprang over her body. There was no mistaking. It was the Seer!

"Hello Given." He said barely above a whisper. "It's been some time since we last met. I see you've found your way from the valley to higher ground."

Given marveled. "Surely many years have passed since I last saw you, but not one shows on your face. You're the Seer, the one who came to our village when I was a little girl, are you not?"

"Let there be no doubt. I warned your people of the coming winter."

"Yes, but I was a child and now stand before you a woman, yet you haven't changed. How is this possible? Why are you here?" Given shook her head. "None of it makes sense."

"Things beyond our experiences often don't. But some of your recent encounters should make this a little easier to understand… Aderyn speaks well of you." And staring into Given's confounded eyes he continued without opening his mouth, projecting his thoughts into Given's mind. *Through your many trials, you have not been forgotten. You have been made strong, and now is your time to fulfill the commitment of your people.*

Given continued to shake her head. Even with Aderyn's stories and demonstration of power, the thought of a practically eternal being standing before her was hard to grasp. *I must be in a dream,* she thought; but it was no dream. The man waved his hand and from nothingness a white fire erupted in front of them. As Given stood hypnotized by the flame's beauty, the Seer continued.

"Long has an ancient power slumbered in the bowels of Earth—a power most thought had been destroyed—but the bones buried deep did not decay. The mind without a head still thinks; eyes out of socket continue to see; apart from the breast a callous heart beats. Daily, I sense his power growing as the beast's spirit is revived by the cunning of evil men."

With every word he spoke, an image appeared in the flame. All were precious gems saturated in fire. All were beautiful but unrecognizable to this poor girl—except one. It was the last one revealed, and when she saw it, she gasped. The *callous heart* was certainly familiar. She had seen it many times but knew not its importance, or origin, or name.

"You know this one?" said the Seer, noticing Given's amazement.

"The others are unfamiliar, but the red one I'd know anywhere. My master, Bledig, now possesses it. At least he did when last I was with him."

"Oh?" said the Seer. "What do you know about it?"

"Only that it is beautiful, and my master is captivated by it, never going anywhere without it."

The Seer grinned. "The stone had come so near to its rightful owner, yet she didn't recognize that which was hers."

Given gave an even bigger look of confusion.

"Did you not desire the gem for yourself?" asked the Seer.

Given sighed. "To the destitute, things of beauty mean little. My only desire was for provision and protection for my son and self...

and I don't understand what you mean. Are you saying it belongs to me?"

"Not only you, but all the heirs of the Gallant tribe."

The mention of Given's tribe pulled her mind from the stone and put it on her family.

"My tribe…do you know how many remain? Is my mother…"

The Seer looked down contemplatively. "The winter that I warned your father about stole much, but I cannot tell how much. Like you, other Gallants were scattered and saved. Only a trickle of tribesmen remained in the Valley." He hesitated and gave a look as though he were delivering bad news. "The answers you seek must be revealed with time I'm afraid."

Though it wasn't the response she'd wished for, Given could still cling to a hope that she would see her mother again, even if it was a fool's hope.

"So what is this red stone anyway?" asked Given. "Why does it concern me?"

"Search your thoughts—your memories. You know the answer."

For a moment, Given did as the Seer told her.

"The Shepherd's Heart." Given declared. "How could I have missed it all this time? The red stone is the Shepherd's Heart, the heart of Derog which Aderyn had spoken of."

"Yes, that is the one. I believe Aderyn explained to you how your tribe came to possess such a gem. Well, after the winter you were taken, the Heart remained with a few who survived. Though terribly distressed by the unnecessary desolation the Chief's decision to stay in the Afon Valley had brought, I was relieved to return and find the Gallants had retained the Heart through the winter. With them, I left it once again. Last autumn, through some act of treachery, the members of your tribe that remained in the valley went missing—along with the Heart.

"Something terrible is happening. The Shepherd's bones buried deep at the roots of the Rebel Mountains have been unearthed and taken, and both the emerald eyes are unaccounted for. The diamond mind remains in its stronghold, but its keeper I have no trust for. And with the other members of your tribe missing, you are the rightful heir of the Heart."

"I don't understand…you are powerful, and I am weak. Why would you leave a thing of such value with me?"

"It is not my duty to lord over the things of man. Let him have the will to choose." The Seer took Given's hand in his. "You may not feel it, but you do have power. Where you lack physical strength, your virtue will be sufficient. Love has always been evil's biggest threat. More than coincidence brought the Heart to you already. You are now its keeper, so with you and your descendants shall it remain." Shaking his head slightly, his eyes narrowed. "But the Heart should not be destroyed unless there is no other way… for if it is, those bound to it—the Deroheed and all of their descendants—may parish. Do not fear: as my father and I have been with you through your many trials, we will continue to be." He ran his hand gently over Grit's head. "The security of many close to you rests with you, daughter. I implore you to return for the Heart. Only with the Gallant will it be safe."

"But what shall I do with it once I have it?"

"Have faith and be not anxious, for when the time comes the answers you seek will be given. But make haste; the deathly howls of war have reached my ears, and I must prepare the warriors." Immediately after saying this, he stepped back, his face and form were encompassed by flames, and he vanished.

73

Given stood in disbelief of the whole encounter. If it wasn't for the charred earth where the Seer had been, she may have denied that it happened. She knelt, plucked a singed dandelion flower and examined it before handing it to Grit. *This is great,* she thought. *The Shepherd of Men wants me to take a valuable stone—with unreckoned power—and keep it safe; and he wants me to return to my former hell to get it back.* "What am I to do Gritsy?" Weighed by thought, she sank to her knees and ran her fingers through her hair. "Why couldn't I have taken it the night we escaped?"

Grit palmed his mother's cheek in a consoling manner.

CHAPTER 8. SUPPER

G*IVEN FINISHED* her trek to Ewe's Delight with Grit snugged tightly in his papoose. She didn't need any more *unexpected delays*. When she arrived at her traps, they were as full as expected —more so. She mindlessly went through her routine of asking if any of the fish were Nataurie before piercing them and stashing them in her tote.

She couldn't help thinking *why me* repeatedly as she went about her chores. *It doesn't make sense, a girl with no family or home, a girl with no fortune or power, the heir to something of such value, the protector of something important.*

She finished harvesting and with Grit walked back across Wether's Field to the forest's edge, too distracted to notice that she was being watched once again by a man on the riverbank.

In a daze she traveled back through the woods toward her village while Grit slept soundly in his papoose. The massive trees she normally wondered at were nothing more than blurs in her vision, and to the woodpeckers and songbirds that tapped beats and sang beautifully she paid no mind. She hardly noticed her arms and shoulders quivering from carrying the large bundle of fish. The Seer's words, "The security of many close to you rests with you," gnawed at her. He, like Aderyn, had implied that Grit was not fully human, and in the deepest wells of her being, she knew it was true. *What could all of this mean for him? Would returning to Bledig for the stone actually protect him? What about the rest of the Shepherd's body? What could be done with the mind and eyes and body if they are held by evil hands?*

Worse than having all of these unanswered questions, was the thought that not listening to the Seer was her father's greatest folly. *If he had listened…and if I don't do as he says, I'm as much a fool as he—more even.*

Heavy thoughts of fear and doubt tugged her one way, while faith in the Seer's words and love for her son pulled the other. She was about to collapse from the anguish when a giant hand appeared before her from seemingly nowhere. It grasped her tote of fish, relieving her of the burden.

"Let me help you with that Miss Given," the deep comforting voice of Orson came smashing through. She'd never been so glad to hear a familiar *masculine* voice. She fell into Orson's barrel chest, surprising herself as much as it did him.

He reluctantly raised his free hand to Given's cheek. "What's the matter? Are you hurt?" He drew her back and looked into her teary eyes.

"No, I'm not hurt." She sniffled.

"Then why—"

"It's nothing," Given interrupted. "I've had a long day is all. I'm just glad to be back here."

"Oh, Miss Given, I can see you're not altogether right. If you aren't up to cooking tonight, you don't have to, or I…I could help you."

Dinner with the two brothers had been driven far from Given's mind, but at Orson's reminder she said, "Oh…oh no, you do too much for me already, let me treat you for once."

He gave a bear-sized smile, and holding up the tote full of fish said, "I think you caught enough. Torben may even be filled by these." After helping Given the rest of the way home, he unloaded the fish outside her door. "You certain you're okay?" He looked into Given's eyes, still swollen with tears.

"Yes, I'll be fine. Bring Torben later, and we'll have a feast."

"Okay, if you're insisting, we'll be here. But at least let me help you unload Grit."

Given smiled and loosened the straps that bound Grit to her back, allowing Orson to catch the tiny swaddled creature in his gargantuan arms.

"You're too kind," said Given as Orson handed Grit delicately to her.

"You're much welcome. I'll be back soon," he replied, unable to hide his blushing.

After laying the still sleepy Grit on a mat, Given busied herself preparing the biggest meal she had ever cooked, glad to have something to distract from the looming decision. By stoking the coals she never really let die, she had a suitable fire going in no time. The fish were skewered and roasted to near perfection. With all that had happened, she had forgotten to eat, and the aroma caused her mouth to water. *This could be my last real dinner* she thought as she pulled the fish from the fire. *Bledig may not let me eat for days if I return to him, or perhaps not at all.* It was difficult to not imagine herself starving to death in the cabin by the lake. Bledig would certainly be unhappy she ran out on him, but maybe her coming back willingly would make it better. What would she say when she first sees him? What would be her excuse for running away? One thing was for certain: she couldn't bear to take Grit back with her. But who would take care of him?

Before she knew it, the sun had sunk below the horizon, and Torben and Orson were at her door looking as clean and hungry as ever.

"Hello, Miss Given," Torben blurted. "Something sure smells good."

"Oh, come in, sit down," Given said, motioning toward the mats that she had prepared on the floor for them. As the two ducked under the threshold and entered Given's home, the one room house seemed to shrink, and room to wiggle became scarce.

"Perhaps we should eat outside where there's a *little* more room." She snickered.

"Whatever you like, we'll do," said Orson with a look of endearment.

"Yes, I think it would be better for us all," she said, trying to coral Grit as he dashed for the opening.

The friends made their way outside into the grayness of twilight, and Given laid down mats for the four of them. She was happy to finally be able to do something nice for the brothers after all the kindness they had shown.

When everyone had found their place, Given uncovered a basketful of broiled fish. Without hesitation, Grit thrust his little paw into the middle, plucked out a choice fish, and put it into his mouth.

"I was going to say guests first, but it's too late for that," said Given.

"I think he has the right idea." Torben chuckled as he reached for a fish of his own.

"You first Miss Given," said Orson, who cared much more about the company than the meal. But after some word wrestling, Given finally convinced him it was more polite for the guest to go first. Orson left the best fish for Given.

The four feasted to their heart's delight while the two brothers shared funny stories about their mother, who was surprisingly small "like Given."

"By the time I was five years old, I had already outgrown her," said Torben. "I remember wanting to be carried, but she couldn't, so I carried her instead."

"At five years old?" Given asked in surprise.

"Don't buy everything Torben's selling," said Orson. "He hadn't outgrown Mama till he was six—maybe seven."

"Biiiiig difference," said Torben. "Anyway, she says I was too heavy for her to hold while I nursed, so Papa would hold me to the breast…and sometimes I would go after his."

Given laughed as Orson rolled his eyes. "What nice dinner talk this is, brother. Why don't we let Given tell us a little about her family."

Her throat immediately tightened. "I…I'm sorry. My stories are not very good. You two should keep going."

"No, Orson's right. We've said more than enough. Tell us more about you."

Given felt the tightness spread. Aderyn was the only other person in the village who knew her story. Could she trust these two to keep her secrets?

"Don't tell anything you don't want," Orson said after noticing Given's apprehension. "We're all friends here."

"Truth be told," Given said. "I don't really know my family, or at least I haven't seen them for years. I remember my mother, who I call Mot, was as beautiful as the full moon. I used to stare at her as a child, hoping I would someday be as pretty. She was so kind to me, always putting me before herself. When last I saw her—the day I was taken—she risked her life to keep me safe. I don't know where she is now or if she's okay…"

Given's mind drifted far from the conversation as she stared into the darkness that had overtaken the landscape. Thinking once again about the Seer and the Shepherd's Heart, about Bledig and going back to the cabin by Coyote Lake, she wondered if she would have the strength to do what was asked of her. *I wish Aderyn was here. She would know what to say.* No sooner did the thought come than a screeching pierced her ears.

"A hawk crying in the nighttime," said Torben. "That can't be a good thing."

Given perked up to listen. Another screech sounded, followed by a faint low whistle, and in the darkness she could make out the silhouette of a person coming toward them. "You couldn't be more wrong Torben," she said excitedly. "That's Freckles's cry, and where Freckles is…Aderyn will be also." She bounced to her feet, snatched Grit, and ran toward the shadowed figure.

Aderyn, seeing her friend coming towards her at an alarming pace, held her arms open and braced herself. She swallowed both Given and Grit with an embrace at first contact.

"I'm so glad you're back!" cried Given. "Much has happened that you must know."

"It's good to be back," said Aderyn with arms still locked around her friends. "I have much to tell as well." Withdrawing a bit she looked at Grit. "How's my boy doing?"

Grit threw his hands out and lunged from Given's arms to Aderyn's.

"Guess I'm not the only one excited you're back," said Given. "He's outgrowing his mother. I can hardly keep up with him when he has a mind to get away…But come now, we have dinner prepared."

After they rejoined Orson and Torben, the five of them devoured the remaining fish while Torben shared more funny stories about growing up in "his neck of the woods." When the two brothers finally said their farewells, the ladies retired with a sleeping Grit into Given's home.

Given laid Grit on his mat and lit a candle as the two friends spoke in hushed tones. Given went first, telling Aderyn all about her successes in trapping, how unexpectedly fast Grit had grown, and of course about the encounter with the Seer.

"What should I do?" Given asked. "I know the Seer's advice should reign, but the fear overwhelms me. We just escaped from that monster only to be sent back to him. What he might do to us is a terrible wonder. I also doubt my purpose for going, and I dare not take Grit."

"I have journeyed long these past weeks searching for some sign of the missing relics," said Aderyn. There is rumor that they are being gathered by one man—the Civitian King. His intentions could not be pure." Aderyn's eyes kindled, and she spoke as one who through centuries of trial had acquired wisdom beyond that of men, "You can hide here and be safe for a time, but evil will find you. Follow the Shepherd's voice. You know where the Heart is, and he has dealt you this task. Recover the stone while it may be found. You mustn't deny his charge, even if obedience means suffering."

The flame in her eyes dimmed as she continued with great concern. "I had a vision of you during my travels. Before my waking eyes you were bathing with Grit in a stream. Your tunic on the shore rested beside the axe and spear. Sounds from the woods nearby startled you, and fright overtook you as out of the trees a wolf with eyes like embers emerged. You raced from the water to your things, and though the spear or axe would have done well in your defense, you reached for the tunic and ran instead. The wolf attacked you both...you trying to flee and cover your shame cost both your lives."

Given sat contemplating what was said. At length she said, "If only you could come too, this would not seem as dreadful...but if the goal is to retrieve the Heart, I fear I must go alone. Bledig would smell you from a league away, surely hiding it long before we could get to him."

"Alas, my remaining may be the wiser choice anyway. I've suffered long under the control of Derog's mind and have much doubt now that his power has been altogether broken. After you retrieve the relic, it must remain concealed—even from me. But what good I wonder...what good would you be alone if you are unable to stand up to Bledig?"

"Before, as his servant, I cared not about the stone. My only concern was survival. Now my only care will be the stone. I will figure a way to take it from him, and when I do, I can only pray to escape with it. But if I am to do this terrible deed, above all else I refuse to take Grit back into the pit I rescued him from. In you I confide. Please take care of him when I'm away...and if I do not return, raise him as a mother would."

"You've become a daughter to me, and Grit a grandson. I'll care for him in your absence, but you will return."

The fire lapped up the last of the candle wax as the friends talked into the night. By the end of their conversation they had devised a *reasonable* plan to rescue the stolen ruby while keeping Given from injury.

The two figured the journey back to Coyote Lake could take a few days longer than the near week it took Given to get to Eurig's village. Though she would be traveling lighter without babe in arms, she would be resting through the night and didn't know the most direct route back. There was no avoiding an encounter with Bledig. In order to find his hiding place, she would need to convince him that she was there to stay, but she couldn't bear to give him more than he had already taken.

CHAPTER 9. THE SORROW OF PARTING

THE DAYS slugged along as the two friends prepared for Given's journey and waited for departure. One sultry day, Orson—by design most likely—found Given and Grit at the well.

"I've been meaning to give thanks for the meal," he said. "But Pa's been working us like rented oxen the past couple days…I figured you'd be out to your traps today—or yesterday even. It's been a handful of days at least since I've seen you leave the village. Those traps are probably overflowing by now. If you're not feeling well, I could check them."

"That's alright, you don't have to—"

Orson held a finger up, "Now Miss Given, I can tell something's not altogether right. We're near finished building for the day, so I'm going to check them for you whether you say it's fine or not."

"You are too kind. I would argue, but I can see there'd be no hope of winning…I will let you help if you promise to share the catch with Aderyn and Grit when I'm away."

"When you're away? I didn't know you were leaving. Where—"

Given motioned to the east: "I must return to my home…to tie up some ends and collect things that I left behind. I hope to be back within the month." Looking back into Orson's eyes she continued, "I do appreciate the help. Aderyn will have Grit to herself as well. She may need a hand."

"If it was anything but watching Grit, I'd say Birdie could handle it," said Orson with a smile. "But it takes more than one set of eyes to track him…and speaking of your little feller, look behind you."

Given turned to find Grit standing atop the well with waist cloth removed aiming his streamline at the water.

"NO, NO...NOT IN THERE!" She screeched.

Grit, seeing his mother coming, bolted on all fours to the other side of the well—not wasting time to stop his stream. After finally coercing him to come back, Given held him and did her best to convince the youngling that it was bad to pee in the well. Grit laughed.

"Then again, maybe Birdie should handle things on her own," Orson jested.

"Oh no," Given laughed. "I've already got you hooked. There's no wiggling your way off now. She held out the small yellow-eyed boy for the behemoth Orson to hold.

"You behave yourself," said Orson ironically as he took the naked child into his arms. Grit wasted no time climbing Orson like a tree.

"I'm happy you two like each other," said Given. "Leaving him here will be easier knowing he'll be in able hands. When I return, you'll have to come for dinner again."

"Th...there's nothing I'd rather do," he said as his face flashed red.

She glanced into his eyes. They were the color of oak leaves in early fall and in them was something she hadn't noticed before—passion. *He actually desires me,* she thought. But unlike all the other men she'd known in her life, he hadn't just smashed and taken what he'd wanted. Since her arrival in his village, he'd been nothing but kind to her.

Given grasped his hand and in an attempt to hide the fire that had consumed her cheeks, looked down. For a moment the two stood together, hands clasped, and said nothing, Grit still atop Orson's head. At length Orson let loose of Given's hand, gently pried the little creature from his thick sable hair, and returned him to his mother. "Well, I've got to get to work. You'd better be back within the month, or I'm coming to find you."

Though he spoke with a smile, Given was fully convinced that he meant what he said. They finished their farewells and went back to their business, Orson to building—and checking Given's traps—Given to tending to Grit.

This would be the final day before she left all that she loved and had begun to love for the last place on earth she'd want to go. She felt like a frog that had escaped the kettle only to land in the fire. Alone with Grit she tried to make the most of what could be their final time together. They played Grit's favorite game, chase, for seemingly hours, splashed around in water pulled from the well, formed mud pies, and sampled them. All Given wanted to do was hold her little boy, but he wouldn't have that for long, so she waited until he was sleeping. Even with all the anxiety, the day flew by much too quickly for her liking.

Night covered the tiny village, but sleep evaded Given as all the maybes and what ifs ran through her head. *What if Aderyn loses Grit or someone takes him? What do I know of her anyway? Can I trust this Seer or Solas, whatever you call him? Maybe Grit and Aderyn should come with me after all, or maybe I should just stay here. Is my son's life really bound to this stone?* Each question brought with it more questions without any definitive answers. She was going to have to trust the only thing she'd ever been able to trust—her gut.

A light tapping on the door startled her as she had begun to doze.

"It's time to get up," said Aderyn in a hushed tone.

"Straight away," said Given, slinking from beside Grit to let Aderyn in. Swinging the door wide, she could see the sun had not yet bounced above the horizon but was up enough to illuminate the landscape in a soft gray.

Aderyn was arrayed in white, looking as beautiful as ever. "You'd better move on if you're going to make it there and back before fall."

"Some of us require sleep," said Given jokingly, pulling her frizzled hair from her face.

"Well, I do sleep— standing up and with one eye open," Aderyn said with a smile. Reaching inside the pack she had brought for Given's journey, she pulled out everything from rope and flint to cured fish and deer meat. "Add this to what you've gathered. There should be enough to get you there. It'll be up to you to get back."

Given cringed thinking of the impossibility of getting in and out unscathed. She turned to Grit. Tears welled as the thought of leaving her helpless baby pierced her heart. But what else was there to do? Caressing his head maybe for the last time, she softly sang her mother's song.

Aderyn stood patiently waiting for her friend to finish saying goodbye. She knew well the pangs of leaving a child behind and wouldn't have dared rush poor Given.

After a long kiss for the sleeping babe, Given stood and whispered, "Be good for Aderyn and remember that I love you." Turning away from Grit, she collapsed in Aderyn's arms. "Please, be a mother to him while I'm away." She sobbed.

"Don't worry, you'll be back in a skip, and Grit will be in caring hands until then…There is one more thing before you go."

Given's eyes widened half-expecting her friend to pile on another difficult task to the mountain already before her.

"Can you whistle?" asked Aderyn.

Given nodded her head in confusion.

"Good, Freckles will be your companion. When you need him, blow; he'll find you."

Given was excited to hear that she wouldn't be completely alone on her journey, but concern quickly shone on her face. "But, I don't know how to care for him."

Aderyn put her hand on Given's shoulder. "Freckles is a big bird; he can take care of himself...*and* he can be a mighty help in a pinch. All you need is a whistle." She put her lips together and blew lowly. A few moments later, the speckled hawk landed outside the threshold.

"Look after her friend," said Aderyn to Freckles, who appeared to respond with a nod before he thrust out of sight.

"Guess there's nothing more holding me back." Given slung her tote over her shoulder and with a wince freed the hair that had gotten caught under the sling of her tote. Taking a handful of hair she said, "Maybe I should cut it off."

"No, though haste is needed," said Aderyn. "There is still time for better. Lay your things back down." She ran her long fingers through Given's fine black hair removing the tangles, twisted it into two tight braids and tied them off with thin strips of cloth. "Now you're set."

Given stroked one of the braids. "My hair's not been like this since I was taken. Mot used to fix my hair and hers. All the Gallant women wore braids." She looked sad both for missing her mother and having to leave her child.

Aderyn stooped and lifted the tote back up to Given then pulled a small leather pouch from between her breast's and jangled the coins inside. "Almost slipped my mind. You'll need these if our plan is to work."

Given shifted the coins into a larger pouch tied about her waist. "No more delays." As she stepped backward through the threshold, she blew her sleeping baby one last kiss and glanced doubtfully at Aderyn. Loaded enough as she was with food, water and supplies, she decided it would be best to take her axe as well and scooped it up outside her house. And east through the sleepy village into the woods she sprang.

It seemed a lifetime had gone by since she'd meandered aimlessly through the woods to Bardorf, though truly only a few weeks had passed. No path had been beaten for Given through the dimly lit forest back to Coyote Lake. If she was going to make it to Bledig's cabin, she would have to rely on her knowledge of the wild and signs in the heavens. It also didn't hurt to have an extra set of eyes in the sky—and some luck for good measure. She plunged through the forest as if she knew exactly the direction she needed to go, but in fact, was only following the rising sun.

The morning wore long but her legs did not tire. She didn't yet feel lonely, for the singing birds and rambunctious squirrels kept her company. Along she traversed deeper into the woods—further from love and closer to danger. Occasionally the dense forest canopy would thin enough for her to peer up and see Freckles circling high above. Though, to Given, he appeared as nothing more than a spot whirling in the sky, she was confident that it was him and knew that he could see her far better than she could see him. "Thanks for coming along, friend."

When the sun had peaked, Given sat for a bite of cured fish and a swallow of water. Her dry mouth and rumbling stomach begged for more, but she knew she must conserve all she had in case there were delays. She had only enough food for about a week of travel

and even less water, as it would have been cumbersome to carry—
and easier to find than food in the forest at any rate.

After only a moment's rest, she was back to a determined pace,
softly humming as she went. The forest grew tired and less playful
as the heat withered all things living, but Given trekked on. The
only thing that slowed her was a longing to see her baby. *I imagine
he's giving Aderyn fits. Well, maybe not. They do love each other. I
hope he'll be okay without me.* She shook her head trying to regain
focus. *The faster I get there and find the Shepherd's Heart, the
faster I get back to my Gritsy.* Her pace redoubled at the thought,
and for the rest of the day until light from the sun vanished, she
was an unstoppable force.

The comforting moonlight was almost enough to convince Given
to move on through the night, but weariness from the day's journey
coupled with the thought of losing Freckles in the dark caused her
to stay put. She whistled lowly as Aderyn had shown her, and
Freckles screeched from a tree nearby in reply.

"Didn't even know you were there. Thanks again for your
company."

Another screech came.

Given spread a woolen blanket over a soft patch of earth and lay
on it, using her tote as a pillow. She breathed blessings toward
Grit, who she imagined was resisting Aderyn's best attempts to put
him to sleep. "May the Creator keep you safe for a high purpose.
May you grow to be kind and always defend the helpless." She
shut her eyes to the melody of crickets chirping through the gloom
and tried to sleep, but the haunting chorus of a whip-poor-will and
the cries of coyotes stirred her fear. "Not to ask too much, keep
watch over me as well," she whispered to the Creator, not knowing
if she was being heard. But not long after her request, a cool wind

rose and whooshed away the ominous sounds of night that pricked her nerves. In no time she was sleeping as if wholly secure.

At first it was a deep sleep, but sometime in the middle of her black slumber, she saw the moon casting its bright reflection on Coyote Lake as she drifted peacefully along in a canoe. But her peace turned to doubt, and doubt to horror, as her canoe crossed the middle of the lake. Two yellow eyes like beacons were set unblinkingly upon her. She tried to paddle away, but their draw was irresistible. Frantically she beat the water without success. It was no use: she was heading straight for the thing she most feared. "SEER! SEER! WHERE ARE YOU? WHY HAVE YOU ABANDONED ME?" As she cried the glowing eyes extinguished and words cut the darkness like a fiery sword, "Never have I left you. Never will I forsake you." Relief like soothing balm spread over her. When she reached the shore, there was no sign of Bledig, only a beautiful red gemstone on the sand. Blackness consumed her mind once again, and she was aware of nothing till dawn.

CHAPTER 10. NO PATH TO TREAD

*L*IGHT SHAFTS broke through the oak canopy as the call of a hawk brought Given back to consciousness. From his roosting place, Freckles spoke to Given that morning had come. "Thank you friend," she said. "You're right, it is well past time to be along." After a quick bite to break the hunger, she rolled her blanket, tucked it away, and slung her tote over her shoulder. The dream from the night before further validated her quest for the Shepherd's Heart. She was on the move once again setting as quick a pace as she had the evening before.

Traveling in the morning was her favorite time, not only because of the happy songs of birds and the coolness, but it was also the easiest time for her to tell direction. Her heading was straight towards the sun, and from what she could guess, she'd done well to stay on the right path the day before. But until she found the Afon or one of its tributaries, there'd be no way to know for sure. Any deviation in direction could take her miles off target.

Thoughts of Grit both comforted and saddened her as she traversed the lively forest. *He's probably had his breakfast by now…I wonder if Aderyn's been able to keep clothes on him. Oh, I hope he knows I didn't abandon him. I'll get back to him…I will…I must.* The undergrowth was thickening as she went along, making it even more difficult to stay a straight course. Snaky vines with thorns like fangs were curled waiting in ambush. The delicate skin on Given's legs paid the price in blood for her haste, but nothing that inconsequential could slow her.

Before her the forest floor sank into a ravine that offered a slight break in the seemingly endless ranks of trees. Hoping to find water there, Given slid down the steep embankment to the bottom. Because of her strict rationing, there was still plenty in her skins, but she was thirsty and hoped for a drink that could satisfy without emptying her stores. The creek bottom was mostly dry, Nothing more than sand with some immature greenery poking through. "Probably hadn't flowed in a couple of weeks," she thought out loud. She followed it for a while. Small puddles of mud were gathered here and there where the tiny creek bent sharply, but there was no water—not suitable for drinking anyway.

She was about to give up and continue east when she noticed the creek go into a straight away and the sandy floor turned to stone and dropped out of sight. Creeping to the edge of what, when it rained, would have been a waterfall nine or ten feet high, she discovered that the crater wallowed out by the cascading flow still held the life-giving substance Given required. She climbed cautiously down the mossy steps beside the fall and knelt beside the pool. The water was surprisingly clear and cool. With cupped hands she scooped a little and tasted. It wasn't as good as Ewe's Delight or Eurig's well perhaps, but it didn't taste bad. Lapping up a little more just to be sure, she decided it was certainly alright. *More favor from the Seer*, she thought as she filled her stomach until her sides split. After topping off her skins she ascended the rocky fall on all fours with pack on her back, seeking to regain the *path* she had abandoned in search of water.

Once atop the fall, she plodded along easily in the dry creek bottom searching for a point of exit, a clearing perchance in the dense pack of thorns and blackjack that lay on the eastern side of the ravine. But her ease was suddenly lost on a not too distant crackle of withered vegetation. She crept forward stopping every couple of steps to listen for what she thought could be her next meal. *Could it have been a deer,* she thought hopefully at first. What a meal a deer would have made. *But without spear or snare there is no way to capture such a prize,* she added to her thoughts. Her second notion was that it was probably an opossum or armadillo. Either one would make a suitable dinner and be easy enough to catch. She was about to slink around the bend in the creek bottom to put an eye on her *prey* when it dashed from hiding. From the noise of it she could tell it was a might larger than an armadillo. It wasn't particularly light of foot like a deer either. Oh no, could it be a BEAR! Gripping her axe and holding her breath, she hoped whatever it was would move on without noticing her. It was retreating, but she stood fast, not about to draw attention to herself. And even as she stood with her ears trained on the fleeing beast, she perceived not the lumbering gallop of a bear but a rhythmic pounding of earth, one big crunch followed by another. She knew of only one creature that ran about on two legs. The crunches faded and fell silent, and Given stood frozen. Suddenly she wished the thing had been a bear. Her stomach knotted with the thought of being followed. "But by whom?" she whispered. After a minute or two of absolute stillness, she inched around the bend and climbed out of the ravine through the bushes. Whoever it may have been was now far out of sight, and all she could do was move on.

For the rest of the day until the sleepy sun retired in the west, she traveled warily. Her pace slackened a bit as she spent more time looking over her shoulder and stopping to listen for unwanted company. She even whistled Freckles down to see if he could share any news. Communication with a hawk was difficult. Before she released him to circle the skies once more, she requested he warn her of any danger that might be seen.

The dull glow of evening faded like embers to ash, and Given took refuge in an ancient willow thats four large branches shot out from the trunk like fingers—all from the same place but in different directions—forming a sort of palm for her to rest in. It was unexpectedly roomy and offered plenty of comfort—as much as the cold earth anyway. But more importantly she felt safe from whatever, or whoever, may stalk through the night. To be sure she wouldn't be caught unawares, she piled all sorts of branches and twigs with leaves around the base of the tree to alert of anything approaching her roost. Of course, she still had Freckles perched a little closer to the willow's peak.

With pack stuffed under her neck and hand still clutching her axe's handle, she began to speak once again into the darkness. Prayers for Grit and Aderyn and for herself went up from her nest like incense, and much like before, comfort like a dense fog fell. Peace about what was behind her and what lay ahead sank into her soul as she slipped into the realm of unconsciousness. Nothing was spoken to her by way of dream that night; black silence was all she knew.

There was no need for Freckles's wake up call the next morning, for Given had already opened her eyes to the twilight an hour or so before sunrise. Not even a bite did she take before she was off into the shadow of the forest. The peace welcomed in her nightly prayers remained with her and her slow cautious pace from yestereve was abandoned. Like a swift westerly wind, she sliced through the undergrowth to regain time lost. *Why concern myself with what follows, when I'm charging towards what I know to be dreadful,* she reasoned.

Trees and undergrowth alike thinned little by little as she went until she came to a clearing. Sitting on the edge of the little field, she rummaged through her pack for meat to break the hunger. It had been more than a day since her last meal, and her stomach's cry could no longer be ignored. *I wonder if Freckles is finding enough food.* She could see her friend wrestling drafts high overhead. *So loyal a friend he is. If ever I'm able, I'll treat him to a feast he won't soon forget.*

After a bit of dried fish and some water, she was back to cutting a trail through the re-thickened wilderness. As she went, the north wind, which had been slowly gaining vigor throughout the day, suddenly brought a great wall of cool air that seemed to collide with the stubborn hot mass that had settled in place. For a while, the two mammoths had a kind of shoving match. Wind swirled in all directions while temperatures swung from cool to hot and back again, until the old man from the north finally triumphed. And as *he* shouldered the heat to the south, angry clouds erupted, blanketing the woods in shadow and sending crashes and booms throughout the land. Given could see rain like curtains being pulled toward her, and in an instant, she was overcome and drenched. Heeding not the waves of rain splashing over her nor the blasts of lightning cutting through the darkness, she continued into the torrent. With no sun in sight to lead her, she used the wind as her guide, keeping the cool north always to her left.

Hours passed, and the storm screamed furiously still, whittling away Given's resolve. The black sky hurled flaming arrows that pierced the earth all around. Each one caused an explosion of sound. Given had never encountered a storm of such ferocity. Panic struck the poor lass, and frantic tears like the rain poured. *Will this storm have an end?* There was another flash, so close she could feel the heat, and the following boom loud enough to physically shake her, unnerving enough to cause an involuntary release down her inner thigh. In a terrible stupor she looked to the south where one final bolt struck, but unlike the others, which vanished in an instant, it lingered. A shape, a figure likened to a man with one leg, formed in the brilliance. It moved alongside her for a moment, and as quickly as it fell, leapt like a ram back into the pitch sky. Not a boom or crash echoed behind it; instead, there was a whisper, "P*ress on daughter, press on.*"

Almost immediately, it seemed the tempest had had his say and moved on to the south. The sun smiled through the canopy, adding warmth to the calm that had suddenly overtaken the forest. Given gave a hesitant smile too as she wrung her tightly braided hair until no more water would come forth. "Always a test it seems," she said, half talking to herself, half intending a prayer. "Not sure I passed that one, crying and piddling on myself and all. But except for the need to dry out, I'm still in fine condition…and on the right path too I hope." And though she was in a secluded forest, she hid in the bushes, removed her buckskin tunic, and squeezed the water from it as best she could. As she stood with her clothes twisted in hand, wearing nothing more than the skin she was born in, she heard once again the footfalls of a man or woman —or something with two legs. Squishing in the wet turf and cracking over fallen twigs and branches, whoever it was approached with caution—stopping after every few steps as though in search of something *or someone.* Given crouched, covered herself with her saturated tunic and focused both ears and eyes toward the incoming stranger in an attempt to solve the riddle of who might be following her. She could perceive little. Stretching her neck this way and that offered no help; The undergrowth was too thick. *It's just as well. Better to not know who stalks than to know and be snagged.* The squishing and cracking had halted completely now as the stranger searched in earnest—or perhaps stopped for a rest. Given waited like a stone for a long while. At last, and all in a hurry as though spooked, the unguessed visitant sprang into motion and ran out of earshot.

Given waited a while longer, squatting and listening in silence, until finally she arose, her thighs aflame from being hunkered so long. *I can wait no more,* she thought. *Surely they've moved on.* She clothed herself with her wet garment and went onward as well. She hadn't a clue how long the storm had raged, but the sun now blazed the western sky behind and dried her as she walked. By now she was all but convinced that she was being followed. There was little chance of encountering anyone in this wilderness, yet to have two encounters in as many days seemed too much for coincidence. *But who and why?* Perhaps one answer could take care of both questions.

Nevertheless, she carried on as before—eyes ahead with little pause for rest—until the sun had sunk and it was too dark to continue. With no tree to perch in as the night before, Given set her back against a sheer rock face about twice her height. To her front and sides she had once again piled all sorts of leaves and branches for noise making; and beneath she had stacked the driest of the nearby forest litter, which was no more dry than the morning grass in the coolness of spring. But her wet bedding did little to rob her of sleep. It was a crime committed mostly by a worrisome mind. Still in the forefront was who could be tracking her. This mystery baffled her. Why would anyone put out such an effort? She also wondered marvelously at the lightning that appeared to skip alongside her. Was it real or imagined? If reality, was the design to comfort her only? And in the bowels of night, as sleep's veil was beginning to cover her, a final question wormed in, *What happened to Freckles*? He had seldom escaped her view since the expedition began, but now she hadn't seen him since the outbreak of the storm, and her whistles were answered only by the sounds of night. Not even her most fervent prayers could lull on this night with so many questions to ponder.

CHAPTER 11. A FRIEND INDEED

GIVEN HAD hardly received a blink of sleep before the blackened sky turned ashen, and though the sun was yet an hour or two below the eastern horizon, she had no need to remain still, tortured in restless thought. So after a double helping of cured fish, Given rose from her soggy nest. She was a little groggy, but at least her aching legs felt rested. Freckles was another tale. Where had he gotten off to? Given let out a long low whistle and listened for a hawk's response. There was none. *Perhaps he'll spot me when I start off again. Doubtless he had enough sense to find shelter from the storm.*

She pulled her pack over her shoulder, and with axe in hand, pushed through the *alarms* she'd set at night. With no stars or shadows to guide, she used the pale eastern glow and moss growth to guess at a heading. "Thank you for the rain," she prayed as she walked. "May today bring blessings in a less…violent way."

The heavy rain did well to restart the flow of many streams and creeks, providing plenty of potable water; yet the parched earth had swallowed much of yesterday's torrent, leaving only a few scattered bogs, which did little to impede the determined traveller. She had made up her mind once again to not fear what was behind and to attack what was ahead. And attack she did: the entire fourth day she hardly slowed for rest, to check her heading, or have a bite to eat. Her pace was a steady trot for a long while.

***

At day's end, Given had gone several leagues through the wild lands, but still she had neither heard screech nor seen feather of Freckles. Her cheeks ached and head was faint from whistling, and worn from haste, she didn't bother setting alarms, reasoning that anyone still tagging her after all the running was too determined to hinder anyway. Bedding in a patch of bunchgrass, she made one more unsuccessful attempt to signal Freckles before darkness blanketed her mind. Her slumber was thorough and long. She slept well into the second hour of her fifth day of travel and would have stayed asleep longer if not for the smashing thud of a rotten oak felled by the enlivened south wind.

"Now you've done it," she said to herself. "Gone and slept half the day away. I guess I'll be running again today. Can't say I prefer it." If she only knew how close she was then to Coyote Lake, she might have started a bit slower. But her food stores were adequate and she decided it was okay to have a double helping for breakfast to fuel a faster pace. She ate enough to satisfy, and after whistling a few more times with no reply, she flew.

By the third hour, the sun was already beating the earth—and Given—with blazing hammer blows, and by the fourth she was flowing more like honey than a mountain stream. There was no breeze, and even the shade provided by the oaks and elms was insufficient. Her parched mouth begged for a draft, so she took out her skins obligingly. The first swallow was too big for her throat which had dried and shriveled from want of liquid. The cool wet raked hard down into her stomach, causing Given to cough and gag. But after her throat was primed, she half emptied her water bag in a couple more gulps. "I needed that one," she said hoarsely.

Coming to a slight clearing in the trees, she shaded her eyes from the intense rays and scanned the sky for her bird friend, wondering at the speck seen circling a mile high. Directing her whistle upward there was no reply from above, nor did the bird stoop any lower. *Perhaps he can't hear from such a distance.*

101

When her dark brown eyes could no longer tolerate the sun's intensity, she closed them tightly and rubbed with her finger and thumb until the burning sensation had been extinguished.

She reopened her eyes to doubles and fuzz, and her vision was recouping quickly but not soon enough. Through the clearing only a few dozen leaps away, she glimpsed the blurry image of someone racing toward her. Her heart bounded, and as she reached for her axe, her stomach sank. It wasn't beside her. She had dropped it to take a drink, and without realizing it, wandered a few dozen steps while looking up at the sky for Freckles. She dashed for her weapon, but it was too late. He was upon her. Like an angry bear, he drove her petite frame into the turf. Lying with face smashed into the grass with the man's knee in her back and hands like talons digging into the flesh on her upper arms, she writhed and screamed to no avail. Straddling her lower back he pulled her head up by her braids as she tried unsuccessfully to buck him.

He bent close to her ear as if to whisper but spoke in a usual tone, "I guess even a snake lucks into a meal now and again." He inhaled deeply through his nose and smacked his lips, "Tasty."

The man paused for a moment, allowing his words to sink in. Given was bathed in rage as she recalled the words she'd exchanged with Gar at their last meeting. Feeling him pressed against her was sickening, and with all her might she twisted to her back to face him. He pinned her arms down at the wrist almost immediately. She conjured the biggest ball of spit she could and launched it into his face before demanding that he remove his filth from atop her. All it gained her was a slap.

"How…how'd you find me—," she grunted and squirmed.

"Like I said, lucky. I was out trapping after visiting an old friend, when down the path came a fox without a hole to hide in….lucky."

Licking his lips with eyes full of lust he scanned her. "I would have paid twice the going price for this, but since you denied the offer, I'll have to take it for free...Then I'll fetch you back to Bledig for a bounty." The lust in his eyes flared to a maddening hunger as he continued, "Or maybe I'll keep you for my own."

Bledig? Given thought. *How does he know...*but as she gazed furiously at her assailant, the fog in her mind lifted, revealing an unexpected memory. She could picture Gar with hair, and with a yellow-eyed monster he came to steal her away. She was young and helpless as they broke her mother, took Given and defiled her. They played a game of chance with beans to see who would keep her, and the yellow-eyed fellow won.

Noticing the mixed display of disgust and fear that came over Given's face, Gar said, "Figured me out, didn't you? I had you pegged the day after I first saw you with Birdie. You seemed too familiar to let my mind rest, but I couldn't remember where I'd seen you. But the way that pup a' yours favors his pa with those yellow eyes helped me remember." Gar licked his lips. "Should have never played that game of beans with Bledig. He cheats and lies every chance he gets. You might have belonged to me this whole time, but I fell a couple beans short. Guess it doesn't matter now though, since fate's paid what was owed...Yeah, I think I'll keep you."

He let go of her wrist, lowered his hand to her thigh, and began pulling up her tunic. But with her left hand now free, Given drove her thumb as far as she could into his eye socket. He snatched her wrist away and delivered another blow to her cheek.

"Don't struggle and I'll leave you in one piece, but I'll be taking what I want whether you're aware or knocked senseless." He struck her a couple more times—once making her see flashes of white—to prove his point. "There's no use resisting."

He raked his grimy paw up her thigh as she flailed wildly. So focused on his mucky deed, Gar didn't see the small shadow gliding swiftly over the landscape toward him. Freckles had found his friend at last, and none too soon. With powerful talons he ripped some flesh from the top of Gar's head before thrusting back into the clear blue. Screaming obscenities he stroked his wounds. He lowered his bloody palm and glared briefly before rising to scan his surroundings for the attacker. With head swiveling in all directions, he searched in desperation, but his assailant had seemingly vanished.

The moment of distraction was what Given needed to slither unnoticed to her axe. Gar was large and strong, and maybe she couldn't win the fight even with a weapon in hand, but she was going to put one up nonetheless. She didn't run. She had had a belly full of that; instead, she charged with the axe raised to her ear and dropped the dull side of it on the back of her enemy's head. His hands flew out in front of him, and with a screech he plopped face first into the grass.

Breathing heavily, Given eyed her foe with disdain. She raised the axe once more above her head to finish the job but couldn't swing. The thought of killing a man—unarmed, unaware, unconscious, no matter what he had done or was attempting to do —stopped her. It went far beyond taking the lives of beasts and didn't require Gallant tribal law to convince her it was wrong. A virtue deep within the wells of her soul was enough to do that. "I am not your judge," said Given, lowering her axe.

"Regardless, a death stroke would have been a just ending for that one," came a hoarse voice from behind her. Startled, she turned to face the newcomer who had his finger still pointing at the fallen Gar. "But if you don't want to end him, I'll at least need to cure him of lust." He unsheathed a long silver knife that flashed in the sun. With eyes wide Given took two steps back and raised her axe.

It was the *Turkey Buzzard* from Wether's Field, Given's fear incarnate. His scarred powerful form towered over her. His crystal eyes peered through his gross disfigurement into her own.

Seeing her terror he said, "Neither fear nor fight me Given the Gallant, for I have been summoned to your aid…which it seems you need little of." He strapped the knife once more in leather and put his hands up as a sign of peace. "And if you can, excuse my appearance for which there is no help." The man appeared to smile —or at least his teeth became more visible—but his face was too disfigured to reveal true expression.

"A…aid? Wh..who sent you to help? How do you know my name?" Given kept her axe high and did not move.

"I am an outcast, scorned by my own people. I have no captain or king to serve. Only to the Shepherd of Men, Solas, will my knee bow. He asked me to help you…"

At the sound of Solas's name a chill struck Given's core and permeated to her extremities. "Why wasn't I told about your coming? Have you been following me the entire time?"

"To answer your second question first, yes, I've been tracking you since your last visit to Wether's Field—the day Solas summoned you in the woods. He called me that day. You were easy enough to follow most of the time, but in the storm I nearly lost you. I prayed for help." He pointed into the sky. "Lightning fell as a beacon." He dropped his hand and looked intently at Given. "And to your first question: to further prepare and test you. You've been dealt a task of uncommon importance that few on the earth could perform. If all goes well, you'll never be at it alone, but the strength to bear the weight without companion may be needed. In the East a menace is rising. Three relics with untold power are unaccounted for." Squeezing his hand into a fist, "The fourth is cradled in the hands of a demented king beyond the wall of Auber Civitas...and *you* are the keeper of the fifth. It is yours to retrieve and protect. Doomed might we all be if you should fail, and the fragments of the Shepherd's Body should be united and possessed by one. Once you retrieve the Heart, none of the Deroheed—or even their offspring—can know where you keep it. Solas believes they might still be subject to their master Derog, no matter how much hate they may have for him. But what to do with the relic and where to keep it, Solas was not clear."

All that the man said turned slowly in Given's mind. With her weapon still held high she pondered his words thoroughly without speaking. At length she reasoned that the man knew too much of her quest—of the Heart and of Solas—to be false; yet she continued to prod his hideousness with untrusting eyes and kept her axe tightly gripped before her.

As if reading her thoughts the man spoke, "Sometimes our own vision can be a veil. If you are to have confidence in me, you'll need to go beyond what you see."

As the two stared at each other, Given thought of their first encounter. She ran, but he didn't follow. She had entered his domain, but he did nothing. This man's intention had never been to harm. The terror inside her subsided as a seed of trust planted itself in her soul and began to grow. She could feel her guard lower and her muscles ease.

"O—okay," she said. "What now?"

"We'd better get along, but first I must oversee his sentence." He motioned toward Gar who had begun to stir. "And it would be best to do it before he wakes." He removed his knife once more.

Given moved between the two men. "I cannot let you kill him in this state. I'll have no part in a slaying."

"Be at peace. I'm not going to kill him." He pointed the blade toward his own loins. "As I said, I'm going to cure him of lust. Perhaps he won't be so vicious as a eunuch."

Given didn't move. The thought of removing body parts as a punishment had never occurred to her, and as far as she could remember had no part in Gallant Law. "I—I'm not sure that's the right thing either."

"This filth would have defiled and enslaved you and will attempt it again with you or another maiden if nothing is done to prevent it. With no dungeon to cast him in and death as no option, it's the only way. It is the way of my former people."

The man was right, thought Given. When Gar wakes and recovers from the blow, he'll return to his treachery if nothing is done to stop him. She sighed, lowering her eyes and head in submission and stepped out of the way. "It's nothing I wish to see."

"Gather your things and be on your way. I'll do what needs to be done and catch up after I've had my say."

Given scooped up her pack and as quickly as she could crossed the little field. Without looking back, she broke through the tree line and headed into the forest before her while humming Mot's song to drown out the sounds of torture she couldn't stand to hear. But as the wails rose from behind her, she paused to cover her ears and hoped that the Turkey Buzzard's cut was quick and clean and that he hadn't changed his mind about killing Gar.

CHAPTER 12. SKELETON WOOD

IT TOOK Given's new traveling companion a little while to do his dreadful deed and catch back up with her. In the meantime, Given had called down Freckles and thanked him the best she knew how without any fresh fish handy. Stroking his speckled brown plumage she said, "I am forever in your debt, mighty one. You have guided me, kept me company, comforted me in my distress, and now rescued me from the evil one. May long life and plentiful prey find you." Freckles screeched his acceptance and propelled into the sky. He was a free bird able to go here and there at his own command held captive only by his loyalty to his friends.

Given waited for Freckles to soar from sight before she continued on her eastward trek. Dipping under a sagging oak branch, she turned to see the *Turkey Buzzard* approaching. For the first time she was able to view him without a veil of fear—at least most of it was gone. He certainly was tall—maybe as tall as Eurig. But unlike Eurig who was sheerly massive, this man was lean and muscular—beneath the terrible scars. She tried to guess his age as he approached, but his disfigurement made it difficult. Judging from his form she thought he had to be around forty years.

"He won't be bothering you again," the man said solemnly when he was closer. "And don't worry about him causing trouble in Bardorf either. He knows the consequences for trying." Crossing under the oak after Given, he walked up beside her. "I might have worried that he would return to harm your youngling, but your son wouldn't be much safer if he were with Solas himself. Aderyn knows how to care for her own."

Given was relieved to hear that the man was true to his word and hadn't slaughtered Gar. And she too had reasoned that Aderyn, who had command of the birds, would have no trouble handling Gar if need be, but the man's mention of her made her ask, "You know Aderyn?"

As if the question took the man by surprise, he hesitated before saying, "For many years."

Given said nothing, hoping he would surrender more information without being prodded, but he walked on. She recalled how Aderyn acted when Given told her of her first encounter with the Turkey Buzzard. She could sense Aderyn knew something about him but hurried to change the subject instead of divulging. Realizing it must be a sore subject, Given changed direction.

"In all the haste, you never gave your name," said Given.

"Aksel." He spoke, but his mind was elsewhere.

"Aksel," Given said with a smile, happy she could finally relate him to a name rather than a big ugly bird. "Even in these pitiful circumstances, it is good to meet you."

Aksel nodded without a word. Given was beginning to think her new companion must not be much for words—a man of action perhaps—but she had had enough silence traveling alone and was determined to start a conversation.

"The lightning that drew you to me, was it Solas?" she asked.

"It was more likely his Father, for Solas cannot be everywhere... but his Father...his Father is in all that is good and will guide the paths of those who'll listen."

Given felt small. Why would this powerful Creator waste even a thought on her let alone pierce the sky with lightning so she could be found? She was but an orphan, a servant, a slave. All was quiet again as she contemplated her purpose in this tale that seemed much too big for her.

At length her mind meandered back to Grit and what Gar said about him looking like his father. Was Bledig the *friend* Gar had gone to visit? Surely that was his real reason for being out here. And if Gar did talk to Bledig, then Bledig may know now that she had been hiding in Bardorf and what she'd been doing to make a living there. Would her plan still work if he knew?

Given looked up at Aksel and pointed behind her. "Did *he* speak to you about my master before you sent him away?"

"No, but we didn't exactly converse. He had too many other… *concerns.* No doubt you know that monster. I'd seen him before in the woods."

"Yes, today wasn't the first time he's tried to force his way. A few weeks ago at Wether's—"

"I was there that day as well," Aksel interrupted. "Thought I might need to intervene, but you handled him well enough."

Given was surprised to hear she was being looked after and a little embarrassed by the praise. "Thanks," she said looking at her feet. "I knew him even before I escaped to Bardorf though—before I was old enough to defend myself. I realized it earlier…I could see his face so clearly when he was on top of me. And his words brought memories flooding back. My old master, Bledig, and he were the ones who took me from my mother." She sighed deeply. "Too bad no one was looking out for us then. I still wonder if Mot survived the night they took me."

"I wish I had the answer," said Aksel. "I know enough of loss: to wonder what has happened to your beloved can be the greatest torment. It's like leaving a wound unbound and letting it fester in the heat. No, I don't have the answer, but maybe we will discover it before this quest ends."

She knew little about Aksel, but she could sense his sincerity. There was nothing fake about him. His words sparked hope once again that Mot could be found. "Do you know of my tribe, the Gallants?" she asked.

"I've roamed the woods west from Auber Civitas's great wall to the Bighorn Mountains for nearly two decades now, meeting more than a man's share of tribesmen, farmers, hunters and trappers. I have forgotten many-a-name and face, but the Gallants I remember well. I was severely maimed and cast out by my people, but I was discovered nearly dead by a most blessed soul and taken to the Gallants in the Afon Valley. In my plight Chief Cynfor and his people cared for me. I had no hope, and in truth no desire to live, but they nursed me to health and their jovial spirits and kind hearts helped heal mine. Though I was filled with hate and wished for death when I arrived, I went away with little interest in revenge and had hope for a long life. About a year after the Gallants took me in, I left the Afon Valley seeking only to find the one who had saved me from death and taken me to the Gallants."

Given's heart skipped upon hearing this revelation. "Cynfor is my Father," she declared in wonderment. "My people brought you back to health! How can it be?"

"It's a marvelous web the Creator weaves," said Aksel. "We are all connected in some way."

"I...I wonder if you met my mother—when you were with the Gallants. Her name is Serenis."

Aksel smiled, and this time Given was sure of it. "Serenis, Cynfor's favored maiden," he said. "No man could glimpse paradise and soon forget. She is a woman of unmeasurable virtue.

111

More than any other, it was she who breathed life back into this deadman. Her lyrics and ointments treated my wounds. Her melodies cured my soul. Some days she would spend hours at my side nursing, singing, praying. I was a stranger. She treated me as a friend.

Love draws friends to thy side
Ever in soul to abide
Even when you are away
In your heart they shall stay

Staring at Given, he drew her eyes to his and said, "I am indebted to the Gallants and to you. My life is your life. If you wish to return to the Afon Valley in search of your mother after we recover the stone, we shall."

Given was beside herself. It was all so much to contemplate. She knew deep down that one day she would return to search for Mot, but to have help offered by someone who knows the Valley—by someone who owes his life—was too good to be true. Thoughts like whirlwinds twisted in her mind as she stood silent.

"You can decide when the time comes," Aksel's voice broke through Given's befuddlement. "It's a lot to think about, I know, but we'd better get along. I want to be through the cursed land before sundown." He pointed towards the blackened trees scattered before them. "This wood was damned long before the assault of the Deroheed began. It was the first great settlement of man west of Auber Civitas, but before it was known as Bella Floris and was Derog's most beloved garden. Lore tells that when he first saw what man had done with his planting—using the trees for homes and walls and tearing through his meadows to build roads—he was enraged and spoke a curse over it in his anger,

Until Lord of Land Returns
Death there will be
All that is green shall burn
With these robbers and these fiends

"Neither weed nor thorn, nor anything desirable has lived there since, and it has since been known as Skeleton Wood, for something in the air has kept the trees as they now stand—like bones in a tomb. It may be imagined, but when I'm in there it's as though life is seeping from my skin."

Given had come through Skeleton Wood on her flight to Bardorf, but it was night at the time, and she thought it had been recently burned. She certainly didn't fear passing through the first time, but now knowing it was cursed—that life could not exist there—made her anxious to get through quickly. Despite the intense evening sun she doubled her pace, Aksel stayed by her side, and about as high above earth as man's eye could see, Freckles circled. Perhaps not even he wanted any part of this doomed land.

It took a couple hours at their enlivened pace to cross through the desolation. When the two travelers finally spotted green on the other side, Given held her breath until she crossed the threshold that separated the living from the dying lands. Under the twisted canopy of an enormous oak she stopped to breathe. "Maybe it was my mind's trick, but the air seemed to grow thick and foul," she panted. "I could no longer bear to take it in."

"If a trick, it is a good one; it was in my head as well," said Aksel. "We'd better get away from this loathsome place as quickly as we can."

Given agreed. They both glanced back at the dead lands in wonder. Derog's dark magic still gripped it tightly, smothering all life. But the land that bordered was a complete contrast, densely packed with vibrant green trees and vines, alive with the melodies of birds. It was like a desert butted against a rainforest. The two turned back toward their destination and trotted a ways before stopping for a drink.

"It does my heart good to hear you speak well of my Father," said Given. "I tell myself that he was a good man, but it feels like a lie. Remembering how he traded me to those monsters still guts me." She held a limb so it wouldn't swat Aksel's face as he went by.

"If he hadn't traded you, where would you be now? Cynfor was not an inadequate man or chief. He cared for his own and helped those he was able. If he let you go, be assured it was out of need."

"My head knows you're right, but the heart mends reluctantly."

"Without doubt," said Aksel, fingering a scar that ran from his temple to the corner of his mouth. "But it *will* mend."

***

Darkness sprawled over the land as Given and Aksel lay side-by-side under star and moon; and Freckles perched above on the branch of a gnarly post oak. It was the first time since her quest began that she felt wholly secure. She pondered if she should continue with her plan to go it alone at first to find the Heart, or maybe Aksel could scare the location out of Bledig. Her thoughts wandered to Grit and Aderyn, and she began to pour out silent prayers for them. And though the only sound coming forth was from the motion of her lips and tongue, Aksel heard.

"Say one for me as well if you don't mind...for guidance in particular."

Given was a little startled by the request and embarrassed that she could be heard, but did as she was asked. After she felt satisfied with praying, she leaned up to look towards Aksel and spoke to the shadowed figure lying beside her.

"I don't like to question what I've been told, but it is difficult. As I lie awake at night the same questions strike me, causing doubt. You asked me to pray for guidance...I wonder why we've been sent on a quest we know no end to. We go after the Shepherd's Heart, but what then? What shall I do with it? I've no power to protect it from evil. And you've been sent to my aid but haven't a notion what to do with it either. Why doesn't Solas protect the relics himself?"

"No doubt he could," said Aksel. "But it is not his place. As gifts to man, he cannot take the relics back...Even if you tried to give them back, he would not take them. Dominion over earth—its mountains and rivers, forests and meadows, plants and beasts—has been given to man. What we do with it is up to us. We can choose to preserve and protect or uproot and destroy. Either way, it is ours. Solas will not take it back, but he does have a plan." Aksel chuckled a little before he said, "Solas's path for us might be filled with pits and snares and riddled with pain, but have faith in his command. He's been doing this a long time, and he knows what he's doing."

Though the answer didn't shine any more light on her future, Given was at least a little reassured. She knew the war between her faith and doubt wasn't over, but for tonight her faith was strong enough to allow her to sleep. There was one more thing she had to know.

"Aksel, might I ask something about you?"

"You might, but I might withhold the answer even though you ask."

"Fair enough," Given said. "What happened to your body and voice? Why would your people treat you thus?"

"The short answer, fire and smoke spoiled my flesh and ruined my voice. Lust and greed drove it to fruition."

He didn't speak for a long while, and Given, judging he had surrendered as much as he was going to, lay back down and closed her eyes. "Until first light, sleep well."

"Apologies," said Aksel. "The long answer is still coming if you desire it." He sighed deeply and continued. "I was reared in Auber Civitas by my mother alone. Father died before I could remember. All I know of him is what mother told me, and what she told me is what I wanted to become. She said he was strong, so I strived for strength. She said he was brave, so I became fearless. She said he had faith, so I believed. That was my downfall. I placed faith in the wrong thing—man.

"I had a brother who I was devoted to. Side-by-side we traversed through life. He was crafty. I was strong and brave—the perfect pair. As we aged we were competitive: racing, wrestling, fighting, scheming. But no competition was as fierce as ours for love. A woman—the most magnificent star in all of Auber Civitas— snagged both our eyes and crippled my heart. We both tried our hardest to win her hand, but in the end I was victorious. After the maiden declared her love for me, my brother was never the same. His envy choked all care he once had for me. I was too blind to see what was happening. He set me up and exposed me as a traitor, *proved* that I was trading Civitian iron to our enemies—the savage tribes west of the city. It was a transgression punishable by death, whether royal or common. As was the custom of my people, I was stripped of all but my weapon and bound to a pyre outside the city gates. The smoke of the fire thrashed my bellows. The flames ravaged my flesh. All went black. I knew nothing until I woke days later under the care of the Gallants.

"All I had known, all that I had loved was taken. My desire to return has not diminished. I still wonder what has become of my mother and brother and city, but my Star shall never see me like this—a monster. 'Tis better she remembers me as I was than her eyes view me as I am now." Aksel fell silent.

Given thought for a while about Aksel's plight. At length she said, "A tragedy it is, to never see those you'd loved. The pain our souls can endure would crush our bodies." Given thought a bit longer and sniggered warmly. "I wonder…does Solas pursue anyone who isn't wounded?"

"Only the broken need mending," replied Aksel. "I shall see you at first light…" He closed his eyes and fell asleep, but Given lay awake for some time thinking about all that had transpired.

***

When dawn came, Aksel was already about the land in search of something fresh to eat. He'd fished a couple of Feather Fins from a brook less than half a mile east of their camp. Given was amazed to see him send sparks flying through the air and into the tinder with only flint and the blade of his knife. "Never would I have turned a stick with bow and string if I had known of this. How does it work?"

117

Aksel slid the blade across the flint a couple more times flinging sparks onto the ground before handing them to her. Given made a few unsuccessful attempts to get a spark.

"Flatten your blade some," said Askel, pressing on Given's hand.

She struck again, this time sending sparks and igniting the tinder. The ease of it was such a surprise that she forgot to nurture the flame. It died. Again she struck successfully igniting more tinder. This time, she blew until it was aflame and shifted it to the kindling.

"Shiny blades that protect *and* make fire, and people who can control the minds of animals." Given chuckled as she piled larger wood pieces onto the fire. "I wonder what other magic I've missed caged at Coyote Lake."

The flame grew and died back down again as Aksel roasted the fish over it. After it was cooked, he served Given her meal piping hot on a skewer. As she ate, Given couldn't help thinking it was a breakfast fit for royalty—one that she neither paid for nor toiled over. "Thank you for this meal and knowledge…and for your companionship. Whatever happens I am most grateful for your help."

Aksel bowed in acknowledgment and stood to gather their supplies. "Our target is near." He said pointing his finger toward the rising sun. "The stream that cradled these fish feeds the Afon directly. Coyote Lake lies only about five leagues to the east of where we now stand."

Given's face drooped. "Only five leagues? You're sure?"

"It has been years since I last passed through, but I remember this valley well," said Aksel. "Be assured: we're less than a day's march now."

"If it be so, we must linger here for a bit. My time to face Bledig has not yet come?"

"Whether we go now or later, you must confront him in due course. Is it fear that restrains you still?"

Given's face flushed red. "If it was only fear, I would be thankful, but what I wait for may be the thing that saves me from defilement." She pulled a bundle of cloth from her pack.

"So that is your plan to stave off his lust," said Aksel. "What if it doesn't work?"

"In all the years as his slave, not once did he approach me when I had an issue of blood. Woman's curse became my blessing and perhaps now will buy me enough time to complete my task unspoiled. But I still fear his fury…can it be restrained?"

Aksel placed his hand on Given's shoulder. "I'm not sure Solas meant for it to happen this way, child. I can't bear to let you go at it alone and be harmed."

The two stood silently as Given contemplated Aksel's offer for help. At length she said, "Though the reason is a mystery, Solas charged me with this task. We may never find Bledig or the Heart with you at my side. I must do this one thing—if nothing else—alone."

"So be it Given the Gallant. May the Creator light your path and guard you from treachery."

CHAPTER 13. INTO THE FLAMES

THE NEXT few days crawled along as Given waited for her *visitor*. Never had she been so anxious for menstruation to begin. The two friends passed some of the time talking but spent a lot longer fishing, which helped relieve their inherent worries and kept their bellies full. Freckles stayed mostly out of sight but could be seen swooping low for a meal on occasion.

Starting a fire with flint and blade continued to amaze Given. Curious as to what other wonders had been concealed from her, she probed Aksel to tell her more of Auber Civitas. The stories of great walls and houses, a palace made of stone, and metal armor resembled fantasy more than reality to a girl who hadn't seen much beyond the Afon Valley. She was delighted to hear Askel speak of swords and shields and training for battle, and her mouth watered as he spoke of the great feasts and festivals. But what grabbed her attention more than all—the thing that sent her heart soaring—was the idea of marriage. She'd never heard of such a thing, a man committing his life to one woman, and she returning the pledge. If there was anything that sounded more fantastical, she hadn't heard it; yet she loved to hear of the Auber marriage ceremonies, and the idea of spending her life with a man—one who she cared deeply for and who reciprocated her love—was incomparable. Her mind wandered to Orson, and she blushed thinking about the possibility of marrying him. She wondered if he ever thought of her the same way, if he would be willing to devote himself to her alone. But now such thoughts were only a distraction from her inevitable confrontation with death.

***

The time came for Given to depart, and though Aksel could predict Given's response, he offered his help one final time.

"Pray for me instead," is all Given replied before turning toward the dreadful uncertainty. Carrying only her pack with dwindled supply and a pouch of coins, Given headed toward the rising sun.

Aksel bowed low but said nothing as his friend faded east. Though he was inclined to follow her, he concluded that now was his time to wait. She was right: If Solas charged her with this task, who was he to contend.

Given traipsed alongside the stream where she and Askel had caught most of their recent meals. It meandered gently back and forth cutting through forest and field ever seeking lower ground. Pressing on through the late summer's heat, she continued without stopping for rest or water. She trusted Askel's judgment of the distance to Coyote lake, believing she could get there before twilight at a slower pace, but she'd had enough waiting. Anticipating the outcome had become more torturous than hurrying to unveil it.

Freckles screeched from the sky's upper limit, reassuring Given that she wasn't alone. Though she was appreciative of his company, she couldn't risk even the slightest chance of Freckles's presence creating suspicion in a man so keenly aware of things in and around his territory. Whistling him down she shook her head and sighed. "You have been my eyes and rear guard, and I am grateful. But for now your duty to me has been fulfilled. You must leave me, lest you place us both in greater peril and jeopardize our purpose. Back to Aderyn you must go…And when you get there, look out for Grit as well." At first Freckles did nothing but stare blankly as though he didn't understand what she was saying; but after a few moments, he screeched a reply and thrust out of sight, leaving Given to wonder if she had done the right thing.

Before her the brook widened, and through the sagging elm and willow branches, she could see its cool clear waters vanish into a murky flow where it merged with a river. It was the Afon. She shuddered as memories, both fond and loathsome, came rushing back. She'd only been out of the valley a month or so, but it felt much longer.

"There'll be no turning back now," Given said aloud as she slashed through a thicket and crept to the river's edge. Tears were welling in her eyes, but she blinked them back. Her nerves—her emotions—battled her resolve but could not master her. "Only a few more miles." She mouthed a silent prayer and flung a stone into the deep. "No turning back."

Continuing east along the south side of the river, she had a mostly clear path to tread. The thinning oaks, elms and willows were replaced by cypress with their *knees* poking out from the water, but their high branches were not a hindrance. After about an hour of walking, Given began to recognize the scenery. To her right was a mammoth poplar she'd retreated to as a girl after her first thrashing by Bledig. A little ahead was a rock jetty where she used to come to pray for relief. The beautiful landscape that should have brought joy to the viewer only conveyed dreadful thoughts to her.

Now, with less than a mile to the cabin, she persisted. She tried to remain quiet and alert, not so she would go unnoticed—with Bledig on guard she knew that would be impossible—rather, she didn't want to be caught unaware. If he was going to hurt her, she wanted to see it coming. The cabin drew near, and there was still no hint of Bledig. *Probably out trapping, or maybe fishing until twilight. He'll show before nightfall.*

Up to the cabin she crept listening and watching. She slid the door to the side and craned her neck to see inside. *Empty,* she thought, taking a couple of steps inside. *But the same as I left it.* Surveying the one room shanty, she could see a mat was still on the floor and the barren shelves had not been restocked. Even without the owner around, being back in the cabin made her quiver. "What am I doing here?" she whispered before stepping outside to see a distant figure coming toward her from the lake.

She tried but couldn't calm her shaking as the man walked steadily nearer. He was empty-handed and wearing nothing but a loin cloth and a grin, his scraggly form a dull bronze in the evening sun.

"Almost gave up on catching anything for supper," announced Bledig. "Almost quit….run outta hope. But this whips anything I could have pulled from that ol' lake." He moved close to Given while eyeing her from head to toe. She shook as Bledig ran his crooked little finger down one of her braids and over her tunic to her thigh. His mouth was close enough she could feel his breath.

"Where've you been off to?"

"I…I had to go," Given said, continuing to shake. "Had to find someone—worthy to take Grit…couldn't let you sell him to just anyone." Given held up the small pouch of coins that Aderyn had Given her. "I got the money, but he had to go to someone who'd not harm him."

Bledig pushed away and snatched the pouch. "Aren't you a cunnin' wench. Thought I'd ruin your mutt did you?" He reached back and delivered an open handed blow to Given's cheek. "This may be enough ta cover the boy…but that's it." Putting his lips near Given's cheek he continued, "You owe me a clump more than the boy's price."

"You're right, I do…but now isn't a good time," said Given as she took a step back knowing well what she *owed* Bledig. But she explained no further, for she knew that like a dog Bledig could already sense her heat and smell the uncleanness of her cycle.

"Huh! You must be wishing for death. More than a month gone, now returning to me in the stink of your filth." He delivered another slap. "I should break you." He pulled her close and pressed his lips over her ear, "Or maybe I'll forget the rules."

Given wanted to pull away, but knew he would still get what he wanted whether she resisted or not. It was only a matter of being beaten first. As he felt his way over her body, squeezing and clawing her most sensitive regions, Given thought of the warrior friend she'd left behind. *If only Aksel were here…He'd cure this monster.*

But Given didn't need Aksel's help on this day, for Bledig's arousal died as quickly as it came when he brought his hand up to Given's rags. "Yech! I can't do it…bet you planned it this way, didn't you?" he said, withdrawing from her. "You'll owe me double after you clean up." Eyeing the tunic Aderyn had given her, he continued, "Make it triple…them clothes didn't come free…Now go fetch me some supper." He walked to the river to wash his hands.

Given sighed, relieved to have survived the first encounter, but was far from the clear. Scrambling to the lake in hope of finding something edible for her master, she was glad to have escaped with only a couple of slaps, but where was the Shepherd's Heart? *Perhaps I spooked him when I arrived, and he hid it*, thought

Given. *He almost never parts from it until nightfall. It'll show...It must!*

Near the shore of Coyote Lake, Given discovered a few crayfish large enough to eat, but to go back with such a meager load would mean a thrashing from her already nettled master. If she had her spear handy, she might have snagged one of the Rhun Gill meandering around the rocks in the shallows, but Bledig wouldn't have eaten it anyway. Like many who called the Afon Valley home, he followed some of the same customs as the Gallants, not allowing women to kill. She scurried down the shore, checking Bledig's lines along the way. All were bare. He had always set a couple of deadfall traps a little deeper in the woods, but they hadn't been triggered. It was useless. Given glanced into her pack at the inadequate catch of crawfish. *I may as well get on with it. I can take whatever's coming my way. Won't be my first time.*

But as she walked back toward the cabin other thoughts tagged along with the acceptance of her forthcoming beating. Thoughts of resentment and of *resistance* sent her heart racing and set her cheeks ablaze. She imagined herself pulling out her axe just as Bledig was upon her, and clubbing him before he could raise a hand in defense; but unlike with Gar, she'd have no pity. She'd end the beast that had brought so much misery to her through the years. A fair end it would be too. But those thoughts, whether just or not, could not be realized, for her son's own life—and countless others —walked on the blade of a knife that she alone gripped. One misstep, one slip by her, and it could've been over for them all. She had to accept. She had to persevere. And deep within she knew she would forgive Bledig whatever he'd done or was to do, for that is who she was.

When Given arrived back at the cabin, Bledig was inside lying on a mat pretending he had been there for a while, when truly he was out watching her from a distance as she searched. She tiptoed next to him, reluctantly placed her catch beside him, and with her head down, took a couple steps backward. She dared not hold his gaze.

"Well, what has my wench caught?" He tore the pack open. Eyeing the crayfish he continued, "Where's the rest?"

"Tha..that's all I could find...I checked every line and trap. Not a thing was to be found—except what you have there."

"Checked every line and trap did ya?" he scoffed. "Wouldn't ya think being 'round all day I would have checked 'em already." He was on his feet in a hurry. "I asked you earlier if you wish for death. Now, I know you do." Pulling Given's head back by her hair, he drove the pack into her nose bringing forth blood. The force caused something to crack, but when Given inspected her nose it was whole. The crayfish weren't so fortunate; their shells were crushed.

"Now go!" Bledig howled. "Fetch me something worth eating!" He grunted curses as Given scurried through the door.

 Tears fell as she returned to the water, but they were not summoned by the pain in her nose, rather from loss. She pondered all she'd left in Bardorf. She never could have imagined having so many friends—and making them so fast. But she didn't realize what any commoner, even the witless ones, could perceive of her: Her kindness was irresistible, her joy contagious. But fools like Bledig and Gar valued not virtue and could only see Given as a tool.

Gazing over the lake wishing she was home, she silently prayed for guidance, for where to find food, for where to find the Heart.

And though she waited and though she searched, not a sign nor a hint of either was discovered on that night. Darkness blanketed the lake and her hunting ground, forcing her back to the cabin empty-handed. The beating she suffered wasn't the worst she'd endured—or maybe she was used to them. Either way, the beating didn't bother her as much as the impression Bledig had Given her. Something wasn't right. She'd been back for much of the day, still there was no sign of the heart. And after Bledig's initial inquiry, he hadn't bothered her with a single question about where she'd been or who she'd been with for the past few weeks. She feared he already knew what her plan was. *But how could he*?

Bledig was *kind* enough to let her sleep inside the cabin. At least that's what he said. Really, he wanted to keep his cold eyes cast upon her. Somehow, she'd slipped away before. It wasn't going to happen again.

Given lay awake on the dirt floor with her eyelids clinched for much of the night, struggling to shut out Bledig's labored breathing and erratic snorting. It was like listening to a couple of pigs at feeding time. But she was worn, and neither the noise nor the pain from her bruises could keep her from sleeping. It was a fine thing that they couldn't, for she dreamt the most pleasant of dreams. Along with their friends, she and Grit returned to Skeleton Wood. In the middle of the desolation, Given sang as the rest danced. With every note and every step, life erupted from death. Brilliant colors sprang from the black until all was joyous and lovely. The scattered bones were restored with flesh.

As with everything—pleasant or nasty—the dream had to come to an end. Given found herself waking to sand being kicked in her face. "Forgot breakfast time already?" said Bledig. "Well, I ain't one to let you off the hook twice in as many days. Get out and find something to eat…you ain't much good for anything else."

Given bounded to her feet spitting granules. "Yes master, I'll be back as fast as I can."

"Make sure you bring back some grub this time!"

She was glad to be sent out for food to get her away from the cabin, and so she might discover a clue of the missing Heart. Though in the back of her mind she knew finding the stone was a hopeless effort without Bledig's help. *He's hiding it from me,* she thought once again. *He knows I'm after it.*

The first fish line she checked brought success in terms of food; a snapping turtle was snagged. Given was careful to avoid its bite when she dragged it ashore. She clutched the creature's shell with both hands and took it back to Bledig. She sensed a hint of pleasure in his cheeks as he took the turtle from her. Wasting no time, he enticed the snapper to bite a stick, and with its neck outstretched, he lopped off its head with a stone blade. "Save the blood," he smiled deplorably as he handed the turtle back to Given.

"Of course, Master," she said, knowing well that he liked to drink the turtle's blood while he feasted on its flesh. It had always confounded her though, how he was happy to guzzle an animal's blood but disgusted by her cycle. She was thankful for the contradiction nonetheless.

Given hung the carcass by the tail over a wooden bowl outside, letting the life-giving fluid drain before she pried the lower shell free and removed what meat she could. After retrieving some water from the river, she boiled the meat in a bear hide *pot* making sure to keep the hide water-filled so it wouldn't burn. She would still need to cook the meat over an open flame after it boiled. Preparing turtle was time consuming. For that she was thankful.

128

Bledig did nothing but wait while Given cooked. He never did anything he didn't think he had to. In his entire life perhaps, there wasn't a single person he'd helped other than himself. When his meal was ready, Given set the bowl of blood before him and the meat beside it. She couldn't watch. Something about drinking blood caused her stomach fluids to curdle.

She wasn't at all disappointed to see Bledig hadn't left her a scrap, for turtle of any kind had always been tough for Given to swallow. Taking the remains—bones and shell—she tossed them into the river. *Maybe the fish could pick something from them.* After her master granted her leave, she reset the line she'd pulled the turtle from and set out to check the other lines and traps. The thought of withholding a catch for herself crossed her mind, but there was nothing to hold back. "Thank you for the turtle at least," she said in prayer. "Surely, it saved me from another thrashing."

Passing much of the day setting new snares and traps near the lake, she had time to think about Grit, and though she missed him terribly, memories of his mischief brought comfort and a smile. "Aderyn didn't know what she was getting into." She chuckled.

***

Given stood looking out over the lake as the western sun sagged behind her. She'd fished and searched all day, but nothing beyond the first line produced anything—and still there was no hint of the Heart. She wondered how Aksel was faring. Was he getting stir crazy? To Given he didn't seem like the type who preferred to sit and wait. It was time to get back to the cabin to tend to the wants of her master, but she waited a while longer, peering across the darkened waters which seemed to go forever in the twilight.

At last she decided she could stay out no longer; she'd be pummeled if she did. But turning toward the cabin she saw just enough of a flash or glare to grip her attention. Focusing on the spot in the water from which the flash had come, she could see floating below the surface a fish, or turtle perhaps, of mass she'd never seen in the lake. Unless the dimness was playing a trick on her vision, the object appeared to easily be the size of a human. It floated, and she stared, thinking maybe it was looking back at her too.

Only seconds went by before the thing in the water thrust itself back into the deep with a splash of its giant tail. At that moment, Given knew for sure that it was no turtle, but an immense fish. And she swore, though difficult for her to believe, that its tail bore the characteristic red and green display of the Rhun Gill.

"Couldn't have been," she thought aloud. "Never have I seen one bigger than my arm, yet had I been in the water, I might have been a snack for that one."

She bolted back to the cabin to find Bledig hardly removed from the place she'd left him. Expecting at least a verbal thrashing, she entered with her eyes cast low, but Bledig said nothing immediately. Glancing up, she could see his eyes upon her and his mouth turned up contemptuously. She'd seen the expression before, the look of suspicion. It made her feel as though a thousand spiders had hatched onto her skin.

"Of all the wenches, I picked the worst. Find what you were looking for?"

Given kept her eyes low. "N—no master. Except for the turtle, the lines and traps were empty."

"Eh, still puttin' on." He scoffed. "I guess since you're pretending, I'll pretend too…It don't bother me none."

His eyes were fixed on her as he waited for her to make a confession, but she said nothing. The minutes he stared were like hours to her. At last, he grew tired of waiting. "To the flames with ya…If I give you what you deserve tonight, I don't think I'll stop." Motioning toward her spot on the floor, "Sleep…but have my breakfast ready tomorrow, or I'll—"

Bledig didn't finish, but from the nasty look he gave in the candle light, Given knew she was in for it the next day. She couldn't risk sleeping much that night—if at all. Having nothing to feed her master, she'd need to wake well before dawn to search.

She rose after a restless night of worry and prayers with the pain from the last beating still fresh upon her. It was the look Bledig gave that concerned her more than another beating. *He won't stop this time. What'll happen to Grit if I die?* He was lying on his mat in the cabin when she left, his eyes tracking her as she exited.

Darkness still hung heavy in the woods as Given set out. When she checked there was nothing in any trap or snare, but there was still hope in the water. Perhaps her prayer for a plentiful catch would be answered. From the lack of resistance on the first line though, she could tell it had been snapped. *Bledig's hastily made lines never last,* she thought. The second line was intact but fruitless. The third and fourth were the same. Her frayed hope now rested alone on the last two lines she'd set the day before. They were a ways down on the southern edge of the lake. *If they yield nothing…I'll have to face him.*

The sun had begun to rise when she arrived at the lines. She was disappointed to find nothing on the first. The second, appeared to have nothing on it as well, but when Given began to drag it in, she could tell there was a catch—a large catch. She struggled as the thing thrashed about in the water seeking the deep. Not wanting her line to snap, she cycled back-and-forth from tugging to no resistance. An hour went by, and she was worn from the tug-of-war. But whatever was on the line had to be tired as well. Slowly, steadily with what little strength remained, she pulled the line toward the shore. The creature had finished fighting.

As it surfaced, Given was amazed. A gleaming red and green fish floated before her. *Could it be the same fish I saw last night? It has to be. A Rhun Gill this large, who'd heard of such a thing? The Creator has surely answered my prayers.* "Perhaps Bledig will overlook his suspicions when I bring him enough food to last half the winter…and in one catch." She spoke to herself.

Dancing about in song, her heart swelled with joy, but when she went to finish the job of dragging the huge fish ashore, she couldn't. A creature so rare and wondrous, whether it would save her life or not, should never be turned over to that monster. "I cannot trade your life for mine, beautiful one," she said, wading out to the fish. "I hope the gorge hasn't done too much damage already." She reached into its mouth to free its bonds only to discover that it hadn't even swallowed the gorge. In fact the fish had been tugging on a line without being snared. Taking a step back she contemplated what it could mean. The fish spit out the gorge and splashed around in the water before swimming away. *It's almost as if…it's trying to tell me something.* "What is it? What do you wish me to know?" she called. But the fish continued east splashing its tail now and again as it went. Given couldn't help feeling regret as the Rhun Gill disappeared, knowing now there was no option but to face a suspicious, hungry beast empty handed. *Just as well be done with it,* she thought as she plodded—maybe for the last time—back to the cabin.

***

Bledig didn't allow her to breach the threshold before he was upon her. A terrible sting on the back of Given's legs brought her to her knees.

"Thought you'd learned," he said, standing over her holding a willow switch. "But here you are again with nothing to eat…don't matter anyhow. I got a bigger bone to pick with you, and I'm sick of waiting for you to fess up." He brought the switch down hard once again, this time landing a blow on the back of her neck.

Given cringed in pain and silence.

"Of all the wenches, of all the wenches," Bledig repeated over-and-over as he paced around her, "I had to get you. And after all I did, saving you from death when you were little and giving you a home, you steal your little mutt from me and run away. If that didn't top everything, you came back to steal from me again…No use in lying, I know you've been looking for it!"

"I don't know what you speak of," said Given, ignoring the warning.

"LIES! LIES! LIES!" Bledig yelled as he unleashed a flurry of lashes onto her legs, and back, and head. She was a crumpled crying mess when the fury had ended.

"Now, tell me you didn't come back for it. Lie to me again. Tell me you haven't been looking for the red rock. I could smell 'em. You had more than your own stink on you when you came back. I could smell one of 'em all over ya. They all smell the same…the Aubs do. Those city folk are all the same. They been round here looking for it too. All over the countryside they've been searching. They got to ya…I figured it, so I've been watching you ever since you got back."

Though battered, Given was aware of what Bledig was saying. Having been in contact with Aksel, her shield, might now cost her

her life. She wanted to reply—to make up some excuse— but her mind was blank. To Given lying was an unknown tongue.

Bledig wasn't listening anyway. "I'm sick of dealing with you," he said, Gripping Given's legs. "Thought I might give you a little more time, but I'm sick of it." He dragged her to the edge of the river and began kicking and stomping her without reserve.

Where was Freckles now when she needed him most? Why had she sent him away? Where were Aksel's blade and strength? She shouldn't have bidden him to stay put. Given was losing consciousness. Her life was slipping—or being pounded—away.

When no hint of reaction or response remained, Bledig rolled her into the river and shoved her lifeless form into the torrent, finally ridding himself of the refuse he'd *rescued* from a dying tribe. He could get another wench—a better wench—anywhere. This one had betrayed him…even after all the *good* he'd done for her.

The rushing waters scooped up Given and cast her into Coyote lake where she sank into the deep. Her body was broken, ribs shattered and lungs filled with blood and water. Ages could have passed without her knowing; her mind was a wasteland. All was still and dark and dead…except for the beating. Her heart never stopped. The Gallant heart the creator had given her to complete her task could not be subdued. Neither man nor beast of the Earth could pound it into submission. As she sank, it kept beating.

CHAPTER 14. WEIGHTS AND MEASURES

ON THE night of his banishment, Dane had been able to overcome the pain of Baird's arrow that remained, in part, protruding from his chest and escape from the shadow of the Civitian Wall. He had whittled away at the shaft with a jagged stone until it could be snapped without much force, but could not wholly remove it. The agony was beyond that which his body would allow and each attempt was trailed by seizures of pain and unconsciousness. Even with an arrow yet buried in his flesh, he trudged aimlessly alongside the Afon hoping to discover someone to free him from his torment.

Weeks had gone by since his clash with Magnus. What little sleep he had gotten since was plagued with visions of his father's treachery. He wondered if it had something to do with the crown Magnus had slipped on his head. Had it somehow poisoned his mind? Perhaps more scarce than his sleep was sustenance. River water was all that filled his belly. Dane was a trained warrior and could wield dagger and spear in battle if need be, but hunter or trapper he was not. Sometimes the pain of hunger rivaled that of the infection that had gripped his chest and arm. It was only a matter of time before one or the other claimed his life, but still he slogged. Every now and again he would peer into the water to see the vibrant red and green flashes of the Rhun Gill antagonizing him, scoffing at his emptiness. Although most of his food in the city had come from sea and farm, he had on occasion partaken in the river's bounty and now longed for it.

When malnourishment and malady had fully seized him, he leaned against a cypress with his eyes closed, hoping if he died he could see his mother again. He stroked the star she had given him that still hung around his neck despite his recent peril. It was the young prince's only remaining earthly comfort.

With strength exhausted, his body slid down the tree trunk and slumped on the ground. The pain from hunger and infection faded, as did the light from the sun. All was still and cold and black. Time passed, ten thousand years times ten thousand or a few seconds perhaps. He didn't know.

Gradually, an awful awareness befell him. All torment of hunger and infirmity returned, and with them came thirst and loneliness and despair. In the distance a colorful light shone and music—or the echo of a song—reached his ear. He tried to move closer, but his weight had increased tenfold and the burden of pain was nearly unbearable. Nevertheless, with immense effort he dragged himself toward the light. As he drew nearer he perceived the great crowd of people responsible for the music he was hearing. They sang a melody he'd never heard, and the singers were unfamiliar. But on the edge of the crowd looking back at him was a woman with beauty he'd only known one person to possess—his mother. Calling out to her garnered no reply. *Perhaps she hasn't guessed it is me*, thought Dane. Moving closer he could see her expression of sadness, and he realized between them lay a great chasm of seemingly infinite depth. He could not reach her, and she couldn't cross to him.

"Mother, is there a bridge to cross somewhere?"

Louder than the crowd with Astrid scarcely moving her lips she spoke to him. "With you I desire to be my son, but repentance first to you must come. The horrors you've been forced to live are now the things you must forgive."

Astounded, Dane pondered his mother's words. *Is she saying I must pardon Magnus for his wrongdoing? Perhaps she doesn't fully know the king's iniquities.*

"After all Magnus has done, I hate him mother…how can such a thing as forgiveness be accomplished?"

"With *Him* all things are possible," Astrid replied. "You must regain the heart you had as a child and be the light you've been called to be." Turning back she rejoined the chorus.

With his face in his hands he sobbed. "How can I? Though I've been commanded, I cannot do this one thing."

He watched as the light vanished and listened as the singing quieted until all was still, cold and black once more. The next he knew pain surged through his arm and shoulder. Feeling with his hand where the arrow had entered, he marveled. The splintered shaft was gone and the hole that would have been was scarred and scabbed over. A delicate hand removed his from the wound. Startled, he glanced up to discover a girl maybe twelve or thirteen years old looking back at him. She quickly diverted her eyes. Dane looked around expecting to find someone of age with the girl, but the river in front and the forest behind him were all that he saw.

"Who are you? Where do you come from?" he said.
The girl, still looking away, replied not.

Dane strained forward to get a closer look and to catch her gaze. "Girl, are you alone?"

A nod revealed that she and Dane spoke the same language, or at least that she understood him, but no words came forth as she motioned for Dane to lie back down. The perplexed prince did as he was told while trying to keep his eyes on her. Neither said anything for a bit as he processed what had happened, his apparent death, encounter in the afterlife, and resurrection.

By-and-by he asked, "Did you mend my wound?"

A nod once more.

"The arrow was deep and the pain was unspeakable when I tried to remove it," he said. "How did you manage without help?"

Forming a circle with her thumb and index finger the girl poked her other index finger through the circle and mimicked pulling it from the other side. Dane patted down his backside opposite the arrow's entry and discovered more scabs on the outside edge of his shoulder blade.

"You pushed the arrow through…it was good to be out for that. How did the bleeding stop?"

The girl held up the arrowhead and motioned toward some embers still glowing near the river. Dane understood and was especially glad to be unconscious for the cauterization, but the pain was still very much present. Checking the mobility of his arm, he nearly passed out once more. The girl shook her head and scowled as she pinned his arm to his side.

"Alright!" Dane cried. "I'll heed the healer's advice."

After his pain had subsided a bit, he took some time to examine the little medicine woman while she searched the river for fish to spear with the arrow she'd pulled from Dane. She was a short girl with straight sable hair twisted into two long braids, her skin so touched by the sun that it was almost black in places. Her looks were not what he was accustomed to in the tall bronze-skinned Civitian girls; nevertheless, he thought her no less beautiful. *How has this girl survived alone out here*? thought Dane. *There must be more of them hidden.*

"Where are your mother and father?"

The girl looked up, but did not reply.

"You do have parents, do you not? Where are they?"

Again no reply, only an expression of great sadness.

"They are gone I suppose." said Dane solemnly.

The girl nodded.

Closing his eyes with his head laid back, Dane thought for a moment of his mother and Magnus and said, "Yes, mine as well."

Both fell silent, contemplating their respective losses for a few minutes.

"Healer," Dane broke the silence, "what are you called?"

The girl looked up and appeared to mouth something without sound.

"Do you not speak little healer?"

Casting her eyes toward the ground, she shook her head.

"Even so, you do have a name?"

She nodded. And moving her mouth slowly and deliberately she expressed what appeared to him to be a two syllable word that starts with "V".

"Forgive me, I've not much skill in lip reading?"

She tried again even slower.

After several unsuccessful guesses, Dane said, "Vivid?"

A smile overcame the sadness that was the girl's countenance, and she nodded.

"Vivid…a fine name it is," said Dane, returning the smile. "I am called Dane. Pleased to meet you…though the circumstances could be better I must say. Thank you for saving me."

Vivid smiled again.

"Where do you stay?"

She pointed at the Afon and spread her arms wide.

"The river basin is your home then?"

She nodded.

"And you're at it alone," Dane said, concerned. "Whatever happened to your people, I am sorry."

Staring at the ground, Vivid shook her head. Dane wanted to hear her story but how could she tell it; instead, he shared his with her —at least what he could with a stomach turned inside out and pain surging through his chest and shoulder. After only a few minutes he said, "You've done much for me already, and I'm bothered to ask, but if I don't eat soon, I will not last."

Vivid looked pityingly upon him, picked up the arrow and waded back into the river. She had seen enough casualties in her few years and wasn't going to allow him to be another. It took until the smoky haze of dusk covered the land, but she snagged a fish and prepared it over the embers for him. She refused to partake in any herself, being more concerned for her neighbor and in fact well fed for a girl of her circumstance. Dane would soon discover that Vivid had an uncommon talent for fishing—among other skills.

"Twice you've saved me now, and it is doubtful I can ever repay. But I will try…when I heal, I shall try."

Vivid's cheeks turned as rosy as her dark complexion would allow. She liked Dane. His genuineness was a comfort, and his appearance, aside from the wound, was fine enough to make any girl giddy.

With no energy for talking and a fuller belly, Dane nodded into a tumultuous sleep, his body still feverish with infection. The evil intent of Magnus still haunted his dreams, and when he would open his eyes from the fright, it was as though he was there with Magnus. Vivid desired to help as she watched him flinch, flail, and on occasion cry out; but after some time, his fits calmed, and the sounds of wind whooshing through the willows and cypresses, chirping crickets, and hooting night birds lulled her to sleep as well.

CHAPTER 15. FROM THE DEPTHS

ON THE lake's sandy floor, Given lay breathless and still for some time, alone in the shadows of the water above. At length she gained awareness. Though her eyes were closed on the bottom of a lake, she perceived light, and even with her ears muffled by the weight of the depths, she heard music. A multitude was singing a familiar song—Mot's song—along with tones and notes and instruments she'd never heard, and occasionally a beautiful voice would rise above all others. The light grew more intense until it surrounded her and the song louder until it permeated. The sound seemed to dance around her in waves of various colors.

Suddenly a hand clasped her own and pulled, and at that moment she became weightless, and her body lifted from the floor. Up and out she flew, her hair flowing wildly behind. Landing moments later, the light dimmed and the music died as pain surged through her battered body once again. She tried to breathe but couldn't; the pain wouldn't allow it, and her blood saturated lungs had no space for air.

A hand stroked her head gently, and a voice soft as down and honey sweet began to sing words she'd heard in another life, far from her present cares in the loving arms of Mot.

All that's broken be made whole
All destroyed be restored
All that's torn shall be sewn
Till all is healthy once more
Till all is healthy once more

The lyrics took life as Given's body was bathed in warmth and from the inside out, seemingly unaided, began to mend. She grew stronger with every line as the song was repeated. When the singer stopped at last, Given was able to breathe deeply without restriction of pain or fluid. Lying on her back with eyes still closed she lifted her hands and twisted them. Even though both had been crushed by Bledig's fury, neither had any discomfort whatsoever. A hand once again touched her forehead, and the same soft voice spoke, "You must rest." Immediately, Given slipped into deep slumber.

***

Day expired, a new began, and still Given slept. When she finally opened her eyes she expected to discover the person who had been singing over her and possibly to view heaven; instead, she found herself surrounded by the stone walls of a small cavern, the lone opening allowing just enough light to see. She peeked out to discover the waters of Coyote Lake she was so familiar with, but where had she been? Where was the crowd who sang Mot's song? She was alone.

Turning her attention toward the cave she wondered why she'd never noticed this hollow before? The barren walls were cold and rough and damp, nothing out of the ordinary for a cave, but looking deeper, she noticed an unusual crevice at the back. With strained eyes she approached, but it was too dark to see inside. Combing the crevice with her fingertips, her heart stopped as she brushed something smooth. She used both hands to remove the mystery from its hiding place and took it to the light of the opening. The discovery made her gasp, for in that little nook in the cold damp hollow she'd never noticed, she found what she'd been hunting. It was the thing she'd abandoned life in Bardorf for, and

143

that which Gallant leaders had protected for generations. Truly, it was the red stone, the ruby Heart of Derog. Goosebumps covered her body and her palms grew sweaty. "So this is where you've been hiding it!"

Someone brought me here knowing its whereabouts, but who… who besides Bledig could've known about this? Wheels of thought turned over what had happened, and she tried to make sense of it all. She was certain Bledig had beaten her and kicked her into the river to drown, but she hadn't a bruise or scratch to prove it. *How?* She looked around a while longer but didn't find any clue to help answer her questions.

She went back to the water's edge and crept in. There was no need to linger, and to do so might put her in harm's way. Bledig could return for his prize at any moment. As she waded out from the cavern, she realized why this hiding place was foreign to her. Being on the opposite end of the lake from Bledig's cabin, she'd only traveled past it a handful of times in her life; and looking back on it from a little ways out, the entrance had already faded into the shade of the surrounding wood. Indeed, Bledig had been clever to hide his most valuable possession there, but his sneakiness hadn't evaded all onlookers.

Now a few miles from Bledig's Cabin, Given sloshed back onto shore clutching the Heart. Seeing where the lake narrowed and the water flowed as the Afon once again, her heart quickened. She hadn't been this far east in years, and never had she been alone. Hoping to see some sign left by the Gallant, she wandered a little downstream, though to find evidence of them this far west would have been a real surprise. As she walked along, sense told her to fetch Aksel and come back later to search for her family, but hope and curiosity encouraged her to keep going. With each bend she rounded she was disappointed to find only more trees and river. There was no sign that anyone had been living there, let alone one of her kin. Finally, more than a mile downstream, she decided to turn back. But before she had fully pivoted, the giant Rhun Gill she'd released, appeared once more, vaulting from the river and landing with a great splash. Given stared at the water as the fish did it again. After the third time she realized, for sure this time, it was trying to say something.

"What is it?" she called. "What do you wish to tell?"

The fish swam closer, half emerged from the lake, its red and green scales shining in the sunlight. Standing motionless, Given admired the creature's beauty.

"What is it, friend?"

The fish made no indication.

"Perhaps you don't understand…"

As Given thought of a way to communicate, it came ever closer. Gradually, its eyes transformed before Given's. The huge black pupils shrank, and the yellow irises faded to the red-brown hue of cinnamon. Given thought she was hallucinating, but when the fish's upper torso and head transformed into those of a woman— brown skinned and black haired—she realized she wasn't. All the stories Mot had told of the girl who'd been turned into a fish came flooding back, and she understood.

"Nataurie, is it you?" Leaning forward, another thought struck Given and she gasped, "It was you who saved me, wasn't it?"

"From the depths I pulled you," Nataurie began. "But you were far gone. Death gripped, and I was powerless to rip you away, but the song, the healing song of Solas, brought you back to life. For hours I sang as I watched your body recover. First your breath returned, then your bones mended, at last your bruises vanished. I

145

sang…but his goodness rescued you. You have been purchased for a purpose."

"What shall I do now?" asked Given.

"We must continue east for a while still. There are those in need of your help downstream." Reaching out a hand, she continued, "I can get you there. I'll hold the Heart so you can cling to me, but grip tight, I swim fast."

Given did as she was commanded, and mounted on Nataurie's back she cut through the water like a shark's fin. Every stroke of Nataurie's powerful tail accelerated them. For a moment, as she skimmed down the Afon at a rate she'd never imagined, Given was too thrilled to remember her cares. She smiled and squinted as the river mists flew into her face, and in the water all around she could see Rhun Gill, Feather Fin, and Blue Scale swimming alongside like a tribe following their chief into battle.

It was as though Nataurie read Given's thoughts as she wondered what it was like under the water, for just a few moments later they began to dive. With her last opportunity Given took in as much air as she could, holding it with her cheeks puffed. Fully submerged racing through the water, Nataurie didn't slow at all. Given's eyes were clinched as water surged over her. They came up a while later long enough and high enough for Given to take a few more breaths before diving back under.

As the river widened and became shallower, Given was forced back to the surface. Her eyes opened to beauty. Three doe were drinking on the river's edge as a buck looked down from a high point. Startled by Given's invasion, they bounced back into the thick and disappeared. About three miles downstream from the lake, worn from her watery sprint, Nataurie emerged and slowed a bit, her tail still flipping hard below the surface.

"We're nearly there." She panted. "I hope they haven't strayed."

"Who?" Given said. "Who are we looking for?"

"Prompted by a vision, I swam downstream as you slept. There I found a girl who resembled your kin and a man with the complexion of those from the city. He had suffered an injury, but the girl had done good to repair it. As I couldn't leave you alone, I cannot leave them. She is young, and he is in no condition to provide for himself. In Solas's name you must help!"

Given would have never purposefully let someone who needed help down, but the urgency in Nataurie's speech and the mention of Solas made her even more anxious to help.

"Get me to them," she said. "I'll do all that I can." She paused for a moment thinking about Nataurie's mention of Solas and her own experiences with him. "Do you know him well? Solas, I mean."

"All who follow the Creator's will do, and I...I've known him since I was...very young." Naturie fell silent in thought.

"Since you were a *girl?*" Given inquired.

"Yes, I was once." Nataurie smiled. "I suppose my past is not as secret as I thought. Many happenings of man, whether or not he wishes, are noticed by my eyes, but rarely am I seen. How do you know about me?" She said with a curious look. "I'm surprised you've heard my name even."

"At least part of your story has become Gallant lore. My mother would tell of a girl named Nataurie who survived a savage tribe's attack by taking refuge in the river, only to be swept away and transformed into fish. Mot said she became the guide for the fishes."

"I've become a part of legend." Nataurie snickered. "The Gallant must be a noble sort, for not even tribal legend wanders far from the paths of truth. That was too long ago though. I don't remember much before my life in the river."

"Even so, do you ever wish to return to the land?"

"Like the land, the waters need a shepherd. I've been given a choice to stay, and for now I shall." Nataurie slowed her thrusts once again and stared into the forest. "To leave is to be with the one who Created, to stay is to do his will. We've been placed here for such a time as this. If we don't do what is needed, who will?"

It was in this statement that Given realized the likeness of Nataurie's story to her own. Through terrible circumstances they'd both been vaulted into a position of importance where no one else would do. Nataurie had graciously accepted the challenge of keeping the waters safe, and now Given must do the same on land.

Nataurie approached the south shore of the Afon where the trees cleared a bit and let Given off on a rock jetty. Handing her the Heart she said, "Someday, I hope to see you again in a brighter place beyond the peril of war, but for now you must shield this with all vigor. Trust your heart and dreams more than your mind and sight, and forget not the songs of Solas—gifts to the Gallant— for they provide healing to all who hear." She smiled brightly. "And save yourself much difficulty. The next time a giant Rhun Gill tries to lead you somewhere, you should probably follow. I'm not one to be hooked on the end of a line." Pointing downstream with a serious look she said, "Now go, those who need your help are around the bend, but hurry; your master may soon be after what's been taken."

Before Given could ask a question or offer thanks, Nataurie had transformed back into a fish and disappeared into the swift. Given was left overwhelmed by the new knowledge, too much so to focus on a single thought.

She peered into the red depths of the Heart. Though extremely beautiful, it didn't appear to be anything more than a jewel. But having it reassured that she had chosen the right path, one being guided by the Shepherd of Men himself.

CHAPTER 16. THICKER THAN WATER

CAUTIOUSLY SHE climbed the small rock face where Nataurie had unloaded her, and not wanting to frighten those she was sent to help, she proceeded through the trees around the river's bend at a snail's pace. Glancing through the dainty leaves of a willow, she set eyes on a scene warm enough to melt the coldest of hearts, a young lady kneeling beside a man, disabled, scarred and scabbed. She was helping him eat, and though his condition was not good, he smiled graciously as the girl tore pieces of fish for him. Studying every aspect of the girl she could from that distance, Given concluded that Nataurie was right: the girl looked much like a Gallant. A hopeful tear rolled down her cheek at the possibility. After nestling the Shepherd's Heart against the willow's trunk, she swam through the sagging branches and emerged into the open.

"Do not be alarmed," Given called from a distance with her hands raised. "I only wish to help."

At first sound Vivid spun and bounded to her feet snatching Dane's arrow as she came up. Clutching it by its splintered shaft, she glared at Given.

"I mean no harm," Given bowed with her hands still up. "Do you need help?"

Dane struggled through the pain to pick his head up from the ground so he could look Given's way.

"Doesn't appear threatening," he whispered. "But we can't be certain she's the only one. Remain on guard."

Given held her submissive posture for a while expecting some response, but Dane and Vivid were too busy scanning the surrounding forest for others. At length she said, "May I approach, or should I stand all day with my hands in the air."

Vivid nodded at Dane who called, "If it's only you, then you are welcome, but we are not fit to fight, so please take not advantage."

"Indeed, you are not fit." Given laughed. "If you worry that someone of my stature could take advantage. Lower your guard, I'm here to help." Approaching the two unfortunates cautiously she continued. "I am Given, what is your name?"

"I am Dane." He strained forward and motioned. "And this is my healer, Vivid. A lady of many talents she is, but speech, she has none."

As Given drew near, Vivid did indeed drop her guard, but she did so unconsciously, for the closer Given got, the more Vivid gaped. Her face displayed a mixture of surprise, as one who had unexpectedly and without searching found something that was lost, and that of great confusion.

Reading her expression, Given said, "Am I familiar to you?"

Vivid stood with a look of disbelief and moved her head in a kind of half-nodding, half shaking circular motion. She squinted a bit longer while shaking her head.

"You have the look of my people," Given said, moving her hand across her face. "As I watched from the trees, I wondered if you could be from the Gallant tribe as well."

Vivid pointed at Given and looked questioningly.

"I am Gallant," said Given affirmatively as tears began to well in her eyes. "And you are as well?"

Vivid smiled and nodded, and tears began to rain as the two embraced.

Dane laughed and said in wonderment, "Sisters reunited on the edge of nowhere, how can such a thing happen?"

His jovial exclamation struck Given as she squeezed Vivid. It was true that her father, the chief, had sired many of the Gallant children through various tribeswomen. "Could it be?" She said. "Was your father Chief Cynfor?"

Vivid looked forward into Given's eyes, though she was much younger the two were of similar height. She nodded and returned the question by pointing back at Given.

Smiling, Given nodded and said, "We are sisters indeed."

Dane didn't feel at all left out as the two young women embraced and laughed, and Given gave thanks.

"Eight years away. With little hope of finding any of my people, and the Creator blesses me with a sister! Are there any others?"

Vivid's smile vanished, and in sadness she looked down.

Given put her hands on Vivid's shoulders. "Perhaps there's still hope…If the Creator has made our unlikely reunion possible, he can do anything."

Vivid glanced up with an unconvincing smile.

"Even so, we have each other now." Given squeezed Vivid once more. "If no other blessing is bestowed, that is enough for me."

Dane watched in admiration at the love the sisters displayed, though they had no recollection of each other. With his good hand he clutched his mother's pendant hiding beneath his tunic and wished too that he could be reunited with family. To scoop little Leif up in embrace or even to shake York's hand and wrestle playfully would be blessing enough, but he longed to talk to his mother. Was it a vision of her he'd witnessed on the borders of life and death, or had he passed into the afterlife altogether? He couldn't know for sure, but the message from Astrid was clear nonetheless. For him to get to where she was, he would need to forgive Magnus. He grew angry at the thought.

152

"So what's your tale?" Given's voice interrupted his sudden turn toward brooding. "I'm sure it must be good. It's not everyday one stumbles upon foreign men in the forest—and in need of aid."

"I suppose not." Dane tried to smile at the jest but was held captive by the disdainful thoughts he was having towards Magnus. "But *good* it is not. It's beyond me to say why, but my own father did this, or he ordered it done at least." Without revealing his princely identity, Dane shared part of his story with Given as she gave full attention. She sympathized when he spoke of his mother's death and was baffled as he told more of his father.

"I see now why you're at a loss. Betrayal by family must be the toughest to take. But I suppose I'm here because of my own father's mistakes as well." Given glanced at Vivid who wore a questioning look. "I'll save that story for later if you all don't mind. It's a might long and plenty painful. I don't wish to turn our time of rejoicing into a funeral…Besides, there are good tidings I shouldn't neglect." She looked at Dane. "At least you might think so. About a day's walk upstream waits a friend of mine who happens to be one of your countrymen, though it's been years since he's been welcome in his homeland. He is the best of men and has been my protector since before I knew him, but like you, he has been wrongfully cast out. When you regain your strength we shall go find him if you will, and perhaps the two of you will discover more in common when you talk."

"I'm certain nothing can fill the hole left by what I've lost," Dane said. "But to meet a fellow Civitian, could be the next best thing to rediscovering family."

"I'm convinced it will be so," said Given before her happy expression changed to that of concern. "But there is one pitfall. On the western edge of Coyote Lake, about two leagues from here, sits the cabin of my master who I've fled. He is a cunning hunter and will surely be after us if we enter his territory; indeed, we may already be in danger. I've taken the thing he values above all else, and I fear he'll be in search soon."

"We might all be in danger waiting here," said Dane. "If this ailment would loosen its grip, I'd have no fear of your master, but if it comes to it and you must leave me to save yourselves, please do not hesitate. I'm in no condition to run."

"You are under my care now," Given said. "If you are to stay, I will too. Whether I run now or stay with you matters not anyway. Like I told you, he is the cleverest of stalkers. What he seeks, he'll find."

"How did you escape such a man in the first place?"

Given thought for a moment and said, "I didn't, at least not this time. He beat me to near death and cast me into the river. Except for help from the Creator, I'd be food for the fishes."

"That's a story I must hear," Dane wore a confused look.

"It's one I still struggle believing myself, but I'll tell it soon, after you've regained a little strength. As for now, rest while Vivid and I fish."

The sisters waded into the river and did just that, taking turns stabbing through the water with the arrow, their only tool. There wasn't much success, for the river was unusually devoid of life. They managed to snag a single bluegill. As they fished, Given did all of the talking, of course, sharing much of what had happened to her since childhood but leaving out her life with the Gallants. She wanted to save the stories for a time of less distraction, perhaps to sooth Vivid before they slept.

With discomfort and troubling visions of vast armies forbidding Dane's rest, he watched the sisters and listened to Given's tale instead. His eyes were drawn to Given, perhaps not consciously at first, but after a while he realized something he hadn't in all the excitement of their meeting; she was exceedingly beautiful. But it wasn't her appearance alone that appealed to him; rather, the kindness she displayed to those she had just met was reminiscent of his mother's. A time or two she turned to see his eyes upon her, but he did not look away. He was not a man of pretense.

***

As the sun rolled west, the first breath of autumn encouraged the sisters to feed the coals and rest before it grew dark. They ate their meager catch, and Given shared more about her time with the Gallants. She spoke of the Afon Valley and the Gallant children and way of life. But when she told of Mot it sparked something, a thought or memory, inside of Vivid. Vivid waved her hands wanting to say something.

"What is it?" asked Given. "Is it Mot, do you know her?"

Vivid nodded.

Given felt foolish for not asking earlier. Knowing many Gallant mothers were called "mot" and wanting to make sure they were talking about the same person she asked, "Serenis, you know her?"

Vivid nodded once more and pointed at Given while flashing her other hand across her face.

"You think I look like her," Given guessed, waited for a nod, and said, "What do you know of her?"

Vivid paused in frustration for a while wanting to express her thoughts but not knowing how with hand gestures. Eventually, she took up the arrow once more and with it began to sketch in the wet sand by the river. In no time she had completed a portrait of surprising clarity.

"It's Mot!" Given said, surprised.

Vivid pointed at the sketch then at Given and held her arms as though cradling a baby. She pointed once again at the sketch, then at herself and made the same gesture with her arms.

Given shook her head in disbelief, "Are you saying that my Mot is yours as well?"

Vivid nodded.

"But how can this be? I was eleven when I was taken and you were not around yet. How old are you?

With the arrow Vivid struck twelve lines in the sand.

"It docsn't add up. You would've already been about four when I was taken. Our mothers could not be the same person."

But Vivid shook her head and drew another picture of a woman holding a baby, pointing at the baby and at herself.

"So this baby is you?" Given asked.

Vivid nodded

"And this woman—"

Vivid stopped Given with a wave and crossed through the woman holding the baby.

"Your mother…died," guessed Given.

Vivid once again nodded and drew a line from the baby to Mot's portrait.

"Mot took you as her own?"

When Vivid nodded at this question, joyful tears streamed once more from their eyes. They were indeed wholly sisters, sired by the same father and raised by the same mother—though at completely different times. Nothing was said for a long while as they remembered the times they'd both had with their wonderful mother.

"She is the best of women," said Given at last. "I never knew if she survived the winter when I was taken. At least now I have the comfort of knowing." She hesitated, afraid of how Vivid might answer her next question. "Is she…gone?"

Dropping her eyes, Vivid made no movement at first and ever so slightly nodded. Given said nothing more, for the sobbing said what words could not. Dane's heart ached for them, knowing the grief caused from such a loss. Now, at least they had each other.

After many tears and much consoling, Given picked up the arrow and said, "Can you show me what happened?"

The drawing that followed amazed both Given and Dane as he craned to see. Even in dirt, the sun Vivid drew seemed to set a village scene in a brilliant light, casting perfectly placed shadows around the characters and tents. No master artist in Auber Civitas could have produced a work of such clarity using an arrow in the mud. She pointed at the people, then at Given and herself.

"These are the Gallants?" Given asked.

Vivid Confirmed before adding to the scene. On a hilltop she sketched soldiers with shields, swords and spears. She pointed from the soldiers to the Gallants and stamped her foot in the middle of the village.

Any who watched Vivid could have understood what had happened. Given gasped.

"Who would have done such a thing?"

Looking at Dane, Vivid stretched out her finger towards him and slowly moved her hand across her face.

"My people did this to yours?" asked Dane.

She nodded.

"What folly drove them to this?" he said angrily. "What purpose could be conjured?"

But before Dane uttered the words, Given knew the answer. "They're searching for it too," she said. "That which I took from my master, they hunt as well."

"What could you mean? What could the Gallants have that my people would desire…enough to kill for?"

Given was reluctant to tell, not knowing if she could trust him, but Vivid's questioning eyes encouraged her to surrender the secret. "The Gallants were entrusted with a red stone of great worth, and some believe of even greater power," she began. "For generations our people have kept it hidden and safe, but many of them perished and still others were scattered; and I've now been charged to keep it from harm. Your people hunt it, believing it holds a power they can wield." She paused in thought for a moment before continuing. "But it is not the only one. I am told there are others like it, each carrying its own significance, and each given to a different tribe or kingdom—"

"The diamond!" Dane interrupted. "The king's circlet contains a diamond." Careful not to give his true relationship to the king away he said, "Ah, many in the kingdom have called it the mind of Derog. He has not kept his interest in the stories a secret, bringing sorcerers and *wisemen* from all over to help him unravel the riddles. But for him to do something so terrible…He's surrendered all reason." Looking at Vivid with admiration, he continued, "No child should have to endure the loss of a mother, and you've lost two. And though my people took one from you, still you have come to my aid." Dane wept as the feeling of responsibility for Vivid and Given's loss overwhelmed him. "Forgive me…forgive my people. They know not what they've done."

Vivid took Dane by the hand, and though she couldn't express her feelings in words, he understood that she didn't hold him at all accountable for the tragedy. Even so, he was moved by her loss and cut to the heart that she would so readily forgive. His mother's words about regaining the heart he had as a child rang in his head. But to hear the words and see them displayed were one thing, to actually forgive Magnus was another all together. Though the conviction was present, the hatred toward his father faltered not.

"The king deserves death for this," Dane said, looking at Given. "But who has the power to stop him? Do you truly possess what he seeks?"

Given nodded, "Though I don't know how, my master Bledig must've acquired the stone before your people attacked the Gallant village. I have taken it from where he hid it." Turning away, she walked back to the willow to retrieve the Heart, cursing it when first she set eyes upon it for the tragedy that had befallen because of it. She desired to cast it into the river where it would sink and be safe at the bottom, and the fish alone would know its whereabouts. But this was not Solas's charge. Though she didn't fully comprehend her call, she knew that tossing the Heart into the deep was against his will. "What shall I do with you?" she whispered before picking up the stone and making her way back to the others.

Given held it up for Vivid who gave no indication that she'd ever seen it. This didn't surprise her. When she was a child, the only evidence she had that it existed were the words of the adults in her tribe.

"It is so delicate in appearance," Dane said. "Why can we not smash it with a rock, scatter its pieces and be finished? Surely, its spell would be broken if we did."

"If it were so simple, it would have already been accomplished," Given answered. "But it should not be destroyed. Countless lives are bound to this stone, and if shattered, they may parish as well. I must guard it with all hope that when the time comes I'll know what to do with it, though at the time I don't haven't the faintest." Staring into the Heart, she thought about what Solas expected of her. "What did your storytellers say of the stones? What were the riddles that needed solved?"

Dane laughed. "I am proven a fool for not paying closer attention as a child. I was more interested in swords and girls than legends of great shepherds." All Dane could recall was the poem Magnus spoke to him after thrusting the crown onto his head. It was one he'd heard a handful of times growing up. "I do remember one rhyme, but I doubt it will shine any more light on your task." He looked down squinting as he tried to think up the correct words before he said, "Take his Mind and control; with his Eyes you will see; mend his Body, make them whole; give his Heart, set them free."

"Give his heart, set them free," Given said softly. "Maybe it will help before the end."

CHAPTER 17: LIKE A CHILD

THEIR FIRST night together lapsed with Given and Vivid reliving their time with the Gallants and trying to figure instances when they might have seen each other before Given was taken. With Vivid's lack of speech there wasn't much success, but to Given there was a vague familiarity to Vivid. Perhaps it was simply their close relatedness, or the fact that they were raised by the same woman. Whether they knew each other in the past did not matter anyway. They were together now, and their hurts, even the recent ones, were far more bearable because of it.

The following day for safe keeping, Given stashed the Heart beside Dane—who wasn't going anywhere unaided for a while. He was happy to keep eyes on it for her. In his condition he wasn't much good for anything else. But the Heart wasn't the only gem his eyes watched; in the morning light, he thought Given even more beautiful than before. Though she took note of his watching once again, it didn't occur to her why. She had far more pressing matters to consider than the fancy of this Civitian. Now that she had recovered the Heart and discovered the unfortunate truth of her mother, it was time to find Aksel and get back to Bardorf to see her little boy. The only things holding her back were the health of her new acquaintance and perhaps crossing paths with Bledig.

Most of the daylight was used up keeping the coals fed and fishing with the spear they had fashioned from Dane's arrow, an oak branch, and some weeds woven into twine. Their work was halted by moans and grunts Dane was making from his resting place. Both desired to help him as he slept fitfully under a tree, but Vivid had done all that she could. Given alone had the ability to do what was now needed. From Nataurie's advice as well as remembering Aksel's story of his own healing, Given knew that she must use the songs—but which. Struggling to recall the lyrics of the healing song Nataurie had sung over her, she climbed from the river and began to sing Mot's song over Dane instead. Whether it helped his body or not they could not tell, but it soothed his fits and soon he slept peacefully.

Vivid listened with delighted heart and tearful eyes as her sister sang the comforting melody she'd grown up on, and by Vivid's expression, Given knew Mot had sung her the same song.

"You know this one." Given said smiling and taking Vivid by the hand. "I wish we could sing it together…perhaps someday we'll get to."

Vivid returned her sister's smile, and leaving Dane to rest, they got back to fishing. Given was more than impressed with Vivid's success catching dinner. It was no wonder she was able to survive alone in the wilderness. She certainly possessed the skilled hands and keen eyes necessary. And though she couldn't express it verbally, one could tell from her look and actions that her wit was as sharp as a Civitian blade as well.

"You're clearly a superior fisher…I'm sure you can handle this alone," said Given. "I'll put myself to better use collecting wood for the fire so we can cook the catch."

Vivid nodded, and Given ambled from the Afon. Night was fast approaching and wanting to collect enough wood before darkness fell, Given went further from the river into the forest than she had the night before. A few hundred paces into the shadows she discovered a hickory with enough broken and scattered limbs to get the job done. Many of the larger limbs had been snapped by strong winds, but there were also many twigs that had been chewed off by beetles. After collecting as much as her short arms could carry, she went back to camp. Vivid was coming out of the water with a large fish on the end of her spear when Given returned.

"What a beauty!" said Given. "With you around no one will go hungry."

Given took the catch, lanced its underbelly with the end of the spear and removed its guts. She built up the fire with the wood she'd gathered and roasted the fish over the flame. The aroma woke Dane. After much objection by him, he was given the entire fish, which he ate mostly without help. Given and Vivid prepared a few more they had caught earlier, and each had plenty.

"A fine meal and a little rest have done miracles," said Dane. "It's been weeks since I've felt this good."

The sisters smiled at each other, knowing more than food and rest were responsible for the way Dane felt. But Given said nothing of Mot's song. Some things are better left for the heart to treasure.

"It is good to hear," said Given. "You'll be well in no time. As long as there are fish to catch, I'm sure they won't escape Vivid." Glancing at the coals she continued, "But we need fire to cook them and it won't feed itself. I'll need to go after another load of wood to last the night."

Leaving Vivid to look after Dane, Given sank back into the woods toward the old hickory and began picking up its litter once more. She was glad to know that even Mot's song had a power to help people, but try as she might, she could not remember the healing song. If she did, Dane would surely have been beyond infirmity already. It was a shame too, for the longer they had to wait, the more likely Bledig would come in search of the Heart. Even now he could be after it. Letting down their guard could be deadly.

With another armload of wood, she trekked back to the fire that burned brightly against the grey sky. Night had all but fallen, and Vivid was bedded down, worn after a long day fishing. Dane was sharing a happy story about his brothers with her when Given arrived. Peering into the sky he said, "May good fortune find them both. Whatever evil my father has accomplished, I wish they have no part in it."

Overhearing his last words, Given said a silent prayer for Dane and his brothers' reunification. "You'll meet them again," she said, piling a couple more branches into the fire. "The Creator will make a way where there is none…After all that has happened in my life, I know at least that much." She paused in thought. "But worry strikes me still. With the fire as a beacon and us holding the treasure he seeks, it's only a matter of time before Bledig comes. We must keep our guard up. I'll take the first and third watch if you are willing to take the second Vivid."

Dane started to insist he get a shift, but Given stopped him after a few words.

"It's better that you sleep; if good health comes faster to you, so might our escape from here."

After taking a quick glance around, she picked up the spear and knelt beside Vivid. "Sleep well. I'll wake you when I can hold my eyes open no longer."

Vivid nodded and closed her eyes as Given began to sing Mot's song, all the while Dane listened in wonder.

"This song," he said, stretching his neck up to look at Given who had finished singing. "I've heard it before, if only in a dream or vision."

"It's the song I sang over you as you slept today. It seemed to calm your fits, but I'm amazed you heard anything. I thought you were asleep."

"I don't remember the song from today, but from days ago, before Vivid revived me. As far as I could reckon, I had slipped from this life into the next—into another world. My mother was there on the other side of a rift that I could not cross, and behind her was a great crowd singing this song. I would recognize it anywhere."

Perhaps Given was even more amazed than Dane as she thought of her own brush with death. "There's no way of knowing how many days ago it was," she said. "But I too nearly died and heard a crowd singing the same song. Whether a vision or reality, I don't know which, but it was this song. The singers were bathed in brilliant light when I approached them. I could feel their love from the song, and the music—the notes—I could see them. I did not want to leave."

"I had also wondered whether it was real or imagined," Dane said. "But now I am certain it was reality. Surely we both passed over at the same time, you to paradise, me to want and pain. If Vivid hadn't rescued me, I would still be trapped there in my longing."

"I think not," said Given. "What have you done to deserve such a fate?"

Dane looked away and swallowed hard. "Mother said to get to where she is, I must become like a child and forgive my father. Is it possible? I yearn to know, but right now I wish him dead."

Given thought of all the pain she'd been subjected to. Although she could have easily hated Bledig or Gar, or Cynfor for that matter, she didn't truly. Beyond the fear of Bledig and Gar and

165

resentment of her father's choices, a love for them lived. Above all else she desired to see them change, to see them become what the Creator had intended them to be. If he could remove her fear and anger, if he could make her useful, he could do a miracle in them. And from Dane he could take all the hatred as well.

Given walked to Dane, and taking him by the hand said, "For you this may be impossible, but with the Creator all things are possible."

Her words like spring showers washed over him as he was bathed in love. It was as if his mother had spoken to him from heaven. None of it was coincidence. A great power had ushered Given to him, so that he might be freed from the bondage of hate—so that he might see his mother on the other side. Dane wept.

CHAPTER 18: A HOPE DEFERRED

THE FOLLOWING day, Dane woke to the first frost of the season, but his heart was warm, thawed by the reviving breath of the one who created him. Still, he lacked the strength to lift his body from its resting place. Given was out collecting more wood for the fire, their lone source of warmth. None of the three possessed garments fit for the cold, each with just a simple tunic. Perhaps now Bledig wasn't the biggest of their worries. If winter did strike early, they'd be in trouble. There would be no way to enter the river for fish without freezing to death, and the fire would need constant attention. Dane's body needed to heal quickly. Mot's song was good for easing the spirit, and even relieving some pain, but for mending a body so broken, it was not.

Given appealed for help, calling out toward the river at different times throughout the day, believing that if Nataurie were there, she could sing Dane back to health. But the shepherd of the waters answered not, and searching her memory for the lyrics was equally as fruitless.

In the evening after Given had spent the day gathering wood and hoping Nataurie would show, she decided on a different course. "Whether or not you're ready, we need to move along before the cold takes us," said Given to Dane. "At first light, I'll gather materials for a stretcher."

"I agree, we must be moving along," said Dane. "But don't waste time on a cot. My legs are not crushed."

"Not crushed but still too weak. I doubt you would make it far, and it would not be good for your healing."

Determined to prove Given wrong, he strained forward and tried to get up, but his stand didn't last long. The effort caused his head to spin, and he collapsed to the turf. Vivid helped him back onto the pile of leaves he was resting upon.

"I am helpless," Dane said angrily. "And my folly has endangered you both."

"Nevertheless, we three will find safety—if not all of us, then none." Given said, placing her hand on his shoulder.

The warmth of her tone and softness of her touch soothed his anger, and looking into her eyes, his heart missed a beat and breath went away. He was dumbstruck. Never had a woman stolen so much from him: first his gaze, now his words…soon his heart.

For the first time, Given recognized the look in Dane's eyes. It was the same passionate look that Orson had bestowed. She recalled the other times she had noticed him staring at her and felt silly for not realizing it before. Embarrassed, she withdrew her hand.

"I—I may start on a stretcher in the morning, but the…the fire requires attention."

Breathing heavily, she scurried to the forest. As she went deeper into the trees, the embarrassment faded and was replaced with a bit of guilt. If ever she did commit herself to a man, it would be Orson, she thought. Now there could be another vying for her love, one she thought extremely handsome, and from what she knew, no less kind than the first. She wondered how she would respond if he did pursue her. What would she say to let him down?

For the next hour she gathered enough wood to last the night and, since for the moment she was trying to avoid Dane, started collecting supplies for a stretcher as well. Returning to camp as the sun went down, she knelt beside Vivid and sang her to sleep.

As he listened and watched, Dane mused that he had found this woman. "Tell me about yourself," he said. "I want to know more. How did you come to this place? My entire life, we were told by my father to fear the people west of Harbor Wall. 'Naught but savages live outside the city,' he would say. Now I know it to be false. Search all of Auber Civitas and you wouldn't discover nobler folk than you and Vivid. What kind of life have you led, I wonder."

"For the most part, not a pleasant one," Given said, still stroking Vivid's head. "But some of it has been a blessing undeserved." And starting with the times she could remember with the Gallants, she told all about her life. Dane was amazed by her determination to secure a better life for her son and disgusted by Bledig's treatment of her and Grit.

"I will try not to despise him," said Dane scowling. "After all he's done, how you still hope for his betterment astounds me."

"There were times I prayed for his death, but now…now knowing what I do, I hope he is transformed instead. It would be a small thing for a Creator that can do all that I've witnessed. I see now even in his wretched condition, he is being used. Without Bledig's cunning, your king would already possess the Heart." Given went on, telling Dane about everything from her time in Bardorf and meeting Aderyn to the charge of Solas and how Nataurie had rescued her and brought her to help them. "Looking back now, it's easier to see a scheme, a design. Was any of it by chance? I think not…yet after all that has happened, I still fear how this story will end."

Dane leaned forward to catch Given's gaze. "From my banishment until Vivid rescued me, I wished for two things: death for me and death for my father. But now your hope has become my hope, your faith my faith. To whatever end you go, I wish to be by your side."

Given's cheeks burned knowing there was more than a sense of duty behind Dane's statement. She wanted to speak, but nervousness bound her tongue. She nodded acceptance instead. Why did he suddenly affect her so? She didn't ask for these feelings, yet now that they were upon her, she didn't shun them either. As she bedded down for the night, both the excitement over gaining Dane's affections and the guilt of not despising them for Orson's sake wrestled for control of her mind, keeping her awake into the morning hours. By daybreak she had decided the right thing to do was tell Dane about Orson. Maybe it would deter his pursuit.

They rose to a cool—not cold—morning with a slight breeze from the north. Vivid was in a nearby field picking water grass to use as the stretcher binding. Given followed, and soon the sisters had all the materials they needed. Using the long stringy grass twisted into twine, they bound two sturdy poles together with eight flexible willow crossbars. It certainly wouldn't be the most comfortable resting place, but it would get the job done, as long as the sisters had the strength to drag Dane along.

"This will have to do until we can get back to Aksel," said Given with a hint of uncertainty. "He should have some skins that we can use instead of these willow branches. With a decent pace, we could get to him in less than two days' walk, though dragging a cot will slow us. We'll need to arch around Bledig's Cabin to give ourselves every chance to avoid an encounter with him, and still we should pray the north wind will cast our scent away from his cabin."

After a small breakfast of broiled fish they'd reserved for their departure, the sisters helped Dane onto the litter. With one lady on each pole, slowly and with great effort, they dragged him as he clutched the Heart and Vivid's spear in his hands. For their size the sisters both possessed tremendous strength, but Dane was a large man and frequent breaks were needed. The first mile, as they made their way out of the river bottom onto smoother land, was treacherous. The sisters' legs were on fire and arms numb, and though they traded sides several times and covered their hands with water skins to ease their pain, blisters formed on their palms and fingers. Dane didn't have it much better, as the willow branches rubbed and cut into his back, and every bump, hole, and branch they overcame jarred his shoulder, causing pain to surge.

Exhausted after the second mile, they decided to rest a bit and take in some water. Leaving the other two in a small clearing, Given took Vivid's skins and cut back through the trees to the Afon to fill them. To walk without the burden of dragging Dane was a relief for her aching body, but her mind was still weighted with thoughts of him. Since the day began, they hadn't spoken much, but delight rippled through her each time they touched or made eye contact. It felt like betrayal, but she couldn't stop the feeling nor find a good time to tell Dane about Orson.

Her thoughts of Dane were interrupted when she noticed footprints in the wet sand as she approached the river. At first she wondered if they might be her own from when she'd passed through the first time, but as she drew near, she realized Naturie had carried her through that stretch of river. Whoever made them had only gone a little further before doubling back anyway. Knowing someone had recently been there was unnerving. Vigilantly she walked to the river's edge. When she stooped to fill the skins, her eyes remained up and her ears trained, but no one was around to be seen or heard. Still her pulse quickened.

Wanting to get back to Vivid and Dane quickly, she high-stepped away from the river. As she jogged through the forest she heard a call, but the crackle of dried leaves and branches and the whooshing of wind through the trees muffled it. Slowing a bit to listen, she heard it again, this time distinctly. Dane was calling for help. Now sprinting, Given burst into the clearing to discover Dane propped against a tree, Vivid in front of him with spear raised. Before them, about forty or fifty paces, Given discovered the object of their concern—her master.

Given went white as her eyes met those of her abuser. For a moment she felt like a gobbet of meat waiting to be devoured. But Bledig didn't approach his former slave as she stood in the knee high grass, for though she was frightened, he appeared doubly so; and as quickly as Given had come to her sister's aid, he fled east into the woods. Given stood in confusion at first, wondering why he had reacted so, but her shock slowly wore away as she thought about Bledig's reason for fleeing.

She turned to Dane who was grimacing in pain. "You held him off well enough, but you must lie back down now. He's gone."

"I don't understand," said Dane. "He was fast approaching us with nothing to stop him, but when you came through the trees—"

Given Chuckled. "A funny thing it was. I don't know for sure, but I believe he thought I was a bad spirit. His old wench, the one he'd murdered, returned from her watery grave for revenge. If I had known his fear I would have played a scarier role as one raised from the dead…An awful thing it must be to see one you butchered staring back at you."

"Indeed, it must." Dane smiled. "May his tail be forever tucked in fear of the one he has tortured."

Vivid and Given helped Dane back to the ground to rest before Given returned for the skins she'd abandoned when Dane called for help. Not wanting to give Bledig more opportunity to realize that Given was truly flesh and bones, they didn't dawdle long. Perhaps it was the easy terrain over the next few miles or the adrenaline that still surged because of the encounter with Bledig, but their pace was surprisingly more enlivened than before. They were a good half-mile south of Coyote Lake when they passed Bledig's cabin, and with the wind still blowing from the North, they weren't concerned with him picking up their scent again. They walked a couple more miles west of the cabin before curving back toward the river.

Except for the tension Given felt about Dane's growing affection toward her, the rest of the day couldn't have gone any better, and Given knew that unless they strayed they should make it back to Aksel sometime the next day. Her hope swelled at the thought of reuniting with her loved ones in Bardorf. How long had it been since she'd held Grit? She didn't know, but she was confident—for the first time since her search for the Heart had begun—it would soon happen. *I'm sure Aderyn had good times with him. But I'll wager she'll be relieved to see him go.* Given chuckled to herself. *And when I see Orson I'm going to...*But Thoughts of a young Civitian cut in. How was she to react to Orson with Dane around? For Orson's sake she desired for Dane to have no effect on her.

Looking back as she walked, she could see he had somehow managed to fall asleep, or perhaps his eyes were only closed. She smiled but not purposefully; something about him forced the smile. Like a tickle inducing a laugh, it was hard for her to resist. Vivid glanced at her sister and smiled too. Given hadn't said a thing to her about Dane, but Vivid knew her sister was smitten.

***

Night was closing in on them as they had dragged Dane nearly three leagues. The Afon trailed off to the north, and they had run into the stream—though nearly drained—Given had followed the day she'd left Aksel behind. Now she knew for certain it would be less than a day.

"Tomorrow we will follow this," she said, pointing at the tributary. "Unless he's been called away or is in search of me, Aksel will be just up this creek. Tomorrow's night should not beat us to him."

"I look forward to meeting your friend," said Dane. "To hear his story. He may have known one of my acquaintances, maybe even mother."

"I would not doubt it." Given winked towards Vivid who was sitting beside her. "Solas has a way of bringing people together. And from what you say of your mother, it would be a shame to not have known her."

"It truly is a pity that you two never met on this side," said Dane. "But I am persuaded that one day you will meet on the other."

Given turned to Dane who had crawled from the stretcher and was lying on the ground, his form a little more than a silhouette in the meager light of the sunken sun. Though she could not see them clearly through the murk, she felt his eyes like fire upon her and knew he desired her to come close. But she would not give in.

"We needn't waste time sparking a fire tonight," she said, mostly as a distraction. "It should be warm enough."

"Agreed," is all Dane replied as he continued to stare at her through the gray, thinking of all he wanted to say.

Given, for the moment at least, ignored the burning of his gaze and began to sing to Vivid as she lay with her head on Given's thigh. Not wanting to face the inevitable, she continued singing longer than usual. *Maybe he'll fall asleep if I sing long enough*, she thought hopefully. When she'd finally sung her last note and Vivid was breathing heavily in deep slumber, Given lay down as well and the immediate silence that followed assured her that she had succeeded. After closing her eyes she mouthed a simple prayer of thanks and was about to nod off when Dane's voice shook her.

"I apologize for the timing," he said quietly. "I know that you are worn from packing me around all day, but I must and don't know the next time we will be alone." His uncharacteristic nervousness caused him to hesitate, but after a hard swallow he proceeded. "Your songs…they are ointment to my injured soul. Your kindness is my remedy. Your beauty grips my eyes without loosening. And though I am stricken by injury and illness, I cannot contemplate my infirmity for you have captivated my thoughts. I passed through hell to get to you, but I would do it again, for you are heaven here with me."

All she had feared yet still hoped for surfaced in this bold proclamation, and for a moment she was speechless, heart pounding.

"Flattered," she said eventually. "There is no better word I can think than flattered, but it doesn't do justice. What you have said goes far beyond flattery and deeply moves me, but we cannot be." Given began to cry.

"I'm sorry," said Dane. "I do not want you to cry, but I must know why?"

"My heart is divided," Given said. "You have brought me to a place I hoped never to be. You are noble and kind. Your words stir me and gaze weakens me…but I cannot commit to you when I've committed to another already. Please, pursue me not, for my desire betrays my conscience."

Dane was stunned. In just a few days, he'd fallen helplessly in love. To hear that Given was pledged to another was the blow of blows. What was he to say? What could he do?

He wanted to tell her he would fight to win her from the other, he'd do anything it took. He wanted to argue that a prior claim was not a good reason to reject his love. But even as his heart ached, he responded instead, "Then he is the luckiest. I wish you both joy." He would not allow his own desire to compromise Given's honor.

CHAPTER 19. LOYALTIES

*T*HEY RESTED uneasily a few feet apart in the pitch darkness of a cloudy night, both wanting to hold the other, but neither willing to compromise Given's original commitment. When they rose in the morning, Given had concluded it a good thing to finally have her interest in Orson out in the open, even if it meant hurting Dane. Dane on the other hand was still confused by the whole thing. He thought, as unlikely a meeting as it was, that he had surely found the woman he'd spend life with.

After poking Vivid awake, they got an early start to the day. There was nothing to eat, and even if there would have been, they had no fire to cook over. So within a few minutes of rising, the sisters were already pulling Dane west. Though tired and sore from the same demanding chore the day before, they made decent time because the terrain was easy. Since the stream was mostly dry and flat along the edges, it made a good path to follow, though the meandering did make the drag a little longer.

Neither Dane nor Given spoke as they went, but now and again she would glance back to see his expression of sadness. It was difficult for her to not console him. Being the source of his pain, how could she help anyway. She tried instead to distract herself with happy thoughts of forthcoming reunions.

At midday, Given caught sight of a massive oak she remembered passing when she'd first set out. "Keep your eyes wide," she said. "Our camp is near."

What she didn't know was that Aksel had already been tracking them for more than a mile, inspecting the two newcomers' behavior. When he'd decided they were harmless, he came out from hiding to welcome Given back and introduce himself.

"I nearly lost hope and had decided to come after you," he said from a distance, his diminished voice barely audible. "But a whisper in the wind told me to stay, that you would be back soon."

"Aksel," Given lowered Dane's litter to the ground, scooped up the relic and ran toward him. "We've got it. We've got the Heart."

When she reached him, they embraced. "My prayers answered— you're safely back and with your prize." He pushed away and looked her over like a father would his child. "Did he hurt you? Heaven help him if he did."

"It is of no consequence now," said Given with a smile. "All has been made new. I'll tell the tale later, but first you must meet Vivid." Joy flashed across her face as she exclaimed, "My sister!"

"Sister," Aksel whispered in astonishment. "How can it be?"

"By the Shepherd of men alone could we be united," said Given. "But truly she is my sister, sired by my father and adopted by my mother after I was taken."

"I am at a loss," said Aksel. "There is no end to his goodness." Turning to Vivid he bowed slightly. "Pleased to meet you."

Vivid nodded and smiled.

"She does not speak," said Dane as he struggled to his feet.

"A blessing disguised," Aksel said, looking at Vivid. "The tongue has a habit of stirring up more wicked than good." He turned toward Dane who was barely standing under his own weight. "And who is this strapping lad?"

"I am Dane from Auber Civitas, and I have been rescued by these maidens fair."

"Rescued?" Aksel asked with a look of distrust. "What finds you this far from the city and in need of a rescuer?"

"I was banished from the city for attacking a high official. Outside of Harbor Wall the King's assassin put an arrow through my shoulder. For leagues I wandered alongside the Afon with no hope to survive. Death was upon me," He looked at Vivid with pride. "But Vivid pulled me from the pit of despair. She removed this arrow." He held up the spear that Vivid had fashioned. "My life is hers. Days later, Given found us…but not by accident. She was ushered to us by the Great Shepherd. My body is mending, but I doubt I can go long without fainting."

Aksel examined the young Civitian and asked, "Was it justified, your attacking the official?"

"At the moment it seemed right…now I think not. If I had mastered my anger, I would've had no need for rescue." His eyes flashed toward Given. "But the Creator has brought forth beauty from the ashes of my foolishness."

Noticing how Dane looked at her made Given's cheeks burn, but for her there seemed to be no remedy. Trying to ignore it, she turned to Aksel. "His story is genuine. Nataurie, the Shepherd of the Waters, brought me to them so that they might be saved. Over the recent days we have shared much of our past. Dane's is not unlike yours, being outcast from Auber Civitas."

Aksel nodded in acceptance. Looking at Dane, he lowered his voice even further than usual, "I apologize for my questioning, but your—our kin have been scouring the woods on the other side of the Afon in search of something. I believe they desire the Heart, and I thought you could be a part of their company, but I trust Given's judgment of you." He pointed toward the arrowhead attached to the spear's shaft. "Not to mention that was Civitian made…They wouldn't have shot their own, not without being commanded." He motioned them all closer. "I fear the drawing has begun. The beasts have been behaving strangely of late, some dazed, others have packed together when normally they wouldn't. Yestereve, a flock of red-tails soared overhead to the east. Has Freckles been near?"

"No," said Given. "He has not been about since the first day we parted. I sent him back to Aderyn, fearful his presence would endanger my quest." Concern raked her face. "But now that you mention it, I have seen many birds flocking east when the season says they should be flying south. Do you reckon he—"

Aksel nodded. "I believe all creatures are bound to Derog's body —including Freckles."

Suddenly, Given looked panic stricken. "If Freckles and the birds, then Aderyn as well." In desperation she said, "We've got to get back to Bardorf. Grit could be in danger." She stared in contemplation for a moment and looked at Aksel with tears in her eyes. "Do you believe Grit—"

Askel put his arm around his friend, "It is possible he has been beckoned as well."

"If this is true, my hopes are a wasteland." She said, "and for me this journey was in vain." As Aksel held her, a thought crept in, one that added insult to her already damaged spirit. Perhaps Bledig wasn't fleeing from her in their last encounter after all. Could it be that he had been called away?

Aksel gave Given a while to gather herself before he said, "For now we don't know what has become of anyone, so hope remains. But you are right. We need to get back to Bardorf. The Heart is not safe here." He retrieved the pack containing broiled fish he'd dropped at their meeting. "I have rationed enough for a couple days, but who knows when we shall find another source." While the others ate, he fashioned Dane's litter with hide so it would be a little more tolerable at least. With his help they'd certainly be able to move faster, but dragging Dane along would still be slow going.

As they went, Given and Aksel did most of the hauling of Dane, while Vivid packed the supplies. She refused to leave behind the arrowhead spear, even though it had no foreseeable purpose since Aksel had constructed a spear as well. Given figured it held some special meaning for her little sister, so she didn't argue. Tucked under the right arm of Dane wrapped in a scrap of deer hide, the Heart rode. They had no real hope of keeping it from the Civitians if they were besieged, even with Aksel now at their side. He was tough enough to rival any five men in a battle, but the Civitian search parties, with fifteen or twenty men in each, were much too large for him and two ladies to handle.

Not stopping for a break and barely speaking, the four trekked west until they reached the edge of Skeleton Wood where they decided to bed for the night. The sun had sunk, but the air remained warm enough that lighting a fire would be an unnecessary risk to their safety. Stars flickered in the half-moon lit sky as Given shared more with Aksel about her journey to Bledig's. She also apologized to Vivid for saying her journey was in vain. "Even if all falls apart and we fail," she said. "I still found you."

As the conversation transitioned to Dane telling tales of his upbringing, echoes of distant voices seemed to whisper in his ears. He lowered his voice, "Did you all hear that?" But when no one else confirmed, he continued with his story. In many long breaths he told of his friends and brothers and childhood hoping to save his favorite topic for last. "It's a joy to tell of these folks, but it is only in my memory that I behold them now." Speaking to Aksel he continued, "The one most dear to me I have not yet mentioned—

my mother—she was the lady of all ladies, never turning a blind eye to those in need. More than any other she taught me to consider my friends before myself." Although he didn't want to reveal himself as royalty by telling his mother's name to Aksel, his curiosity and desire to speak of her persisted. "I wonder if you knew her…Astrid was her name."

"Astrid," Aksel whispered and paused. "Astrid," he whispered again. "A beautiful name…beautiful and unusual for a Civitian I think." He hesitated once more, and if any of the other three could have seen a little better through night, the look of curiosity and concern on his face would have revealed much more than his words as he said, "She sounds like the fairest of women. What has become of her? Does she yet live in Auber Civitas?"

"Only her body rests behind Harbor Wall now," said Dane in sadness. "Her spirit now rejoices beyond the realm of man and beast."

"Sorrowful," is all Aksel said for a while. He shut his eyes tightly trying to hold back tears. Somehow one managed to slip through to the ground. He never expected to see his beloved Astrid again, but hope that she was leading a happy life had always brought him contentment. Now, that hope was in heaven. His thoughts of love lost ran a long course through his weary mind, but soon another thought stole his attention. If Astrid was Dane's mother, then Dane must be Prince of Auber Civitas. But why would the son of a king have been shot with an arrow and cast into the wilderness? "Your father," he said at last. "Who is he?"

Dane didn't answer. Before he opened his mouth to speak, a voice loud enough for all of them to hear echoed through the night. It was followed by the sound of many feet falling on dried foliage. An invisible company cloaked by darkness fast approached.

"Run," said Dane. "Leave me and hide yourselves."

"We will not," replied Given. "I've sworn not to abandon you."

They scrambled to get Dane on his litter and crossed the edge of the cursed land. With as much speed as they could muster dragging Dane, they went. The increasing sound of feet pounding the surface drove them further into the black wood. They hoped in vain that the pursuers would not follow them there, but louder and louder the pounding grew until they knew fleeing further was of no use. Hiding in the barrenness was impossible.

"There is no hope of escape now," said Aksel. "Whatever approaches does so at a speed not even I can match."

Soon, shadows of men mounted on beasts whirled around them in dim moonlight. They were being surrounded but by whom? They could not see. Aksel drew his blade while Given gripped Aksel's spear and Vivid lifted her own, the three forming a protective circle around Dane and the stone. Dane tucked the Heart beneath his litter and sat on it. He was prepared to die for the cause if need be, but knew he offered little by way of fighting.

When the beating of feet finally ended, men dismounted their beasts and a booming voice called through the darkness, "TORCHES!" The command was followed by the sound of metal scraping together. Small sparks floated to the ground all around, but soon some of them hit their target. A torch blazed from a soldier's left hand; a dull sword could be seen clutched in his right. More strikes and another torch burst into flames, and another, all three at different locations around the travelers. "You are surrounded with archers trained on you," the commanding soldier said. "But with cooperation no harm will befall you."

"What is it you seek?" Aksel responded. "We are but four drifters trying to get back to loved ones, one of us injured. We possess no riches."

"We shall see," said the officer. "Lower your weapons for me to approach."

"Do as he commands," Aksel said, placing his blade on the earth before him. "They are of no use anyway." He looked up toward the commander. "Again I ask, what is it you seek?"

"It is my business to decide and not yours to know. I will search. If I discover not what I'm looking for, I will leave you in peace."

As the commander drew near, his torch illuminated Aksel's face, and he paused with a look of horror. "What sins were committed to earn such a fate?" he whispered.

Aksel answered not and remained silent as the soldier searched him. Given and Vivid cooperated fully, allowing the soldiers to search the pack and their person; but when it came time to search Dane, he held his head down and would not look up.

"I will not ask you again," said the commander. "All have been searched but you. We will have our way no matter—But the commander's jaw froze when Dane finally turned his eyes up, the torchlight revealing his identity.

"How long has it been, Roar?" said Dane. "It is odd to see you so far from Harbor Wall."

"Yes, it is uh—odd," Roar stammered. "Dane? No doubt it is you. How—"

"Father put me in exile," Dane began. "You probably knew that. Well, that wasn't enough to quench his anger. The night I was cast out, he sent someone to make sure I never came back to the city. My wound from his archer's arrow has been mended, but I have not recovered from the infection. I know your allegiance lies with the king but please consider his intentions. What he seeks is beyond what any man should possess. You are too good a man to offer blind obedience."

"I—I can't," Roar lowered to one knee. "I mean, it is difficult to believe, but it is you. What do you know of what your father seeks?"

"I was present long enough to know…to see his passion for the relics. He seeks them and believes the legends. The Minister of the Wild may still have power, and Father wants it. Even if you find it, do not take it to him. For one man to possess this power—" Dane shook his head.

"Indeed, his intentions have not gone unnoticed by his son, but I am still sworn to obey; and I hope to be rewarded for my allegiance. But larger than my hope for reward is my fear of his wrath—if the king would do this to his own son. He has certainly not been just of late, arresting any who challenge his opinions. Even Erlend has been locked away. Never could I have imagined my captain in chains, yet he is."

"But he is alive?" asked Dane, concerned.

"Yes, I have seen him, talked to him even. Not in good spirits, but alive nonetheless."

"And what of my brothers, are they well?"

"As you did, York has gone into training. So far he seems inept in handling weaponry, but I've been told he is a master tactician. Leif still grieves for you and your mother, but the beasts have helped."

"Beasts?" said Dane. "What beasts?"

"They'd been gathering outside Harbor Wall for a while when we set out a few days ago, some in herds and some alone. All different kinds of birds, dogs, wildcats, and rodents had arrived—strange beasts I'd never imagined too. Some seemed more human than beast…but still not fully human. Leif has taken a liking to them, one little fellow in particular. For him I am glad."

Roar's eyes narrowed. "Everyone agrees the strangest and most terrifying is Magnus's new guard, an immense creature with the head and wings of an eagle and the body of a great cat. It would be folly for a hundred men with as many beasts to challenge him."

Wings? Could it be, Given thought. *Could this creature be… Aderyn's son?*

"Feeding them all has been a constant chore for the city folk," Roar continued, "but I won't complain. Getting about on the horses that have come beats walking. A good steed can carry a soldier thrice as far as he could walk in a day, which makes searching for the relics easier."

"So horses have come too," Dane said. "From stories alone, have I imagined their beauty."

"I will bring one over if you wish," said Roar. "but don't get attached. I have none to lend, and even if I did, they follow the will of the king alone. He whispers to them, and by some magic I do not understand, they are entranced. They carry us about already knowing the direction his Majesty has chosen. I believe they can see through darkness, for it was not I or any man in my company who spotted you here."

Dane recalled the time Magnus placed the crown on his head, how it seemed there was an entire army he could control, but at that point he could not see. Perhaps by now Magnus had discovered the solution to that problem as well. Dane reasoned that his father might be able to see him through the horses eyes if they were to be brought closer. "Someday, when my strength returns I will gaze upon their beauty and hope to ride fast and free, but not tonight. Tonight, I desire only rest and healing, so keep your beasts thither and finish your search of us."

"As you wish," said Roar. He bowed, and in a voice barely audible even to Dane, he said, "But I will not shame myself by searching you, my prince." He pretended to pat around on Dane's litter before springing to his feet and announcing, "I see nothing here that we should desire. Let's ride." He bowed slightly to Dane once more and fetched his horse. After extinguishing his torch, he mounted and rode with his company into the night.

Given was the first to speak after the riders were gone, "What happened? Who are you that the commander would treat you with such respect? Is your father truly the king?"

Dane thought for a moment before saying, "It could be that I don't know. I was raised by a man who all my life I reckoned to be my father, but in the end disowned me, alleging my illegitimacy. I had no grounds to argue, nor could I contest his decision to cast me out. Who in Auber Civitas has the right to defy the king?" Dane could feel a fresh anger rising in him but breathed deeply to soothe it.

"It is odd that a king would toss out his son like refuse," said Aksel. "Were you his firstborn?"

"Yes, I am the eldest of three, but have never been favored. In fact, though I was raised under his roof, Magnus has always treated me as a bastard. After Mother died he told me he had only kept me around for her sake and that my real father was a rapist. It is still difficult to believe."

"Partial truths are easier to sell," said Aksel.

"What do you mean?"

"Perhaps there's some truth in the king's claim about you. Maybe you're not his son, but maybe you're not the son of a rapist either. Could it be that your mother had a lover before Magnus?"

Dane thought for a moment about the conversation he'd had with Astrid the night she died. "She never mentioned another lover, only a dear friend."

"And what became of her friend?"

"She said that tragedy took him away." Dane clutched the star pendant beneath his tunic and thought about the way his mother spoke about her friend. "She didn't say it, but listening to her speak, one might have believed that she loved him. Is it possible?"

"I believe it is more than possible," is all Aksel replied.

CHAPTER 20. LORD OF LAND RETURNS

AFTER SPENDING the night huddled with her companions more than a mile within Skeleton Wood's border, Given rose feeling surprisingly well rested. Something was different from the last time she'd passed through with Aksel. The foul air that seemed to choke life from everything had been replaced with a freshness that welcomed the living. Given wondered about this as she took a stroll around.

Walking out to where Roar's company had surrounded, she knelt to inspect the tracks. Like Dane, she'd only heard of the great mounted beasts in stories and was disappointed when he turned down Roar's offer to have a horse brought over. *Perhaps one day I'll gaze upon their beauty in the daylight* she thought as she fingered a hoof print. Recalling her time ripping through the water upon Nataurie's back, she wondered if riding a horse was similar.

Glancing up, Given saw Aksel walking in the distance over the grayness that was the cursed land. *Couldn't be hunting,* she thought, going out to him. *There is no life here but us…and water is just as scarce.* When she came close enough to be heard without yelling she said, "they were strange tidings to hear that I have been dragging around the prince of the Civitains on a litter." Even stranger to her was the thought that the Prince had become enamored with her, but she didn't dare mention it.

"Strange indeed," said Aksel, staring at the ground. "I'm not sure what it all means, but there must be purpose in it." He lifted his hands, in one was a bow and a quiver of arrows and in the other a pack. "Whether or not we will discover that purpose I don't know, but it has brought provisions regardless."

"Things forgotten?" asked Given.

"Intentionally, no doubt—a soldier aiding his prince…they are welcome." Aksel opened up the pack to reveal enough jerky to last the journey back to Bardorf and pointing toward some items lying beside a blackened stump he said, "Four skins of fresh water."

Given smiled. "More than welcome I'd say." But a look of concern flashed across her face. "When Roar mentioned the creature that now guards the king…I thought of Aderyn. Do you believe he could be related—even her son?"

"It was a thought that crossed my mind, and it worries me as well."

After scooping up the water skins, they started back toward the others. "Have you noticed the air?" asked Given. "It has changed since the last time we passed through."

"Yes, I've noticed," said Aksel. "Breathing was drudgery before; now it flows with ease. All feels lighter, more alive." Kneeling, he put the pack down, scooped some soil and sniffed it. "Even the earth is different. There's warmth, and the stench is not as it was."

Given paused watching him. "Normally, I would welcome life and think the opposite bad, but knowing what you've said of this place makes me wonder what evil could be at work. What is being brought to life?"

"You are not alone," Aksel stood up with pack in hand. "This land was doomed by Derog. He alone can free it."

When they returned to the others Vivid was opening her eyes. Upon seeing the bow and arrows she marveled.

"They were left by the soldiers for us," said Aksel. "I could teach you a few things while Dane still rests if you'd like. You may require some skill with weaponry before long."

Vivid nodded excitedly and bounced to her feet. Taking the bow from Aksel, she admired the sturdy ash and sinew stave, moving her fingers over the arch. She plucked the string a couple times and turned her attention to one of the dogwood arrows, looking down its length. Afterward, she stroked the turkey feather fletching and touched the sharp point of the iron arrowhead with the tip of her finger. Impressed, she smiled at Given and Aksel. The three walked to a nearby stump and stepped off twenty paces. Aksel showed Vivid how to nock, aim and shoot before turning her loose to practice. She was a natural, hitting her target dead on after a couple of tries, and every time thereafter. After about a dozen shots, Aksel taught her how to hold more than one arrow in her drawing hand for rapid fire. This feat didn't go as smoothly.

"It took much effort for me as well," said Aksel, taking three arrows in his drawing hand and the bow in his left. "It is a skill developed over time." Without another word he ran toward the stump, vaulted from it and let all three arrows fly, one after the other, before striking a foot on the ground. Vivid and Given were both amazed to see each of the arrows had hit its mark in a shriveled oak several paces away.

Aksel retrieved the arrows and took them with the bow back to Vivid. "Your hands are gifted. Train and soon your skill will surpass mine."

Vivid nodded acceptance of the new task she was charged with and mouthed *thank you* to Aksel, who bowed slightly in return.

When Dane woke in the second hour he felt as good as he had in a long time, so good in fact that he rose to his feet under his own power without a shudder. "Incredible, this is incredible." He whirled his wounded arm jogging around his litter. "Something has happened. Solas himself must've healed me in the night; almost no pain remains."

"It is incredible," Aksel said perplexedly. "An invisible power is at work here and except for my knowledge of this place, I'd think it was Solas as well."

Something on the ground next to Dane's litter caught Aksel's eye, and he squatted for a closer look. "Curious," he said, fingering a tiny green sprout before noticing others encircling where Dane had slept. He lightly brushed over them with his hand. "Perhaps the curse *has* been lifted." Flipping over Dane's litter, he was astonished to find a sapling, of a type none present could figure, springing up from the gray earth.

"I could have sworn something was growing into my back through the night," said Dane. "But I reckoned it was the stone."

"The stone!" gasped Given. "Where is it?"

Aksel held up his hand. "Do not be anxious. I believe it is still here." Brushing back some of the soil beneath the sapling he proved his assumption correct. In fact, the little tree seemed to have sprouted from the Heart itself, as if the ruby were an acorn or seed. He stood and fixed his eyes on Given. "Until lord of land returns, death there will be. The curse of Derog has been lifted, at least in part. Skeleton Wood may well become Bella Floris once more, if only while the stone remains here."

"Bella Floris," Given whispered. Her eyes were wide as she crouched beside the tree and touched its roots and branches. She raked the Heart with her fingernails to test its authenticity. Convinced that it was indeed the Heart, she looked up at Aksel. "I hate to supplant the Lord of this land a second time, but the Heart cannot stay here—not yet anyway." She crouched, clutched the sapling in both hands, and gave a hard tug, ripping it from the earth. The tree immediately withered and the roots and stem fell to the ground, returning the stone to its prior form—albeit dustier. She stashed it in her pack.

"Let us waste no more time here," said Aksel. "We must return to Bardorf for Grit, and warn all we can of the forthcoming doom." He snatched up his spear and two skins of water. Looking at Dane while pointing toward the litter he said, "You'd better bring that along. Healing came unexpectedly to you in this place, but like the sapling, your health may diminish as rapidly as it came."

Dane did as he was told and took up the litter while Vivid clung to her bow, quiver and pack and Given toted the Heart and remaining supplies. Racing through skeleton wood, even loaded as they were, it took them little time to cross, and by the end of the day, after realizing not a single symptom had returned, Dane abandoned his litter. For the next few days nothing crippled their flight, and the rations Aksel had saved added to those Roar had left them kept their energy up and bellies full enough. Now that Dane was able and knowing the danger that hastened behind them, Aksel demanded that they travel by night as well. The stars guided them. Given was more than okay with this. She was anxious to see Grit. Her mind constantly teetered back and forth from fear that he was lost in the wilderness to faith that Aderyn was still looking out for him.

On the fourth night after reuniting with Aksel, as they trudged sleepily along, the tree line to the northwest seemed to split as a row of beasts the size of Bledig's cabin lumbered through, their shadows long cast by the gibbous moon. Hunkering down in a cluster of sumac, the travelers gazed in wonder as the creatures with their scraggly coats and ivory tusks paraded by, close enough to perceive the moonlight gleaming in their dark eyes and to feel the rumblings of the earth beneath giant furry feet. Billows of steam rose as their hot breath intermingled with the cold night air.

"Mammoths," whispered Aksel from beneath the leafy cover. "How can man contend?"

When the herd had passed, they came out of hiding and went on their way, walking a few more hours through the dead of night before resting. They said little as much weighed on their minds now that they had witnessed a small portion of the strength that Magnus could so easily muster.

Given wondered if she was doing the right thing keeping the Heart intact. *Destroying it may be our only hope*, she thought. *But what would happen if I did*? As though he sensed her distress, Dane grasped her hand. He vowed silently to accompany both Given and Vivid through whatever trials they faced, whether Given was ever to be his or not. She did not withdraw, for even through the peril her heart yearned for him.

***

When dawn arrived, Aksel, not having slept, was the only one awake. He poked the others to their feet, "We should make it to Baredorf before nightfall."

The day felt shortened as the sun sped west along with them. Herds and flocks of beasts rushed past toward Auber Civitas, but the travelers didn't slow down to watch. If anything, they went faster, knowing that these creatures would soon be gathering to make war against them. It was bright with few clouds, but the air was cool as the north wind whispered of the cold night to come. In the early evening they spotted evidence of their destination in the distance as smoke swirled from the welcoming fires outside Bardorf's dwellings.

Aksel, who was leading the group, hesitated. "I have guided you safely back, but perhaps…perhaps I shouldn't go with you into the village."

Given looked questioningly at her troubled guide for a moment and believing she figured his conflict, said, "Do not let your appearance stop you. No one there will judge."

Aksel sighed. "If it were only that, I'd happily accompany you. But my true fear is hurting a dear friend."

"What do you mean?" Given asked.

"No doubt you've wondered how I know Aderyn. In truth, she was my savior. Sent by Solas himself, she descended from the heavens to draw me from the flames outside Harbor Wall. It was her who flew me to the Gallants for healing; it was her who I found in the Bighorn Mountains on Mount Eyrie; and it was her who gripped my heart—my heart which belonged to another. Aderyn looked beyond the scars, and loved me unconditionally, confessing her desire for me to remain with her. I wounded her deeply when I left, and I wish for it to never happen again. To remind her of that pain, to cause her grief…I'd sooner surrender my life."

Given wondered how she hadn't realized it before. Only someone with Aderyn's ability could have rescued Aksel from the pyre. As Aderyn had explained to Given when she revealed her true identity as Bird Guide, it must've been the one time since Derog's uprising that she'd flown. "I'm sorry. I didn't realize," Given said, knowing what it was to have a heart torn by love. "But for both your sakes I must speak…you are my friends and I wish you happiness. What heights you both overcame to find each other, what depths you crossed…only to deny love. You torture yourself by being away, lingering outside her village wishing to go in. Whatever hurt you've caused her can be healed, and your own reservations vanquished…" Given looked down, embarrassed she'd overstepped. "I mean no ill-regard toward your Star…if hope remains for your reunion—"

Aksel appeared wounded, "There is no hope. I despise the thought, but never again shall I see my Star shine on earth." He looked away, tormented with the thought. "I will enter with you, if only to beg Aderyn's pardon…but she deserves much more than I can offer."

CHAPTER 21. BENEATH THE VEIL

*E*URIG WAS feeding logs to a small fire outside his house as Given and company approached—Aksel trailing far behind. Not knowing who it was sprinting his way, Eurig called his two sons out before taking up an axe for defense. "Come no closer! I don't welcome a fight, but I'll do as needed."

"Neither do we come to battle." Given dropped everything but the pack containing the Heart. "At least not you. I only wish to see my son."

"Given, is it you?" Orson called, stepping beside his father to see. When he confirmed the fact with his eyes he set out toward her, and she to him. They met in embrace. His gargantuan arms swallowed her small figure.

"Where is he?" Given said eagerly. "I need to see him."

Orson lowered her. Guilt overtook him as he confessed, "He's gone Miss Given. Something took him…I tried all that I could to stop it, but it was stronger." He spun, revealing a chunk of flesh missing from his shoulder. His face and arms were scratched and scabbed over. "I tried to stop it…but it took him and flew away."

Given melted from his arms.

He followed her to the ground. "I'm sorry, I'm sorry. I tried…"

After shedding many tears, a thought struck Given and to Orson she said, "But it flew? You said it flew away? It was Aderyn. The thing that took Grit was Aderyn, and there may still be hope that they're well."

"No, it wasn't even human. It was like a bird—a huge bird."

By now Vivid and Dane had made it to them, and Eurig had come with Torben from the village.

"The explanation could take longer than we now have, but I speak the truth. Grit was taken by Aderyn, and I must go after them."

Orson shook his head. "It couldn't have been—"

"Her words are more than ramblings." Aksel had crept beside the gathering, startling Eurig and sons. "There is a power that has long been sleeping, but has awakened. Aderyn is part of that power. She has the ability to change form."

Orson stood between Given and Aksel, "Who are you?"

"He is Aksel, my guide and friend," Given answered before Aksel could. "And he knows the truth which I speak."

"But I'm not the only one here who can bear out," Aksel said, his gaze fixed on Eurig. "There is one with weightier testimony than mine perhaps."

Wanting to remain silent, Eurig looked away. But Orson pressed him. "What does he mean Papa? What do you know?"

Eurig growled. "Less than this man believes I do." His tone softened as he said, "But more than I've told you. They speak the truth about one thing at least: Birdie does have the power to transform. She is a Skin Walker."

"Can't be," Orson said. "Is she not a harlot and aren't the stories about people changing form make-believe, told to scare children?"

"What she does for bread makes no difference, even Walkers need to eat," said Eurig. "And I wish the stories were made up... But the truth is that Skin Walkers are real. My eyes be a witness."

Aksel, still staring at Eurig, said, "And having known the atrocities in the past I realize why you are wary to speak the truth to your kin, but it is time for you to make a choice. By some devilry of man, the ancient power of Derog has returned, and we must unite against him. I've seen enough to know there is more to your story than you let on, and if the legends lend to the truth, perhaps you are one freed from Derog's enchantment. Don't squander the gift...make a choice!"

Eurig seemed to ponderAksel's words for a moment and said, "Having so few possessions and no one to love, it must be easy for you to exchange sense for folly, but I have much to live for. Nay, it is not my business to get involved, nor would there be any more hope for your cause if I did." He stared at Aksel in irritation. "I will say no more."

"As you wish," Aksel spat. "But know that soon your only choices will be to flee or fight." He cast his gaze back toward Given. "I must go now to muster what little help I can before the clash that could be our end. I know you're anxious to find Grit but please wait. If I have not returned by dawn on the sixth day, go in search of him without me. My heart tells me he is safe. Aderyn took him, and they will be together, even behind the wall of Auber Civitas." Pressing his mouth to Given's ear, he whispered, "Tell no one of the Heart, for it is where it belongs, safe with the Gallants."

Given clutched the pack containing the Heart and reluctantly agreed to not go immediately in search of Grit, knowing their only real hope now was in Solas's wisdom. Where was he? she wondered. She prayed for guidance.

Dane on the other hand refused to sit idle while something so important was transpiring and volunteered instead to accompany Aksel. Hugging Vivid tightly he said, "I leave you in capable hands," before grasping Given's hand and shaking it awkwardly. He turned his eyes to Orson, "Defend them."

The two Civitian's borrowed a few supplies, including warmer garments, from the brothers and darted south to alert the folks residing in the small fortified village of Bockdorf, while the others gathered near a fire outside of Eurig's house. Not wanting Orson to be burdened with guilt, Given tried her hardest to hide the distress of losing Grit yet again as she spent the next hour telling Torben and him what had happened—excluding the part about the stone of course.

"I've never heard a bigger tale," Torben said, amazed. "Not even Papa tells them that big. But even after seeing that giant bird and hearing what Papa said about it, it is still difficult to believe."

Resting her hand on his, Given said, "Before long you will see enough to convince."

Torben shook his head with nothing to say for once.

"You must be worn from your travels," Orson broke the silence. "You're welcome to your old house. It hasn't been touched since Birdie—since she left."

Given was heartsick. She didn't know how she'd react to Grit's things left behind, but she was glad to have somewhere to sleep. "I thank your father for keeping it for me. I know there are others in need of a house that could have taken it, and I have fallen behind on rent."

Torben scoffed, "Papa didn't save it for you. Orson's been working until dark every day—even later many times—so he can pay Papa for you, so you'd have a place here when you returned... Ms. Given you've got him hooked."

Embarrassed, Orson nudged Torben. "You say too much little brother." But there was certainly no hiding the fact that he was indeed hooked.

"Even when I'm away, you look after me," said Given. Compelled by his kindness she kissed him softly.

Vivid smiled as she watched the two, no doubt wondering which man, Orson or Dane, would win her sister's heart in the end. At least for the time being, it appeared Orson would be victorious.

Orson pulled Given close and kissed her again. Caressing her cheek, he said, "It may not be the best time to say it." He sighed deeply searching for the right words, "But Torben is right, I—I do these things because I want you to stay here—with me."

Given froze in the moment, surprised by the usually timid Orson's candor and not knowing how to respond. It was the second profession of love she'd received in only a few days, and although she wanted to reciprocate his expression, a gnawing deep within stopped her. There was too much going on, and still she felt the guilt of being smitten with another.

"My belly's nearly full of this," Torben said to Vivid, breaking the silence. "Maybe we should leave these two to it."

"No, you should not go," said Given. It was the opportunity needed to change the subject. "These days have been hard enough on us. It's time we rest." She kissed Orson once more. "I will see you in the morning." She smiled as she rose, slowly pulling her hand away from his. When she turned to go, a thought she'd had earlier suddenly struck her again. "Before we go, there is something I hope one of you can answer. It would ease my mind to know what became of Gar."

"Ol' Gar," Torben laughed. "Last I saw of him, he limped into the village, packed what he could carry and headed west. He didn't seem himself though—said little."

"It wasn't long after you left," said Orson. "No one has seen him since. It is just as well, I hate the way he talked to you and Birdie, whether Papa appreciated his hard work or not."

"Thank you, it is a comfort to know." Given bowed, gathered her supplies, and scurried to her house alongside Vivid who was holding her bow in one hand and a borrowed candle in the other.

Upon entering, they barricaded the door behind them. When she caught sight of Grit's papoose wadded in the corner, she nearly broke down. She lifted it up, pressed her cheek against the softened deer skin and thought of the many times she'd carried her son in it. "I miss him." She grasped Vivid's hand. "Please pray we are united soon. I don't know how much more my heart can bear." Given stashed the Heart, still in her pack, in a basket and instructed Vivid to keep it hidden and secret no matter what happened. They bedded together on the same mat, comforting each other through the chill of night.

***

Aksel and Dane had spent the first night and day instructing those in Bockdorf and other surrounding villages and tribes that they needed to unite. There was little success, yet they managed to summon a small band of warriors at least. They told them to meet in a few days in Bardorf where they might devise a suitable plan of defense. It was not until their second night that the two Civitians were able to stop for a rest, and after striking a fire, they sat to warm themselves and talk. It was the first time they'd truly been alone together in stillness. At first, their conversation focused mostly on Aksel's plan to take a stand against Magnus, which he said was the main charge of Solas—after retrieving the Heart.

"Our chances are poor, especially with the number we've gathered thus far; but if we can rally villagers from Holzhagen and Faber Glen, together we might make a worthy stand. They are men learned in war and battle tested—although mostly against each other. They must realize their unification is vital. Let us hope their leaders are more understanding than Bardorf's. Eurig has become a greedy fool."

"What do you know of him?" asked Dane. "You seemed to guess secrets not even his sons knew."

"I don't *know* a lot," Aksel tossed a log into the fire, sending sparks flurrying into the night. "But I can assume much from what I've seen and what Civitian legend lends me. From watching Eurig working in the woods on occasion, I know that he possesses great strength. He tosses trees about as though they were branches. A gift of strength such as that was not bestowed on men. But on the Deroheed? Yes, they have been gifted—"

"If part of the Deroheed," said Dane. "Why hasn't he been summoned as Aderyn and the others have? Would he not be under the control of the same power?"

"I would reckon as much too, if not for—" Aksel paused, pondering his words. "If not for legend…" He waved his hand as if to dismiss his thought, "But it may amount to nothing."

"What legend?" Dane insisted. "Why mention it if nothing? I have come to help, I must know."

Aksel sighed, "You of all people have the right to know. I have hoped for a good time to tell you." He stared contemplatively at the fire. "For generations the Civitians have protected the Diamond mind of Derog—you know that at least—but only a few know there's more. There was a fragment, a smaller chunk of his Mind that broke away when Solas defeated his brother. It had become tradition that the first born to the throne of Auber Civitas would always possess this fragment."

Dane gripped the Star beneath his skins wondering if Aksel had somehow seen it. "And how do you know about it…if only royals should know the secret?"

"That is the peculiar thing; I only know of it because I am royalty. In fact, Ingeborg's Star as it is called, was rightly mine." Aksel watched as confusion consumed Dane's countenance. "But I have given it to another—one that I loved."

"You speak in riddles…tell me plainly what you will."

"I am Aksel, first born of Haskell and heir to the Civitian crown. My brother, who by means of treachery now sits enthroned, is Magnus. Out of jealousy he set me up as a traitor and our courts sentenced me to death by burning. It was all for a woman—one whose love had fallen on me instead of him." Aksel paused, allowing Dane time to turn the information over in his head. "He desired my lover…he desired—"

"My mother," Dane bounced to his feet and shook his head. "Can it be true? What proof do you have?" He sank to his knees, "I need to know."

Aksel placed his hand on Dane's shoulder. "Perhaps the best evidence is the Star itself. I had given it to Astrid our last night together. Have you seen it?"

Upon hearing his words, Dane had little doubt that Aksel was being truthful in all things. He reached under his skins and beneath his tunic and brought forth the fractured diamond pendant, Ingeborg's Star.

At the sight numbness gripped Aksel. This thing had haunted his thoughts for a score of years, and having the Star before him without his beloved Astrid only echoed his loss of her. His desire, as it had been for some time, was to reach out and claim Dane as his son, but Dane needed to reckon the truth for himself. All Aksel could think to speak was Ingeborg's Verse—the poem he'd shared with Astrid when last they conversed:

Sun shaded by cloud
Ready to shine but for this shroud
Tis darkness without
But within this light
Yearns to radiate the suffering night

"It was you!" cried Dane, throwing his arms around Aksel. "What else can there be?" But he knew what else there could be already, and having no easy way to ask the question that pricked his mind, Dane said plainly, "Did you lie with her? Be not modest; I know what it could mean."

Aksel nodded, "We were lovers indeed."

Love emanated as they embraced. Never had a father been so glad to discover his son, nor a son his father.

Having years to catch up on, Dane told of what had happened in Auber Civitas after his father's banishment. Aksel was saddened to hear of his own mother's death, but happy that Dane had at least gotten to know his grandmother.

"She was good to us," said Dane, smiling. "Perhaps *too* good…or so mother said." His smile vanished as he stared into the flames. "I miss them."

"We are both doomed to that end." Aksel squeezed his son's shoulder.

Silence took them for a long while as they thought of all that had come about. At length Dane took the Star into his hand and said, "You should have this back. It is rightfully yours."

"No," said Aksel, "not so long as you are here. It would have become yours at manhood regardless."

"Then I shall wear it with double pride now, knowing it's significance." He slipped the chain over his neck and tucked the pendant under his clothes once more.

Aksel looked thoughtfully at Dane as he did so. "I wonder," he said, pointing toward the covered pendant. "You've worn this through all our travels together, have you not?"

Dane nodded, "Only to keep it hidden from Magnus have I removed it since mother gave it to me."

"Could it be possible that this stone is part of your cure? The life being restored to Bella Floris by the relics—from the Heart to the mind—could have passed through you, bringing about your healing."

"One can only guess," said Dane, "but the idea has much reason." He stroked his forehead with both hands in thought. "There is yet more of the Star to question though. I see visions…I have dreams that cannot be stopped, frightful ones. It is like thinking with another's mind—seeing with someone else's eyes. Memories of experiences I never had spring forth…and beasts… there are always beasts awaiting command. Sometimes I see my brothers surrounded by odd company, York with great cats, Leif with a young boy—one with yellow eyes. I cannot stop the visions —even with eyes open."

Aksel said what Dane was thinking. "The Star must still be linked to the Mind…you are seeing Magnus's thoughts." A look of panic struck Aksel. "And if you can see his thoughts—"

"He may know mine as well," Dane was on his feet in a hurry. "I shouldn't have left her. We must fly!" After shedding their outerwear, they snatched their weapons and sprang into the cold darkness.

CHAPTER 22. WINGS AND FURY

WHATEVER ATTEMPT Dane might have made to fulfill his promise to protect Given would not be realized on that night, for Magnus had already dispatched his best to tiny Bardorf; and unlike men who are restricted by land's obstacles, these creatures could not be hindered, as they soared far above the mud pits and thorny tangles of earth.

Torben was the first to herald their coming. At about midnight while piddling under an elm canopy, he saw the shadows—large ones at first—eclipsing the light of the moon at times. Back-and-forth they glided over the village. They were followed by a flurry of smaller shadows skimming the surface. He ran to Eurig and shook him, "Papa, get up! It's back, get up! The giant bird is here with many!"

Eurig pushed him away. "They search only for the stone, which we do not have. Rest easy. This is not our fight if we do as they ask."

Awoken by the clamor, Orson was to his feet. "I'm going to Given, she will need me."

Eurig tried to grab hold of his son, but he was out the door, running toward his love. When he arrived the door was still bolted, and not wanting to draw attention from the invaders, he tapped lightly and whispered, "Given, Given get up. Birdie has come."

Vivid was the first to hear the tapping as Given was enveloped in deep sleep and a dream of flying. She woke with a start when Vivid violently shook her.

"What—what is it? Who's there?" she mumbled as the haze of sleep wore off. Going to the door she listened for a moment to the tapping. "Who calls?"

"It's Orson. I think Birdie is back. Many creatures circle in the sky with her."

Fright seized Given. *They're here for it...they've come for the Heart.* She snatched the pack and felt inside for the stone. It was there, nestled in safety. "What should I do?" she repeated in prayer. A familiar voice, likely one from her memory, came to her, but it could have just as easily been audible. "*Only with the Gallant will it be safe.*" From these words there was only one thing she had a mind to do. Thrusting the pack into Vivid's arms, she said, "Hide this until they are gone, and afterwards let no one know you have it —not even friends. If it seems right to do so and there's no other way, destroy it." She swallowed hard, almost choking on her words. "Come not after me, even in my despair." Given unbarred the door to let Orson inside, and when she embraced him, Vivid slipped through the opening and darted west toward Wether's Field, evading the eyes of all the stalkers—save one.

"Where will she run in such an hour?" Orson turned in pursuit. "I will bring her back—"

But Given gripped his hand, "She has gone because I sent her to hide. They are here for me, not her."

"They will not hurt you," Orson said as he peered through the open door, holding Given behind him. "Whatever may come, it will not harm you."

The sound of splintering wood tore through the night, followed by cries for help, and Eurig's voice rang above the noise. "What is your business here?"

A familiar voice, albeit hollow and lifeless, responded, "We have found eyes of emerald and a mind of diamond, our bones of gold have been restored as well…but a heart we lack. The Gallant has come here with it. Give her to us."

Given didn't wait for Eurig to give her up; instead, she twisted free of Orson's grasp and ran to face her brainwashed friend who'd taken human form once more. Aderyn turned, and though it was difficult to see through the dark, her expression was like her voice, hollow and lifeless.

"Do you not recognize me Aderyn, friend?"

"So, you are its keeper?" Aderyn made no indication that she remembered Given. "Give the Heart to us and you shall go free."

"Even if it were here I would die rather than grant it, but search as you might, and still you will not find the Heart. But know this: if you should tear through this village for it, it will be destroyed."

Aderyn's expression changed not as she stepped toward Given. "Your courage be your folly and damnation, Gallant. You must come with me if it is as you say."

Given stood in awe and terror as her friend transformed before her. Aderyn's brown skin and silky black hair was replaced with feathers, gray like storm clouds. Her eyes were lightning in the darkness.

But snatching Given from the beast's frightful gaze was Orson. "You will not have her." He shoved Aderyn back and stood between her and Given, prepared to surrender all for the one he loved.

Aderyn thrust from the ground over Orson and clasped Given's arms with unyielding force. Given screamed in agony as the talons ripped her flesh, but Orson would not be slighted. He leapt on Aderyn's back and wrenched hard on the giant bird's head until she loosened her hold. It was his undoing, for in all the ruckus, he had become unaware of the beast that yet hovered above the village. It's fury was swift; it's rage nearly painless for Orson as the beast —half-lion, half-eagle—sank its claws into the back of the hero's neck, severing his spinal cord. After dragging the drooping mass free, the beast cast it to the earth and soared up and away alongside its mother, who had recaptured a screaming, writhing, heartbroken Given. To the east they soared through the cold blackness at a speed the fastest of stallions could only hope to match, but still not fast enough to dry Given's tearful eyes, her first love slain.

Back in Bardorf mourning began immediately for Torben and his mother as they gathered Orson's body in linen and took it to their home for preparation. But rage and regret gripped Eurig's heart and through the forest he galloped—no longer in the form of man —toward the east, hoping to overtake his son's murderer. Though his black eyes were well suited for the darkest of nights and his thick fur and padded paws could not be penetrated by the sharpest thorns, he grew winded from the sprint and could not keep pace, but he swore not to take on human likeness again until his son's death was avenged.

***

Vivid however, continued with the Heart in the opposite direction, ignorant of all happenings in Bardorf. Her prayerful thoughts went up like steam as she ran through the wilderness, and she wondered if she could be the final hope. *How far should I go? Should I return to Bardorf with the Heart or should I hide it first? Should I return to Bardorf at all?*

The underbrush thickened and running through the shadowy forest grew ever more difficult. She needed to slow, to breathe, to think clearly, but fear of what could happen if the Heart fell into evil hands spurred her on. At last when all energy was exhausted and she was simply stumbling along, a root or vine snagged her foot and she tumbled over. Her pack with the heart flew from her hand into the weeds. After twisting to her back, she lay catching her breath and staring up into the dense oak canopy. The lively tumult of summer nights was long gone, and other than the occasional rattling of leaves, Vivid heard only her own panting and heartbeat for some time. But a faint crackling in the forest a distance behind alerted her that she wasn't alone. The footfalls were slow and calculated—heel to toe—like those of an experienced hunter. She leaned forward to see, but shadows of branches and leaves, and silhouettes of trunks and bushes were all that she perceived. The crackling grew louder as the hunter drew near. Vivid started for the pack she'd dropped, but froze with a thought. *This stalker, whoever it may be, probably flew in with the others seeking the Heart and has followed me from Bardorf. If I take up the pack and it gets me, it will have what it wants. I must not let it happen.*

She abandoned the pack to the weeds and scanned her surroundings for a suitable weapon, all the while cursing herself for rushing off without her bow. She kicked a branch. Lifting it she could see. It was large enough to do some damage but not so large that she couldn't swing it. It would make a proper club, or so she thought, as she turned to face the stalker. But what she saw when she turned both terrified and enraged her as Given's stories of her sister's master rushed into her mind. Her pursuer's yellow eyes seemed to shine through the blackness upon her. There was nowhere she could hide now even if she had the thought. Her mind screamed for him to stop, warning him of the repercussions if he didn't, but of course no such thing came from her lips. As she raised her club in confidence, she was all but ready to strike when her pursuer stopped and turned his eyes to the north. At first Vivid couldn't see why and wondered about it, even considering coming at the stalker while he was distracted. But after a lengthy moment's wait, a whooshing sound reached her ear as an axe flew end-over-end through the air and slammed against a tree behind the fellow with yellow eyes.

"That one'll cost nothing," a voice unfamiliar to Vivid called. The fellow burst into a hardy chuckle.

"Mind your business," the yellow-eyed fellow hissed. "I'm after the rock, and I'll be taking it if no one's to be hurt."

"Bledig, you mangy mutt." The other fellow laughed. "Is that you? Don't you recognize me?"

Bledig ignored the newcomer, focusing his attention back on Vivid, "Give it to me."

Vivid shook her head in defiance with club still raised. Bledig advanced. Vivid's arms twitched and heart raced as he came within reach, and with all her might she swung, dealing a great blow to his temple, splintering her club. The stroke was enough to spin Bledig completely around, but it was not enduring. He shook his head, grabbed her hair, and flung her down.

"Where is it?" Bledig screamed.

"You shouldn't play with your food, you old dog," the other fellow chimed in once more.

"Leave me be." Bledig growled, swinging his fist toward Vivid, who ducked in time to dodge the blow.

"I thought I could be nice about it," the other fellow yelled before wrapping his arm around Bledig's neck. "But I can see it ain't gonna work." Bledig kicked and flailed as the larger man cut off his air by lifting him from the ground by the throat. After a few

212

seconds the man said, "I'm going to have mercy and release you, but you have to behave yourself. Leave the girl be."

It was a terrible misjudgment on his part. When he loosened his grip, Bledig turned on him, and with much fury, clawed, bit and gouged. Though he tried, the man could not dislodge the little beast, who soon worked his way behind and gripped the man's throat. The man dropped to his knees, pried, butted, and elbowed with no effect. The blood supply to his head had been cut off, and for him all was going black. Except for the young Gallant girl's mettle, the man would have been killed. After quickly seizing the axe that had struck the tree, Vivid came back to the two men who were wallowing on the ground. Seeing that Bledig was on top, she swung with all the strength she could muster. The stone blade slashed through Bledig's flesh, shattering his ribs and puncturing lungs. His death grip loosened. He would not recover from the stroke.

The other man tried to comfort him as he writhed on the ground for a long while. At last, when he stopped squirming and opened his eyes, Derog's Mind no longer had control of him, and he recognized the man who had come.

"Gar?" Bledig wheezed. "Is it you?"

"It is." Gar knelt beside his old partner. "This wasn't supposed to happen, not like this."

"I couldn't help it," said Bledig, "couldn't control it. The Auber King…"

Gar squeezed Bledig's hand. "There's no time for it now. You will soon bow before the judge, and all you've done will be weighed on scales. Unless you've changed since last I saw, you will be found wanting. But there's hope, the same that I found. Call out for forgiveness. The Maker shows mercy and can forget what you've done."

"Mine are too many." Bledig spat. "I'll face the pit that I earned. I ain't turning yella' now." Even at the end and in his darkest hour, pride, hate, lust, envy and greed were Bledig's masters. "Go yonder away feeling you did right by me." He closed his eyes, ignoring Gar's pleas for him to repent, and after only a few more minutes, he left his battered earthly vessel behind to meet his Maker.

Vivid had the axe trained on Gar when he finally let his friend go. From Given's stories of him, she knew that he was rotten. Still, she wondered why he tried to help her and pondered his appeal to his dying friend.

"You won't be needing that for me," he said. "There was a time not too long ago you would have but not now." He walked to a nearby oak and sat leaned against its trunk. "In the morning I'll bury the dead, but you can go now if you'd like."

Vivid would have taken him up on his offer, but didn't want him to see her retrieve the pack with the Heart in it. So she stood her ground instead.

"What's a lass doing out here with Bledig anyway? It makes no sense." After waiting for a reply that didn't come, he said, "Yeah, I wouldn't talk to me either."

Gar waited a while for Vivid to move or speak, but she did neither.

"Well, come to think of it, if you're wanting to get back to the village, I reckon I should take you. I can't in good sense let a little girl alone in these parts at night."

When he said this, a couple thoughts struck Vivid. The first was that she could take care of herself just fine in these parts—even being a little girl. The second was what she reckoned from Given's tales: that Gar would never leave a little girl alone in the woods, because his want was to defile her. She grew red-faced with anger at the thought and tightened her grip on the axe handle.

"I suppose you ain't gonna go? Well, if we're staying and you ain't going to speak, I suppose I'll have to do the talking." Gar cleared his throat. "That fella there is Bledig, and we used to run together. Wouldn't say we were friends—more like business partners. The problem was that all our dealings were dirty. Plain bad. We split ways several years back. He kept a cabin at Coyote Lake, but I went to work in Bardorf. For me it was honest work— hard work—building and fixing and the lot, but inside I was still rotten. Not too many months ago, something happened to change that—to change me." Gar fell silent for a moment. "Well, after an incident in the woods east of here, which I'm gonna pass over cause it…it got a bit messy." He grimaced. "Anyhow, after that incident I came out here to live by the meadow and the stream. I wanted nothing but to be alone. One day when I was fishing, a fella came to me. At first I thought, what is this fella doing here? Can't he see I ain't here cause I want to talk to folks? But when I looked up at his face—into his eyes—I could see something I've never seen before. There was a passion for me no one ever had. It's hard to explain, but that's how it felt. He started telling me all kinds of things about myself, things I did wrong, things I was ashamed of, even thoughts no one else knew. He told me to stop those things and do what was right. I cried at his feet and promised to do what he told me. Now—now I can't do the bad things anymore—won't do 'em. One look into his eyes gave me hope, one word from him changed who I was. In the end he said that the old had washed away, and since I was a new man, he'd give me a new name. He called me Dom, said I was now the Creator's child. He never told me his name, but I've heard the tales…I know who it was. 'Twas Solas…No other could do what he did."

Listening to his tale of redemption, Vivid wanted to take him at his word, but she'd seen enough in her short life to not buy in completely to what he was selling, though she did ease her grip some and lower the axe. Dom, as he was now called, couldn't see it, but she now wore a smile too as she thought of the goodness of this person, Solas, she hoped to someday meet. *The stony heart is but clay in his hands*, she thought.

CHAPTER 23. ENTOMBED

DO I still have arms? That was Given's thought as she hung from Aderyn's sturdy talons, her tears no longer flowing. She had lost all sensation in her hands, and the throbbing and pain of her upper arms had been replaced with numbness. Her only proof she still had upper limbs was that she yet soared through the night at a height she could only guess, for all below was dark and scarcely visible. The wind was chill and her face, like her arms, was senseless. Her eyes burned and heart stung from the loss of love. Out to her right Orson's killer glided effortlessly, peacefully, without notion of his own treachery—or so Given thought at first —but the tale of Derog's first uprising came to mind, and she realized that these creatures were as much a victim as her. Blame wasn't theirs. That belonged to the Civitian King alone.

After a few more miles of Given hanging, the beast to her right swooped suddenly below her dangling feet, and Aderyn released her squeeze. Though it was a coordinated effort, not a word was spoken between the creatures. The two were controlled by one mind. The beast below gave little as Given dropped into the fluffy mane that poured over his wide powerful shoulders. To either side she could see a sable wing so smooth and waxy that it seemed to glow in the moonlight. Her heart beat fiercely, restoring the life giving fluid through her arms and hands and into her fingertips. Albeit welcoming, the stinging pressure was not pleasant. When at last she could feel again, she examined the wounds inflicted by the claws of Aderyn. They bled still, but being little more than flesh wounds, scabs would cover them quickly.

Gripping tightly the creature's long black tufts, she sat for the remainder of their flight with her legs together to one side or the other, for the beast was too broad to straddle. The stars blew past her like leaves in the wind, and she was reminded of the dream she was having before all the terror of that night had begun, and of a more joyful time upon Nataurie's back racing down the Afon. Except for all the terrible things that had transpired, this ride would have been even more thrilling, but intense mourning and bouts of anger hindered any enjoyment, and the hours passed like days. At least, wearing furs borrowed from Aderyn and being almost encompassed by thick hair, she was not too cold. A few times during the flight, she appealed to Aderyn as a friend to let her go, but whatever pleas did reach the giant bird's ears had no effect.

From a league out and until they reached Harbor Wall, Given could make out hundreds, if not thousands, of darkened clusters, not much more than shadows on the ground. She wondered if they were only trees, or if they could be the large gatherings of beasts she and her companions had witnessed migrating east.

Other than the stars and moon the first lights Given noticed were the torches the watchmen carried to and fro atop the wall. From her height they appeared small as smoldering twigs pulled from a campfire. Her eyes were wide as they floated into the realm of the Civitians. She could see smoke curling up from the chimneys of tiny rock houses that speckled the further countryside. In a matter of seconds the creature she rode dove frighteningly low, swooping between huge oaks—perhaps ancient as the city—that lined the Golden Highway, the stone road which ran through the King's Gate all the way to the palace.

A dull gray hung about the city as sunrise was not for another hour, but already people trading goods packed the streets and market. Torches burned at every corner and on market stands and in many hands. Great commotion stirred as folk caught sight of the two giants carrying Given through the city, but it wasn't only the beasts they gawked at but the Gallant as well. Many had never set eyes on any of the "wild ones" who lived west of their wall. Aderyn seemed to lead her son past the palace and over a stony path to giant rocks that jetted up from the otherwise flat terrain that bordered the king's dwelling. In the rocks were many cracks and hollows, some formed from weathering, others carved by man. Given could see Aderyn land and immediately transform into the beauty she'd grown accustomed to. The beast Given rode, didn't bother to so much as set a paw on the ground before he bucked her off onto the rocky path below.

Crashing onto her buttocks was no more painful than the other brutalities she'd endured that night but added just another bruise to the battered heroin. "Why?" cried Given. "Would it have been too difficult to land?"

The beast heeded not her words as it flew toward the palace without turning its head.

"Come with me," Aderyn said.

Given groaned as she struggled through the pain to her feet looking at her old friend. Except for the blankness in her eyes and the chilly expression, Aderyn didn't look any different, but she was. There was no warmth, nor feeling, nor love; she was devoid of all her usual character.

"Do you not remember," Given pleaded in tears. "We are friends. You took me into your home and we supped together. You were a mother to my son while I was away. What about him?" She said more frantically, "Do you know of Grit? Can you tell me if he's safe?"

Aderyn led Given by the arm past two guards to one of the cells carved in the rock, shoved her in, and rolled a large stone in front of the entrance, never uttering a word. Only a smidgen of gray light wormed through the slit where the stone met the side of the hollow. Straining her eyes to see, she went to the stone and pushed with all remaining strength. It did not stir. Again she squatted low pushing, straining, grunting.

"Not with ten strongmen could you budge the stone from within," a sturdy voice came from the darkness. "It has been wedged and barred from without."

Startled, Given turned but could not make out even a silhouette. "Who's there? I reckoned to be alone."

"Be glad you are not, for lonely you would be. I am Erlend, formerly royal captain, and if you could see through the pitch you might take my hand. I have extended it in welcome."

Given waved her hands slowly through the air and was surprised when it struck Erlend's. "Oh, apologies." Taking his hand in hers, she shook it. "I am Given the Gallant, and I've been thrown into this cell because I have something the king desires…" She paused in thought for a moment. "You've probably never heard my name or of my tribe even, I know of you."

"And how could that be." Erlend chuckled. "Surely the names of Civitian prisoners are not declared amongst the tribes and villages."

"No," Given said, "but yours has been on the lips of Dane, the Civitian Prince. Not only his, but also a soldier called Roar, who I'd met in the cursed land."

"You were right in saying I would be amazed." Erlend tugged gently on Given's hand. "Come, sit. I will lead. From the sound of it, there are tales you must share."

He led her along the far wall to the left. Groping his way down the rough cold surface, he found a pile of clothes where he'd made his dwelling. "This is where I sleep and waste most of my day. At least it is not without comfort." He pulled Given's hand down to the garments and helped her sit. "Meals and freshwater have been provided twice a day since my imprisonment." Guiding her hand back to the wall he said, "If you feel your way the opposite, you'll find a relief bucket, its contents the guards have been kind enough to empty once a day. But unless you like to hob and nob with the dead, do not go far past the bucket. This is not your usual prison cell but a tomb. Auber Civitas has no prison. Her magistrate keeps few prisoners. Exile or death are her usual means of justice. Why they have kept me alive thus far, I can only guess is for Leif's, the king's youngest, sake. He is dear to me, and I to him. Once he has forgotten me, I will be…forgotten."

Given could sense the sadness in his tone and prayed a silent prayer of comfort over him. "Before I share my story with you, which is lengthy, I wonder if you might ease my curiosity. What do you know of the beasts that have come to this city?"

"I've seen little of them," said Erlend. " I have been in this cell for weeks, ever since the king branded me a traitor for lending Dane a dagger outside the wall. But I have seen some, and others I've heard…and from asking, and listening, and being in the king's confidence some months ago, I know how they've come to be here. It is an ancient evil awakened by men. Magnus has gathered the fragments from a fallen power's body, the mind, eyes, and skeleton…and maybe his heart too. With the bones and precious metal skeleton, the king's servant, Baird, both refined and formed the king's circlet and inlaid the diamond mind, and later the emerald eyes. They say that the spirit of Derog, the shepherd of all beasts, yet lived in the bones and was transferred to the crown during purification. When Magnus dons the crown, he is likened to the legends of Derog in power and ability."

"The legend I have heard," Given said, "but how Magnus gained Derog's power I had not…it is a pity you have not seen more of the creatures." She sighed. "I had hoped you glimpsed my son who is of their number. As for the Heart, be comforted. The king does not yet possess it. That is why I am here. It belongs to my people, and he has taken me captive with hope of acquiring it. By what means? I quiver to think."

Given continued to talk until the pale gray smidgen became a beam casting enough light for them to see throughout the tomb. Erlend was captivated by all she had to tell and as much so by her beauty when first he perceived it. She was not at all how the women of western tribes had been described to him when he was a boy, and he felt foolish for believing the lies. When Given had said all she could think, and Erlend exhausted his questions, they both fell silent in thought. It was then that a crumpled mass in the corner —that Given reckoned was only a rock or pile of cloth—started to rouse.

"What is that?" asked Given, guessing it to be a raccoon or cluster of rats in the moment.

"Apologies for not mentioning," Erlend said. "I didn't want to overwhelm you with the thought of too much male company, but *that* is Berthorn. Poor soul was cast in even before me, but counting his name, he has only uttered about nine words since first we met." Erlend lowered to a whisper, "Odd lad…and only has one leg too, but he's a fine listener." Erlend laughed

The mass jolted straight and twisted, and from it a raspy but kindly voice came, "I speak solely to ears fit to hear, and nine words be a fair ration for you, Erlend." Berthorn hopped to his feet as though someone had jabbed him with a stick. "And I only say what needs saying, but he is right: I am a fine listener...pleased to meet you Given the Gallant."

"Likewise," Given responded. "I suppose you heard my story. Do you have one of your own?"

"Nay—well, perhaps—that is to say, not like that one," Berthorn pointed his finger toward Given. "Not as good as yours, I mean." He fell silent and began tidying his pallet as though he had said all he intended to say.

"Is that all," Given asked, thinking Berthorn was jesting. "Will you tell me no more?"

"Like I said," Berthorn used the wall to steady himself as he rose on his one leg, "I only say what needs saying." He bounced past Given and Erlend and to the far side of the tomb where the bucket lay. Pushing it into the shadows, he relieved himself of yesterday's cares before hopping back, whistling a merry melody.

"Odd lad indeed," Erlend whispered.

***

At around the second hour, an unpleasant voice came from outside the tomb, "Be clear of the portal. The hour to break fast has come." At that, the stone was rolled just wide enough to slip a couple wooden plates through with a bowl of water. They weren't terrible rations, albeit only enough for two rather than three, but Berthorn refused food even at the others' insistence, claiming he had meat they didn't know of.

"He mostly drinks the water, but rarely takes bread," Erlend whispered. "I wonder if he means to starve himself."

Given had another thought. Perhaps he was placing his neighbor's well-being above his own.

After breakfast they sat mostly silent, each delving into their own mind. Given prayed that Vivid had escaped with the Heart unscathed and that she would have the wisdom to know what to do with it now. *She is only a girl*, thought Given, *but she is mature beyond her years. She'll fair.*

At the third hour there came a scraping on the stone door. Light burst into the cave as the stone was rolled to the side. A youthful soldier clad in rudimentary iron armor with blade unsheathed peered inside at Given. "His highness, King Magnus, has sent for you. Come."

Given hesitated, looking at Erlend as if for advice.

"Be strengthened," said Erlend. "Do not give him what he desires, and you will live." He glared at the soldier. "You are not obligated to fulfill your oath in treachery. Our king's aim and demands are madness, Steen." The soldier did not acknowledge Erlend's words, and averted his eyes as he led Given from the tomb.

After rolling the stone back into place, Steen led Given down the rocky path toward the palace with three other soldiers trailing, all clad similarly in iron and with weapons naked, as though she were a threat. Given glanced around at the kingdom and nearly forgot her fear for all the beauty. To the north and south in the distance jagged peaks stretched for leagues on end, and before her she could see the Afon, shimmering in the sun, split the range, pass through the portal under Harbor wall, and race east, chasing its finish—the sea. The city itself was cradled in a large valley that seemed to grow ever wider toward the east, where the Sawtooths had been worn away by millennia of flow and overflow from the mighty river. Ancient trees with falling leaves and yellow meadow lined her path, the only visible beasts were livestock and birds.

As they neared the palace, Given tried to concentrate on what she would say to the evil king—what lie or threat she could conjure—but all focus was abandoned when she glimpsed two boys playing in a pile of leaves under the oaks. The larger of the two was a thin framed, bronze skinned boy, handsome and joyful, tossing leaves all around. The other was scrawny but cute. By his size, he couldn't have been a day over a year. He crawled about on all fours, but it was natural for him, like it would be for any beast. Given gaped. *Could it be Grit?* she thought, but the boy was too distant to know for sure. She called, "Grit, Grit it's Mot," but the boy, whoever he was, disappeared into the leaf mound. Given gasped and her heart beat fiercely. She started for the boy, but Steen stepped in front, brandishing his sword.

"FALL BACK!" He shouted. "If you shall go unharmed, fall back!"

Like the stone that blocked her prison cell, Given didn't budge but stared through Steen towards the potential prize—her little boy.

"FALL BACK!" Steen repeated.

But when Given took a step towards him instead, he motioned to the other guards.

The older boy noticed the commotion and darted through the meadow toward Given to see what was happening, leaving the other still covered in leaves. "Is she trying to escape?" he asked, startling Steen.

"No, master." Steen kept his eyes on Given, who was still gazing past him. "We were on our way to your father with this one. She stopped without command and appeared to be advancing your way. I was keeping her in line."

"What has she done?" the boy asked in a low tone. "She doesn't look like a bad one."

"Nothing," Given said before Steen could speak. "Nothing deserving of imprisonment. I just want my son back. Is that him?" She pointed to the leaf mound. "I need to see him."

Steen thrust his blade toward Given. "You shall not address the prince without permission."

Prince? Thought Given. The names of Dane's brothers ran through her mind as she took a step back.

The boy touched Steen's shoulder, "It's fine. Let her speak."

"There is no time," Steen said, annoyed. "Your father desires her now."

The prince ignored Steen. Casting his smiling eyes on Given he said, "I am Leif, thir—second Prince of Auber Civitas. What's yours?"

It was difficult for Given to focus as she wondered if Grit was only steps away. She wanted to run and sift through the leaves in search, but with Steen's weapon in her face and soldiers to either side, she thought better of it. "I—I am Given—The Gallant."

"And what would my Father want with you if you have done nothing?"

"It is not what I've done, but what he believes I possess that interests him. My people—"

"YOU'VE HAD YOUR SAY!" Steen almost gagged on his words. "Let the king's business with her be his own." He lowered his sword and gripped Given's arm where Aderyn had spiked her, forcing a yelp. Though she was determined to meet the boy in the leaves, Steen's strength persuaded otherwise as he tossed her over his shoulder and toted her halfway to the palace before tossing her like a sack of meal. He kicked into the air and flung his hands shooing her along as if she were a dog. "There'll be no more trouble from you. Move along!"

Given yet stared with hope of spotting Grit, but both boys had vanished. She scrambled to her feet and complied with Steen's demand, walking the rest of the way without stopping. Peeking over her shoulder every few steps rendered no view of her boy along the way, and before she knew it, the palace's high stone walls had surrounded her. Its huge timber beams hung above.

"So, this is her?" a voice with accent Given had never heard echoed. "She's the keeper?" The speaker asked confusedly. He started to laugh, a deep, robust chuckle. "You have given more trouble than all the others—together...and you're nothing but a little girl." A tall, willowy man wearing a wood carved mask resembling an owl stepped from behind one of the oak posts that supported the roof beams. He wore several layers of skins and in his right hand was a stick topped with the feathers of various birds. He motioned for Given's escorts to leave. The hefty wooden planked door slammed shut behind.

The edge of his furs swept the stone floor as he slithered toward Given. He glided around her examining—intimidating. When he drew near enough for her to feel his warmth, she glanced up into his eyes. They were cold gray and hollow. A chill raked her spine.

He scoffed, "You are not what I imagined you to be. Frightened are you not?"

Given gave no response, though she was indeed terrified.

"Where is it?" he hissed. "Where is the relic?"

She remained silent even as she could smell his foul breath from beneath the mask.

He reared back with open hand and delivered a stinging slap across Given's right cheek. "SPEAK!"

But when she said nothing, he struck her again. This time with his fist and double the force. It was as hard a hit as she'd ever taken, knocking her to the floor. The masked man stood over her laughing. "You will tell." His fist was raised above her like a hammer ready to strike when another voice stole in.

"Baird! leave her be." A fellow, handsome and stately, clothed in royal garb and crowned with a gold and silver circlet with a giant diamond in the middle and emeralds to either side had entered the hall. "Let me talk some sense before you ruin her." Standing behind him was Orson's killer, the winged beast—Aderyn's son— even more frightening in the light.

"Apologies for my advisor's gestures," he continued as he came closer and Baird stepped away. "Guests aren't dealt kindly in his country. I am Magnus, King of the Civitians, and you are indeed my guest." He extended his hand to her.

Given ignored his offer to help, struggling to her feet unaided. She glanced from Magnus to the beast behind him.

"Don't concern yourself too much with Cadoc," said Magnus with a smile. "He is well trained and will not attack…unless I desire."

Rage was growing inside Given as a flashback of Orson's limp body dangling from the beast's claws ran through her mind. Breathing deeply she tried to calm herself, to focus on what needed to be done. "You used him to murder my friend, steal me through the cold night, and cast me into a tomb." She clenched and unclenched her fists, wishing she could rip the crown from his head. "You abandon your own kin to despair and death and destroy the innocent. There is no measure to your evil. Kill me if you will, but do not pretend I am your guest." She spat on him.

Magnus turned and wiped his face with his back to Given. She saw her opportunity. If she could only remove the crown from his head, perhaps Cadoc's mind would be free enough for rebellion. It was the best chance she had—her only chance. She lunged with hand outreached toward the circlet, but Cadoc stretched his wings around Magnus, shielding him, and threw her down with a flick as if she were a rain droplet off his back.

"It could be a bad thing to get excited around him." Magnus laughed as he came from beneath his protective covering. "I would not…Indeed, you should stay seated until we are finished." He rubbed his hands together. "Legend speaks of a giant ruby called the Heart of Derog that your forebears, the Gallants, were gifted. It's no secret that I desire it. And knowing your people have inhabited the Afon Valley for hundreds of years, we searched the villages, tangles and ravines there for months. No matter how hard we've looked, no matter how many villages we've raided and people we've threatened and killed, the ruby has not been found, but now I have help." He pointed to the crown. "I can see what they see and think their thoughts, and I know that you have it. Somewhere in your village perhaps, or hiding in the fringes, it is there." He stood, towering over her sunken form. "You will tell me where it is."

Given once again fell silent, vowing in her heart to say nothing no matter the threat. And the threats did come, threats of beatings and death and the torture of friends, threats of destroying whole villages, and even threats of rape and other filth; but she would not be moved. When Magnus could see plainly he would not have his way with mere words, Steen and the other guards were summoned.

"She refuses to speak," he told one. "Fetch some rope and bind her hands." To another he sent for a whip, and still the other a rod.

229

When they returned she was stripped of all garments and bound to the king post. Baird took the whip in hand, held it high above his head, and brought it down on her naked back. The sting sent her to her knees, where she would stay for the remainder of her flogging, her face pressed against the rough wood. Steen and Baird alternated blows with whip and rod while Magnus questioned. In the end no more than cries of agony came from Given's lips. She was loosed, clothed, and escorted back to the tomb.

CHAPTER 24. THE CLOAK OF GUILT

THE NIGHT Given was taken slugged along for Vivid as she waited anxiously for Dom to leave her be, wondering what had become of her sister. Though his stories about Solas and the good deeds he'd done since his encounter had mostly torn down the wall of distrust, she still could not allow him, or anyone other than Given, to know that she possessed the Heart.

The next day Dom was out before sunup surveying the land for a place to bury his old partner. He decided under a pecan tree in Wether's Field would be best, in part for its beauty but mostly because of the soft soil. With many words he convinced Vivid to lend his axe back to him to make digging a little easier. And since she felt somewhat responsible for Bledig's death, she even helped him dig. When the pit had been fully made and the body deposited, Dom spoke to the Creator on behalf of his friend.

"I know he wasn't a good man, but maybe—maybe he never had the chance to be. When you judge him, if you haven't already done it, keep that in mind. He was born into filth and that's all he ever knew. No love did he see. Please forgive him for doing what he'd seen." When he'd had his say, he began scooping dirt into the shallow hole, trying to cover the body as quickly as he could. Vivid didn't help, shunning any possible contact with the man she'd killed. The finished work was a small dirt mound that would surely bear grass and flowers come springtime.

"I want to stay here a bit if it's alright with you," said Dom. "I need time to myself. He was a bad one, but still losing him…it doesn't feel good." He sat down beside the dirt pile and thought for a moment. "But if you need help getting somewhere, I could—"

Vivid shook her head vigorously, seeing it as the opportunity she needed to escape with the Heart unseen. As she was leaving Dom to mourn, she bowed low to him and mouthed thank you. After all, he had saved her. Closing his eyes he bowed in return and in a low solemn tone began to sing to the dead, "Go home, go home, good friend go home; Away from here, good friend go home. Don't look back, good friend go home; to open arms, good friend go home."

Vivid walked away in sadness, sensing the pain in his lyrics; but for her it was no time to mourn. She shook off the melancholy, retrieved the pack, and trekked back toward Bardorf. On the western outskirts of the village, she spotted a large knothole about halfway up the trunk of a leaning white oak, climbed the tree's branches, and stashed the Heart inside, making certain she was not being watched—by man or beast. She thought a prayer of protection over the relic as she dashed into the village.

Bardorf was burdened with mourners when Vivid entered. On the North end of the village in a small clearing where no homes had been erected, a funeral pyre had been built with Orson's body on top. She had not a clue what'd happened after she'd fled the night before and seeing Orson lifeless threw her into dismay. She frantically scanned the small gathering for Given. *Where is she? What could have happened?* When she didn't see her, she searched for other familiar faces. Torben's was the only she saw, twisted by agony and stained with tears and ashes. His wide shoulders, usually upright, hung low. Even his fluffy brown hair sagged. Next to him, beneath his right arm, a tiny woman—his mother—wept. A torchbearer, probably one of their kin, split the mourners and thrust the flame into the pyre. All were silent watching Orson's body being devoured by fire.

As the flames faded away, so did the mourners, until all that remained of the crowd were Torben and his mother. Though Vivid desired to know what had become of Given, she didn't dare approach them in their distress. At last, when Torben's mother retired to her home, Vivid went to him and grasped his hand.

He looked down. "Apologies Vivid. Orson tried...he tried to help her, but they killed him. If she's alright, I do not know."

Vivid nodded and squeezed Torben's hand, letting him know she understood and was sorry for both of their losses. She sighed deeply, hopeful still that she would see her sister again but knowing the security of the Heart for the time being was up to her.

Aksel and Dane arrived only moments later, gasping for air. They had been running for long stretches through the night and morning with little rest. Seeing the pile of ashes and the two mourners, Dane went to them and pleaded for information. He seethed in anger when Torben told him what had happened.

"I should have stayed, they may still—"

"If you would have stayed, I would likely be mourning the loss of a son as well. No, the cloak of guilt is not yours to wear," Aksel gripped his son's shoulders. "Orson's blood is on Magnus's hands, and now we must pray Given is well—that the relic is safe. Regardless, the time has come for war." He pointed to a small band of warriors wandering into the village. "Our allies."

By midday warriors from all around had begun to trickle into Bardorf, some summoned by Aksel, others by Solas himself. By evening the trickle became a downpour. Burly, heavily clothed spearmen of the Gogledd, a tribe several thousand members strong, came from as far north as the Wooly Mountains. They had been tracking the mammoth herds south when Solas caught up to them

233

and informed them of what was happening with the beasts and in turn what had to be done.

Soldiers—swordsmen and archers—about seven hundred in all, from the Hidden City had come for a different reason. Thieves from Auber Civitas had infiltrated their highest ranks and stolen the emerald Eye of Derog from them. They had trekked over mountain and valley and through desert and forest to get it back, having sworn an oath to return with the relic or not at all.

When the last ally had arrived, Solas emerged from the thick and spoke to them, "We mustn't wait, for the enemy's number grows by the hour and will soon be overwhelming. But take heart knowing my father has not forgotten you. He will fight by your side even when I cannot, for the oath I have taken to abstain cannot be broken."

Vivid had climbed a blackjack behind the ranks so she could see and was listening intently to Solas's instruction. In truth she planned to follow behind the warriors in secret with bow and arrow, since she was not allowed to be in their number. But as he spoke to the crowd, it seemed to Vivid that she had caught his gaze. And though he uttered plans of attack to the men, something different was spoken to her mind. "Vivid the Gallant, strong and brave, follow them into battle...but abandon not the Heart, their hope for victory."

***

It was past midday when Given landed back in her cell, but the sunlight was still plentiful. Erlend came to her aid. "Did they assault you?" He stooped down to her. "Can I help?"

"I don't know," Given cried. "My back is aflame. For hours I have been questioned, for hours I've been beaten. My flesh is split and bleeding."

"Stay here in the light," Erlend said. "I'll fetch water and cloth."

He returned also with some furs for her to lie on and cover with. Peeling up her garments he could see the wounds were still oozing, but they were not too deep. He tore a piece of cloth, soaked it in water and patted them. Given jolted from the initial shock of cold and pain.

"Easy," Erlend whispered. "They have to be cleansed."

When all was cleaned and the bleeding had stopped, Erlend covered her in furs and she rested.

Berthorn hopped up behind Erlend. "Injured, is she?" he said in a tone more of interest than caring. "How bad could it be?"

Erlend waved for Berthorn to go, "Leave her be, she has enough cares, the least of which satisfying your curiosity."

"Curiosity," he shook his head. "No, no it's not that. I can help her...if injured I can help."

"What can you do?" Erlend asked in annoyance. "We have no medicine and hardly enough water to keep the wounds clean. Nay, all there is to do now is leave her be."

"Okay, okay," Berthorn stammered. "If that's the way you see it." He hopped back into his corner and was silent.

Evening was chased away by night and darkness filled their cell while Given slept with Erlend at her side. At length slumber overtook him as well. Berthorn, however, did not sleep for his concern of Given; and in the early reaches his voice came gently in melody through the darkness from where he lay in the corner. The song was indeed the same Nataurie had sung to heal Given, but his lyrics commanded such authority that one verse was all that was needed. When dawn came, Given woke painless and confused, wondering if she had even been flogged or if it was all a terrible dream. When she questioned Berthorn he said that it was good that she felt better and was silent once more.

Breakfast time came and went without a morsel to share between them. Later they were informed that Given would have to give up the relic if they were to eat again.

"If it's well with you," Erlend said. "I'd rather starve than give Magnus what he wants. Keep your secret."

"*Starve*, no," said Berthorn. "Why would you want that? You're not the best fellow around, but you don't deserve to starve." He pointed a crooked finger toward Given, "Nor does she…you should give it to him. Give it to them. Give the Heart." His eyes widened as if he remembered a very important thing. "That's the rhyme…er—something—something else…Give his Heart and uh —set them free."

"You fool," Erlend spouted. "We cannot base our actions on old rhymes you can't remember. If she gives it to him, he will have all he needs. Nothing would there be to stop him, and all men would kneel before Magnus—if not worse." He shook his head. "But to help your memory, the rhyme says: Take his Mind and control, With his Eyes you will see, Mend his Body make them whole, Give his Heart set them free." He looked at Given. It's a poem taught to Civitian children and means nothing."

"Yes, I've heard it." Given said. "It was what Dane could remember of the stories about Derog." She bowed to Berthorn. "I'm grateful for the advice, but I believe Erlend is right. If I give it to him, there will be nothing left to stop him."

"If that's the way you see it," he said, "but that's how we got into the mess to start. Be assured Magnus believed the rhymes. Along with that, starving hurts." He waved his hands through the air in annoyance. "Ah, you'll see soon enough." Hopping back to his corner, he plopped onto his pallet.

Given didn't want to upset Berthorn. Despite his oddities, she liked him. But the idea of giving the Heart to Magnus seemed ridiculous. Still, in the quiet she considered the rhyme. *Wouldn't that beat everything,* she smiled. *All our problems solved by giving.* She imagined herself bowing before Magnus presenting the relic to him and shook her head, *absurd.*

***

The rest of the day moved like cold molasses as Given contemplated all she'd lost, and her gurgling belly called every now and then for her to listen to Berthorn; but a new hope blew in with twilight's chill winds. Roar, along with a small band of soldiers who had decided they owed no fealty to a murderous king, came to free them. The tomb was watched still by only a couple of guards camped about a small fire, neither willing to risk his life to stop Roar and company. At the point of their swords, Roar and four of his best forced the guards into the cell and made them shed their outer garments of wool, which he gave to Given and Erlend to wear. Given was happy to have the extra cloak, hat and gloves, but in them she looked like a child that had robbed her father's wardrobe, sagging all around.

"Perhaps night will lend us enough cover," she said, knowing she looked silly and not much disguised.

"Likely from man," said Roar, "but the creatures…they will not be fooled so easily. We must avoid their gaze. There are only a few within the city but along Harbor wall and for miles out, there are scattered thousands."

"Is it possible to get past them?" asked Erlend.

"While the mind sleeps," Roar tapped his temple. "But we cannot rely on that. Slumber evades Magnus as he contemplates evil deeds. There is hope still. The beasts are on the move, being organized for battle. Magnus has seen far, discovering the Shepherd of Men has rallied tribes and kingdoms to march against him. He plans to meet them as they cross the cursed lands. In that desert there will be no place for men to hide. The mammoths will crush them like grapes in a press."

"What is our hope," said Erlend, "if their number and strength be so?"

"For those of foreign blood," Roar said sadly, "there is little, and since I am helping you, I give myself even less."

Given thought of all her friends marching to their death. Aksel must be part of their number, fearlessly leading them, and Torben must've gone out to avenge his brother. Dane with them as well, aching to battle his father, the king. And what of her sister? She wasn't the sort to linger behind, and her bow skills would be useful. But Given hoped for the sake of the Heart and Vivid's own safety, she would avoid this soon to be tragedy. *I sent her away with only one charge. I pray she has kept it and is well.*

Given's thoughts were broken by Roar's voice. "I am sick with grief thinking of Magnus's intentions. In the beginning it seemed he planned only to gain more of the valley for farming, now his schemes are madness. He speaks of the purification of man. I have heard that with Derog's army he wishes to sweep this land clean of all wild men, and after he's done this vile deed, he plans on destroying those he used—the SkinWalkers and their kin. One pure Civitian race is his desire, not tainted by the blood of foreigners or half-beasts.

Given couldn't believe what she was hearing, and if it were all true, there was only one course she could now take. She had to get back the Heart and destroy it, even if it meant never seeing her son again. Tears streamed at the realization. *And Aderyn,* she thought, *would be killed too.* Of all that could be done, it made the most sense to her, but her heart despised the idea.

When they had fully discussed their way of escape and were prepared to leave, Given realized that Berthorn hadn't added to the discussion, not a single word of it. Though usually he didn't say much anyway, he did have a habit of speaking his mind. Surely he'd have something to say about these important matters. *Must be sleeping,* thought Given, *even through all this.* But when she went to stir him, all she found was a pile of furs. *Where'd he get off to? Surely he couldn't have given us the slip.* "Berthorn?" she called. "We're leaving and you should come too." There was no reply.

Erlend felt his way over. "The fool must have gotten past us in the dark and gone his way. We're better for it. With his one leg and half brain, he would have only hindered our journey."

Given reckoned Erlend was right but felt regretful he had wandered off alone. He was nice enough, and though his advice was not the best, it was well intended. She prayed that he would find his way to a better life.

After the seven had cleared the portal, Erlend and Roar rolled the stone back into place, shutting Magnus's guards inside. Two more of Roar's men, who had been keeping watch by the campfire, were summoned and the nine strode into the darkness together. As they trekked north, Given questioned the two watchmen about Berthorn, thinking surely they would have seen him exit, but they had not a clue either.

"Our concern was what could have come from the palace," one said, "not who was coming out of the tomb."

"He could have rolled behind us," the other laughed. "And we wouldn't have turned our heads."

Given was happy with the thought that perhaps he could make it out to the country, and with all that was happening, no one would ever go after him. *Why would the king be concerned with a one-legged man when there is a war to be won?*

The nine neared the Afon, and Given began to wonder how they intended to cross. But soon enough she spotted the crossing through the darkness. It was a wood planked bridge—wide enough for men pulling carts both directions—that arced up and over the river. Given had never seen anything like it, being accustomed to rope or vine bridges. Before she set foot on the first plank, she stopped to inspect the craftsmanship.

"It is called Suther's Ladder," whispered Erlend after noticing her curiosity. "Its construction was ordered by Queen Saga after her son, Suther, drowned trying to herd his goats across the Afon. Aside from Harbor Wall, it stands as the only Civitian overpass for the river. Most folks downstream use rafts to get to-and-fro. Others yet risk their lives as Suther had."

With Roar in the lead, the others followed two by two across the bridge in as much stealth as they could manage with a creaky ancient structure beneath their feet. Once across they curved back toward the west and headed for their escape. So they didn't have to make the impossible climb through the mountains, Roar, at the risk of being betrayed, had arranged for the night guards to hang a rope for his company at the north end of Harbor Wall, just before the wall crashed into the great cliffs of the Sawtooths. When they made it to the rope, all was going as planned, and one-by-one like worms they inched to the top of the wall. But once atop, things took a horrible turn. A multitude of soldiers bearing swords appeared from behind the watchtower. Roar had been double-crossed. Even armed as they were, fighting was futile, for they were grossly outnumbered; and with their backs against the stony cliffs and a deadly fall to either side, trying to escape would have been disastrous.

"If your life is of value," the stony voice of the commander called. "Cast your weapons down and surrender."

"Be not hasty," Erlend said. "We shall do your bidding, but you must swear to spare at least one of our company. The bearer of the relic is with us, and I doubt the king wishes her dead."

"I am not so dull that she has evaded my eyes," said the commander. "And be glad she is with you. If it weren't for the Gallant girl, your company would be razed already."

"I see no way out of this," Roar whispered as he laid his sword down and raised his hands. "The fault is mine."

The soldiers followed their leader. Given on the other hand had been shoved back by the others for protection and was leaning against the cliff. She felt something like a hand rub the top of her head and firmly grasp and pull her hair. Suppressing the screech of pain, she looked up into the noble face of a mighty ram, one of the Bighorns, that appeared to be gripping the wall of the cliff with its hooves. The ram rocked its head up and down, beckoning Given. Unlike with Nataurie, she would not miss the obvious sign. Shoving back against the surrounding soldiers, she cleared enough space for the beast to pounce from the cliff onto the level ground of the wall top. The ram wavered not as she mounted behind its sturdy shoulders. With Given clinging with all her might, it bounded back up the cliff's steepness as though it was without burden.

The commander shouted angrily from below, but the ram gave no attention. As they climbed higher, something like a strong wind gusted past and Given could hear the beating of hooves on the stone. She glanced back. Though it was dark, she could still see well enough. More bighorns had come to help and were now standing amongst Roar's company prepared for battle. There was clashing metal—sword on sword—and loud cracks and whacks—sword against horn. Shouts and cries of men rang out, as did bleating. Frantically, Given prayed for her rescuers and friends. In a sudden the mighty ram that bore her stopped on a tiny ledge, turned and opened his mouth, but what came forth was not the bleating of a sheep or goat but the roar of a mighty beast. Below there was a loud crash, so loud that Given reckoned part of the wall had collapsed. In truth, most of Magnus's men had fallen in unison, petrified by the ram's boom.

Not one of the nine was captured that night, for the bighorns saved them. They bore the nine up the cliffs and along the ledges and back down again, until they were on flat earth about a league north and west of Harbor Wall. Never did any bighorn speak an intelligible word—not even the one that carried Given—but they understood human speech and acknowledged the nine's gratitude with bows of acceptance before bouncing back into the steeps.

Given beamed, awed by their size, strength, and grace as they vanished into the cliff's blackness, how effortlessly they climbed after bearing men on their backs for so long. Not even their battle wounds hindered them, and the mighty ram that had borne Given, though missing a hoof, floated up the cliffs like steam. Given hoped to see them again and wondered why they had not fallen under control of Derog's mind. Of course she didn't know yet the secret which Dane carried.

Coming up beside her, Erlend grasped Given's hand. "In all my days I have not been as thrilled and terrified," he laughed. "They snatched us from death's withered hand. With the commander's sword at my throat, they charged our enemy and pushed them back. Then—*then*—the crack of thunder from cloudless sky finished the job, driving Magnus's men to their backsides." He faced Given with eyes wide. "Where did it come from? I wonder."

"The sound you heard was not thunder, but the shout of the ram who bore me away," Given shook her head in disbelief. "A sheep that speaks as a lion."

As they spoke, Roar came before them and bowed toward Erlend, "I give back what was stolen from you by Magnus. This regiment is yours to command."

"A noble gesture," Erlend said, placing his hand on Roar's shoulder. "But out here we are brothers, and you know these lands better than most. You shall lead us."

Roar bowed lower. Wasting no time, he began to tell all that he knew of the wilder lands west of the wall. "The beasts have mostly gathered south of the river. The further along we stay to this side, the better our chances of survival will be." He pointed to the west and motioned to his right. "Where the Afon curves north, we will cross."

With haste Roar led them into the wilderness, all weaponless, for they had dropped them in order to grasp the bighorns' backs. They were well clothed though, and the night chill did little to penetrate their woolen outer garments and furs. As they sprinted, Given thought back to the boys playing in the leaf pile. *Could it have been?* She smiled at the memory, knowing in her heart it was Grit.

But her happiness soon vanished when she remembered Magnus's plan to purify. Was she truly willing to end her son's life for the sake of many? She resolved to think she was.

CHAPTER 25. THE DEEP BREATH

COOL NIGHTS and mild days passed over them like the wind as they sped hungry and worn through the wilderness toward their friends. On occasion they would stop to listen for the movement of Magnus's army, which at first was a great tumult. Eventually the noise quieted though, proving that Given and company were outpacing the beasts and Deroheed. When at last they came to Skeleton Wood, they were all on the verge of collapse, but the echo of a shofar stirred them.

"A herald of welcome perhaps," said Roar, shielding his eyes from the intense morning sun as he glanced back at Given and the others.

"No," said Erlend. "Likely a call to arms. A lookout has spotted us, probably mistaking us for scouts of Magnus. We must move cautiously, inoffensively, letting them know we are friends."

Onward they trekked into the dead lands at a snail's pace. The soldiers had formed a protective circle around Given and now and again Roar or Erlend would call out, announcing their peaceful intentions. The air was foul as ever, gagging the nine, making Given wish she was holding the Heart once more—if for no other reason—to lessen the stink of death as they crossed.

Toward the end of their trudge through the wood before they plunged back into the living lands, Erlend called out, "If any can hear, let him hear that we are servants of Solas the Shepherd of Men. We mean only to escape the atrocities of Magnus."

"And to fight him," said a man concealed, "would you be willing?"

Upon hearing, Given grew anxious. "It is Dane," she whispered. She wanted to run to him, abandoning all care of death and war, but stayed behind the guards as amends were made.

As Given continued in her thoughts, Erlend stepped forward, kneeling with his head low. "Dane," he called. "Forgive a soldier his foolishness. With deep regret I have realized my error and denounced loyalty to the king. My service is now yours."

With Aksel at his side, Dane stepped from the thick that hid him. "Rise friend," he said, "no forgiveness is needed. Your oath was to Magnus. What's more, the dagger you offered was my salvation, and I have heard from a good friend that you suffered greatly for its offering." Dane glanced at Roar and bowed his head slightly before returning his attention to Erlend. "Above all, there is a greater detail, one that you have not yet perceived. The Lord of Auber Civitas, the king by right, is here with us, and he has already declared your innocence."

"Erlend, old friend," said Aksel as he approached the kneeling captain, "long has it been since my eyes beheld such a sturdy warrior. I have missed you."

Erlend stared in disbelief. "Is it you Aksel, or does my mind play a trick?"

Aksel extended his hand, "Your mind has discerned what your eyes have not…Albeit less comely, it is me indeed." The two embraced. "I've been away too long and missed much, but I nurture little regret. Thank you for caring for my son. You were a father to him when I could not be."

Erlend pushed away from Aksel with a questioning look. "Son? Who do you mean?"

Aksel motioned toward Dane. "Through many long stories and much time together. We have figured that Dane is *my* son, not Magnus's."

Erlend looked at Dane who nodded. "With little doubt, I believe it too. Truly, it does not surprise me," Erlend laughed. "Your mother's love for Aksel was no secret, and you have his look... Nay, I am not in the least surprised."

Given on the other hand was in awe of this new revelation, and could no longer remain out of sight. Stepping from behind her rescuers and protectors her eyes met Dane's. He stared in wonder.

"Throughout our march, I prayed in earnest." He swallowed hard. "I called out for your security, and here you stand in perfect health—a miracle."

"It is that." Glancing around at her company she said, "Much thanks is due to the men who rescued Erlend and me...and still more to the beasts who saw the job through."

Dane approached her and glancing down said, "Do you know of Orson? He—"

"Yes, I saw and will forever be burdened with the memory and guilt. It was for me that he gave his life." In tears, Given looked away.

"He was honorable," said Dane reaching for her hand, "and his cause just." He pulled her close. "I'm sorry I wasn't there to help. The blame is mine." Sighing deeply he said. "But casting fault does nothing to fix what's been broken. Now with the Heart, Magnus holds all the advantage." Motioning all around, "We will challenge him—likely forfeiting our lives." He looked into her eyes. "You mustn't stay. Return to Bardorf for Vivid, and together flee to the west. Perhaps you will survive."

Given pondered with relief what Dane was saying. Vivid was alive in Bardorf, which surely meant that the Heart was there too, that she had been able to escape with it the night Given was taken. And It seemed she had followed Given's instructions, not even telling Dane the truth of the Heart's whereabouts. *I need to get to her*, she thought. *This must end…I must end it.* Realizing Dane desired a response, she nodded. "I'll do what is needed…I'll do as you say."

Pulling her close, Dane said, "If never again my eyes behold your beauty, I hope you fill my dreams." He kissed her forehead, pressing his cheek against her. "Do not stop praying for us."

Dane and Given's embrace ended only after Aksel insisted they must be getting along. Knowing that Magnus's army was fast approaching, Aksel thought it best to be beyond the cursed land when they clashed. "The winged beasts may at least be hindered by the branches," he said. "And behind the trunks and in the pits and ravines of yonder land, we may at least evade the Mammoths. We will want to engage them in daylight, for many of the beasts see better by night. Magnus will be somewhere in their number. We must get to him." It wasn't much of a plan, and one spoken with little hope at that, but it was better than going at the beasts naked.

Aksel escorted Given through the ranks and into the woods behind. "You have become a daughter to me, and without you I wouldn't know my son." He squeezed her hand. "The fight is not over. There is much for you to do yet." Squeezing tighter he said, "To you the quest was given. Only you can decide what needs to be done."

Given wondered if Aksel had figured her secret—that the Heart had not fallen into evil hands—but said nothing of it. She nodded, and stretching forward onto her toes she kissed his scarred cheek.

He bowed low before turning to resume his command. Given watched as her shield and protector, the nearest she'd known to a father, vanished into the ranks. Moments later a shofar sounded, calling the warriors to attention; after a second blast the lines headed east.

As the final soldiers waddled into the dead lands, a hand brushed Given's shoulder, causing her to jump. Vivid stepped out smiling.

"You nearly took my skin," Given gasped. "What are you doing out here?"

Vivid motioned for her to step behind the tree where she revealed the Heart stashed in her pack.

Given hugged her and said, "You have done everything I asked, but why are you following the army? It isn't safe."

Vivid stepped back and did her best to mouth and motion that which she couldn't speak. Pointing to her heart and head, she moved her lips to the name that was above all others on Earth, and though Given didn't fully understand what had happened to Vivid from the motions, she reckoned that Solas had told her to follow the army. *Why?* She couldn't know for sure. Perhaps only to get to Given faster.

Given took the pack and stared at the Heart within. Her gut tangled at the thought of shattering it, at the thought of killing those she loved. What else was there now? If she didn't, *everyone* she loved would perish. Tears blocked her vision. Vivid closed the flap over the Heart, and shaking her head, she grasped Given's hand and tugged her forward toward the moving army.

"For now we will follow," Given said, wiping her eyes. "But soon it will be destroyed."

Vivid nodded and tossed onto her shoulder the bow and quiver of arrows Roar had left, then gripped the spear she'd fastened with

Dane's arrow. She and Given trailed in the army's wake back through the cursed land, a longbow's shot away from the nearest warrior. Breathing was easy once more since the Heart and part of the mind were present, and Vivid listened with smiling eyes as Given shared all that had happened to her since being snatched away from Bardorf. Vivid's smile vanished toward the end of the tale as Given explained to her why the Heart could not remain whole. Perhaps more so than any other person that had embarked on the quest, Vivid remained hopeful, but even she began to feel burdened trailing behind the warriors. Like a prairie creek on a mild winter's day, they—hungry and exhausted—traversed the landscape toward their finish. But the pains of life no longer mattered to them, for they realized the truth—they marched to their deaths. The sparkling waters of the creek were soon to be swallowed by the mud red flow of a savage river.

***

Soaring kites, hundreds of them, were the first indication of Magnus's fast approaching army. They were skilled flyers, nearly impossible to strike with an arrow from any distance. At first they flew high above, scouting their enemy, or so Aksel said. But when they began to dive into the crowd of men taking chunks of flesh back up into the sky with them, he changed his mind. "With these fowl Magnus means to cause terror before the onslaught," he said. "We are at their mercy in the field." He pointed toward a line of trees before them. "To the hedges. Shield your eyes."

Once in the shadows of the grove, the soldiers did their best to reform ranks, and the kites stopped their assault for the time being, returning to the heights. Aksel and company now knew there would be no element of surprise. The enemy's eyes were too many and could see from most angles. Their only hope was to charge the middle of the enemy's army, however thick, and get to the mind of the beasts.

It was evening and since Magnus knew their whereabouts already, there was no use going any further. "From this location we shall stab," Aksel told a group of commanders and friends. "But keep your guard through the night and pray that they do not approach us until dawn. When the time comes, I will be the point of the sword. All who have courage shall follow. Though our blade be small, it is sharp. We will get to him. If only with the hilt of our sword, we *will* get to him."

"If you are the point," said Dane, placing a fist over his chest, "I will be the edge and your rear guard."

Aksel nodded, proud of his son's mettle.

"Our sword will be two-edged then," said Erlend. "Old friends will fight together."

"You shan't go without me," said Roar. "I am treasonous as far as Magnus is concerned and should just as well face my judge sooner than later."

The four shook hands laughing, joyful in their camaraderie. If all others fainted, they would fight to their end.

CHAPTER 26. MUD AND BLOOD

*N*IGHT FELL hard and fast, and the rumble of thousands of feet
and hooves pounding the earth came into hearing. Given and Vivid
hid in the branches beneath a huge cedar, Vivid with spear readied
and Given with the Heart sandwiched between two stones,
prepared to smash the relic at any time. Eventually the hoof beats
ceased and for a while quiet reigned. In the quiet, the most terrible
noises—groans of pain, screeches and cries for help—began to
sound throughout the camp. Given raised the wedged stone above
the Heart, preparing for the shattering stroke, but Vivid gripped her
hand preventing the death blow. The panic in the camp had calmed.
All that could be heard was the silence of an early winter's night
once more.

The ladies clung together leaning against the cedar's fragrant
trunk deep into the night. Given's soft hums soothed them both.
The moon, fat and bright, was veiled by dark clouds that warned of
a coming storm, while the confused wind whirled in all directions.

A few hours past midnight the crackling of dried tree litter put
the ladies on guard. Both leaned forward in hope of discovering the
source. At first it sounded like one or maybe two beasts swishing
through the leaves, but after a while Given could tell there were
many more; and when the moon peeked from behind the clouds, it
lit up the creatures enough to see that they were large and four
legged. Her heart raced and mind screamed. *The beasts must have
creeped behind Aksel's warriors with them unaware.* She wanted to
cry out, but to do so would put her and the Heart in danger. More
swishing of leaves sounded, and more shadows accompanied. They
were surrounded. Given clinched the stone, thinking all would be

lost if she didn't act, but over the crackles and swishes Given heard a voice, one she'd known before but couldn't place. Because of the circumstance, her mind wouldn't allow it, but hearing it calmed her nonetheless. She knew deep inside that whoever the voice belonged to was good, and she needn't worry. The man spoke to the beasts, which in turn responded with grunts and snorts. After a few minutes they quieted as well, abandoning Given to her thoughts for the rest of the night.

By morning the wind had decided to blow from one direction—the south—and storm clouds packed the heavens, blocking the sun. Rolling thunder resounded after occasional lightning spread like a spider's web across the blackened sky. It was right before the battle, and Given could see now what her heart already knew. The beasts that had arrived hours earlier were friends. It was the bighorns that had saved them, but there were now hundreds instead of a few, their leader, the one that had rescued her from Harbor Wall. She recognized him, in part because his size was greater than the rest—though many of them were as big as bison—but mostly by his missing hoof.

Through the sagging branches, Given could see that Aksel had come to speak with the Bighorn captain, and though she could not make out what they were saying, she could tell it was a two-way conversation. "Indeed, he does speak," she whispered to Vivid, feeling silly for believing he didn't. *Why wouldn't he? Aderyn does and Nataurie too. He is of their number is he not. He must be one of the Deroheed.* After much gesturing and many words, the bighorn with his herd followed Aksel through the trees and out of sight. "He is placing them for battle," whispered Given. Having their help ignited her hope, and for the time being she put the plan to smash the relic out of her mind.

253

***

Thunder boomed and cold rain soaked the earth, but the sisters stayed mostly dry under their evergreen canopy. Vivid plucked her bow string deep in thought as Given grew more anxious. The tune played by the storm was all she'd heard for more than an hour. If a battle was to be fought, why hadn't it begun? Suddenly, the blast of a shofar cut through the wind. Her heart stopped. *That was it. The battle is here.*

Vivid perked and crawled from under the cedar to get a better view. Given followed. The rain fell harder, drenching their furs and hindering their view. Vivid gripped her bow in one hand, spear in the other, and eyed the field expectantly. By now, Given knew her sister well enough. She couldn't speak her desires but Given knew Vivid wanted to fight. Vivid wasn't one to let her friends go unaided. Never again would she sit back and wait to see if her loved ones would be alright. With Vivid Looking at her with a question, Given nodded permission, knowing she may never see Vivid alive again. But her duty was the Heart—that wretched thing. What could she do but wait and see?

Given walked with Vivid to the edge of the battle, careful to remain in the thick. After a final embrace Vivid handed Given her spear and slinked away into the pouring rain with an arrow drawn. Unable to bear the not knowing, Given searched for a high point— a lookout. Discovering a cottonwood taller than the surrounding trees, she glanced around for enemies but saw none. With the Heart secured in the pack over her shoulder and Vivid's spear in her left hand, she began to struggle up the slippery tree, halting the ascent every few branches to check for enemies. She expected winged beasts to be on the attack, but the rain had proved too much for all but the best flyers.

A few branches from the top where the tree was just strong enough to support her weight, she looked down to horror. Bodies of men and beasts littered the ground. Their blood mixing with the flow of rain created red streams through the mud. Her eyes scanned in panic for loved ones, for Vivid or Dane or Aksel, but they could not be seen. The first person she recognized was unexpected, so much so she thought her eyes were fibbing. He was a tall man, bald and pointy headed, swinging a short axe through the air to fend off a wildcat. Blinking heavily she shook her head trying to right what her eyes were seeing that her mind said she shouldn't, but nothing changed her knowing. It was Gar, and at his feet was a fallen brother in arms whom he protected. When Gar helped his friend to his feet, Given knew him as well. Though covered from head to foot as if he had wallowed in mud, the gargantuan Torben was easy enough to peg. With one giant arm flung over Gar's shoulder, he limped from the battle to potential safety.

The next person Given knew was her sister. Stealthy and precise, she meandered from cover to cover letting arrows fly at the sight of danger and fetching them for reuse. Given's heart stopped when she saw three coyotes had taken notice of Vivid. She cried out to warn her, but her voice was drowned by the dull howl of rain and bellowing thunder. Given thought her sister dead for sure, but when the coyotes had drawn to striking distance, Vivid sprung her trap, pivoting toward them and letting three arrows fly from her string, one after the other. Two of the coyotes dropped immediately. The third took a few more steps toward Vivid before she drew another arrow from her quiver and sent it through the coyote's head.

Given's attention was drawn away by a shofar blast in the distance. Shielding her eyes from the rain, she strained to see warriors rallying together as a line of enormous creatures charged, smashing many into the mire. Some of the men crept forward still, fighting with all fortitude, only to be driven back in retreat. The men stood no chance head-to-head against the mammoths. Given winced hoping against hope that her friends weren't part of the number that were now crushed.

Past all the lines and over a ravine on a hilltop, Given could see a great crowd of men and beasts who muddied themselves not with the ongoing battle. They appeared only to be observing the onslaught. *It is him,* thought Given. *It is Magnus. Without a miracle no warrior will get to him. What can be done?*

***

Beneath Given all around, the battle churned harder, and the warriors like leaves in the wind were blown and scattered by the beast army's might. Some ran for cover, still others surrendered to death. As frantically as she searched, Given could no longer see anyone she knew. *Are they lost? Is all lost?* She needed to climb down and end this before even she was overwhelmed. Resolving to destroy the Heart she began her descent. It would be simple now. All she needed to do was land where she'd left the stones at the tree's base and smash the relic with them; but halfway down the tree, a dead branch snapped beneath her foot. Though she tried, she could not keep hold of the slippery branch above. Crashing through the timber like a hailstone thrown from the heavens, her body bounced from branch to branch, landing with a thud in the mire, her head colliding with the stones she'd left. She saw a flash of light before all went black.

The next she knew, she was back in Coyote Lake fighting to keep her head up. Her back stung as though she was bathing in the sea after being beaten with the nine-tails. As she struggled she realized that the lake was no longer the clear cool water she was accustomed to but a warm crimson pool, and all around floated corpses of men and beasts. This was her darkest hour, darker than losing her mother when she was a young girl, darker than the flogging by Magnus's henchmen, even darker still than the beatings and rape she endured at Bledig's cabin. It was the death of everyone she adored—her friends and son—and she drowning in a lake of their blood. In the pit of her despair she cried for help, and like so many other times, a man in a boat appeared. Grasping her hand, he pulled her to safety. At his feet the pain in her back ceased and her fear vanished, but unlike all the other times she'd dreamt the similar dream, she was able to see his face—kind and somewhat familiar. Yes, she reckoned she'd seen him before—if only in the darkness—but it wasn't Solas as she'd expected.

She heard voices. First, Aksel's rough warming tone permeated "To you the quest was given. Only you can decide what needs to be done." Then Nataurie's, "Trust your heart and dreams more than your mind and sight." Her heart all along had clung to the hope Grit was alive and she could somehow save her little boy. But how? Dane's poem came to remembrance, "Give the Heart, set them free." Was there something to it? Berthorn thought there was, but who was that funny man anyway? Memories of her captivity began to flood back, and questions like the heavy rains washed over her. How had she been healed after her flogging? How could a crippled man have disappeared into the night? How did the bighorn know where to find her? The voice she'd heard the night the bighorn arrived at the battle front, who did it belong to?

She looked up at her rescuer once more and suddenly realized the answer to all the questions.

Her body started to shake, but she didn't feel cold or scared. She was shaking hard but couldn't figure why. Someone was shoving, rocking, trying to rouse her. A hand touched her cheek. She opened her eyes but could see only raindrops and tears. Blinking them away revealed the most welcome sight—Vivid. Next to her was Gar, but his presence did not startle her. He was different than she remembered. Glancing to her left and right at the battle yet raging, she realized that she'd been unconscious—dreaming—but knew now, here at the end of it all, what she must do.

Gripping Vivid's shoulders, she said, "I need to give it to him...I must give the Heart to Magnus."

As Gar and Vivid helped her to her feet, men came battling toward them—a group of four that fought as one. They seemed to move smoothly through the packs, herds, and hoards. And when they had drawn close enough to recognize, hope that the battle would end well was restored in Given, for the four were none other than Dane, Aksel, Erlend and Roar. She tried to take a step toward them, but pain surged from her ankle nearly bringing her to her knees. It was broken, but she couldn't stop. She would crawl if need be.

Seeing her sister struggle, Vivid flung her bow and quiver into the mud and fetched her spear Given had dropped. Using it as a staff for balance she propped Given on her shoulder while Gar readied his axe. The three plunged back into the heart of the struggle, beasts and men, blood and mud surrounding them, and screams of agony resounding. Given hopped on one foot, splashing up brown and red with every bounce. Gar swung, slashed and shouted, guarding all their angles until more help could arrive.

When the four reached them there was no time for proper reunion or questioning. Aksel started to give direction, but Given silenced him with the wave of her hand.

"Through a dream I have been shown what to do," she said loudly over the clamor. "I am to give Magnus the Heart, and though it would seem an easy thing, I need your help to get there."

Erlend wanted to argue the foolishness of the idea, but Aksel interrupted, "Sometimes the wisdom of our Maker is folly in man's hearing. Regardless, there is little hope in any other plan. We will do as she says."

With no more words they went, an entire army of beasts before them. Like legend, Dane, Erlend, Roar and Aksel fought, cutting their way through Magnus's defenses as Given, Vivid and Gar trailed. The witless beasts and brainwashed half-bloods could neither hinder their charge nor tear them asunder; but when they reached the mammoth line even they were outmatched. The four had tried and failed earlier to penetrate, fortunate to escape. Beasts with such power and size could not be overcome by man's skill. The hope of making it through was for fools and the odds impossible, but it didn't stop them. They plunged forward, Aksel leading the charge, but with a swipe of its head a mammoth caught him with its ivory spike and hurled him into the mud.

Dane went to his aid, but the mammoth allowed no time for recovery, charging while Aksel yet lay in the mire. Seeing the peril his Civitian brothers were in, Roar, clutching his sword, sprang toward the charging bull. When he had drawn near he stooped beneath the giant with blade up, tearing through the beast's fur and flesh, spilling its bowels. The mammoth's charge ended as it fell headlong, its tusks cutting into the earth like willow roots. But the joy of Aksel and Dane surviving the assault was short lived. Roar lay motionless with his face turned toward the falling rain. When the others arrived, they could tell from the muddy print that covered his tunic he'd been trampled. Like branches in a gale, his ribs were snapped—heart crushed.

"To the Creator's blessed assembly," said Aksel with his head low. "He shall not go naked. He was a good man."

Further lamentations would have to wait though. Even as he spoke, more mammoths prepared to charge. Looking north, south, and behind to the west, the company saw no path of escape. With Given hobbled as she was, running would have only delayed their destruction anyhow. So they steadied their weapons, stiffened their footholds and waited as the herd tramped forward. When their death had become as sure as the sunrise, salvation came. Led by their captain, the bighorns rushed into battle and met the mammoths head on, shattering tusks and horns in an unsightly collision of mass and muscle. Although the bighorns were grossly outweighed and had little chance of success, their captain spoke the language of thunder and urged his troops forward.

The company saw their chance and rushed into the bighorns' wake. Dane led the way with Given cradled against his chest. The mammoths were large, but the bighorn captain by strength unseen pushed through. After the company had cleared the final beast, Gar and the bighorn captain turned back to guard the rear against attackers. The others ran toward their goal.

They slid into the final ravine and clawed their way out on the other side. When they reached the base of the hill where Magnus perched, he was surprised but not in the least bit alarmed by their presence. The king's guard was mighty, one hundred of Auber Civitas's best, well-armed and shielded. Behind them were the most dreaded of the Deroheed, a fierce sabertooth, an enormous bison, a savage bear, and a terrible bird of prey—Aderyn. Still, the worst of them, Cadoc, stood warily at the king's side, claws like swords, spearhead teeth, and wings as a shield of iron.

Knowing she now held the king's gaze, Given removed the Heart from her pack and held it aloft. From the hilltop came laughter too wretched to strike from remembrance, and with it clapping. Moments later, Steen and several spear bearers seized Given, Dane, and Aksel, and heeding not Given's injuries, shoved them through the ranks of men and beasts up the hill, leaving Vivid and Erlend at the base under guard. When Given could climb no further without crawling, Dane lifted her from the mire once again and carried her the remaining steps.

Magnus's laughter sounded again as they approached. "So, the rumor is true," he shouted in amusement. "The wayward son *has* returned, and he has come bearing a gift." He stepped closer, Cadoc his shadow. Glancing at Given still in Dane's arms he said, "Wayward indeed…so this is what has become of Auber's beloved bastard? Do you now fellowship with savages?" Looking at Aksel his lip curled in disgust, "And sup with the vile? The most noble of your company may be the traitor below." He motioned toward Erlend.

Dane didn't reply, for he knew Magnus's game—one in which he'd never been able to win. Breathing heavily he kept his anger caged.

"Though, your company does not bemuse when I consider your heritage," Magnus continued with a smile. "Your father *was* a rapist."

"No," said Dane, calmly. "You know it isn't true. The story was an invention to gain what you wanted, but your lies, hate, and greed I have forgiven. My wish is that you would turn from this wickedness and share the hope that I have found. Even now Solas can heal what has been done."

The king smirked, waving his hand, "Do not speak to me of your forgiveness or hope." Rubbing his shoulder where Dane's dagger had struck, "They are but hollow words from deceitful lips." A vile look shone in his eyes. "My only interest in you now is watching you strapped to the pyre as the flames slowly purify through agony." With his eyes set on Aksel he said, "But there is something about this one that interests me. His bearing seems familiar."

"Indeed, to you my bearing should be familiar," said Aksel. "It is shameful that it is all you recognize, but it's what remains of a body marred, ravaged by fire. Except for the scars, to you my face might be more familiar than thine own, for you have glimpsed it more than your own reflection—though a score of years lay betwixt your viewings." Aksel sighed, "After all you did to me, I hope you treated Astrid well at least. She deserved the world... brother." There was a deep sadness in his eyes as he stared at Magnus, his emotional scars opened afresh.

Magnus's smile straightened as Aksel's words settled. He said nothing for a while, just shook his head scrutinizing his brother's appearance. "Yes," he said at length, "I treated her well." Looking blankly away, "but she is gone now."

"Yes, that I have heard, and it torments me," Aksel said. "Like Dane, I have excused your transgressions. Your wickedness I hold not against you, but still at times I wonder, was it worth it? Was her forced loyalty to you worth what you did to me?"

"Her loyalty?" Magnus scoffed. "Your sight is too small brother. Any dolt could see that I stood to gain much more than Astrid's loyalty." Spreading his arms wide, he said, "All that would have been yours became mine when *you* betrayed your people."

"Then your true reason for treachery is more sorrowful," Aksel said. "All that would have been mine, I would have gladly shared with you. Though I loved Auber Civitas, I had no desire to rule her, and still I do not, but now seeing your wretchedness, I know my generosity would have been folly. When will your want for more end?"

Magnus seemed to ponder the question for a moment. Anger flashed across his face, "Never, I suppose." Weary of the conversation, he motioned to the guards that surrounded and ordered Dane and Aksel be brought low. With the shafts of their spears the soldiers struck them across the backs of the legs causing their knees to buckle. Aksel fell where he stood. Dane, however, stumbled forward and dropped Given into the mud. At the tips of their weapons the spearmen forced Aksel and Dane facedown. Steen grasped the backside of Given's skins, dragged her through the mud, and laid her at the king's feet. Stooping, Magnus snatched the Heart from her hand and for a moment stared into it, eyes full of lust. "You should have saved yourself much pain and surrendered it the first time, stupid girl," He spat on her, returning the favor from their first meeting.

Given looked up with fire in her eyes but said nothing in reply. She wanted to strike, to end this, but it would have gained nothing. The Deroheed guards—the bear and Bird—had moved behind her, and Cadoc stood in front to Magnus's right. One swipe of paw or claw or talon would be her end.

She surveyed the surroundings. To Magnus's left his esquire Seamus and sorcerer Baird had positioned themselves, and beyond them was another group of soldiers with weapons ready. There seemed to be neither help nor path of escape, only beasts and soldiers all around. But to the left of the back row of Civitian soldiers, a curious couple of folk had crept, and except for their relation to the king, they would've had no business at this battle. York, Magnus's eldest, and Leif, the younger, had wandered out from behind the guards to see what their father was to do with the newcomers. On Leif's shoulders rested the scrawny yellow-eyed fellow he'd been playing in the leaves with as Given was being escorted to the palace.

When Given saw Grit, she wondered at first if he was imagined, if in all the calamity her mind was taunting her. Only while he slept had she seen him so docile, not moving from Leif's shoulders though his mother was directly before him. He needed only to bound down and run to her, but his mind was captivated by a force seemingly more powerful than the love he held for her, and his stare was as empty as the other beasts.

Magnus looked down at the brave Gallant lass with disdain. "You have caused me much grief, savage, but this gift will be of some recompense." He raised the Heart. "Lower your eyes before me, and I may grant you a dignified end, swift and without torture."

But seeing Grit held captive behind him, the fire in her eyes exploded like lightning and she stared at Magnus with the scorn of ten thousand slaves toward a ruthless master.

He smiled, "Knowing how your weak, ridiculous tribe withstood as the soldiers of Auber Civitas surrounded them, I expect as much from you." Motioning to his guards, he commanded them to not interfere, and calling his two sons to his side he said, "Too long have the wild men of the west crippled our nation. Fear of their savagery has kept us locked behind Harbor Wall for generations." Glaring at Given he raised his voice, "I say, never more!" With his right hand he struck her cheek and with his heel drove her into the mud. Lifting her mud covered face, still she stared. Another strike came, this time from Magnus left fist, sending her dazed to the earth once again.

Dane and Aksel struggled to move—to intervene—but the spears pressing into their flesh prevented action. All they could do was beg for the king's mercy.

Leif with a heart for justice joined their appeal. Stepping forward, he cried, "Father, stop please! What has she done to deserve this." Magnus pushed him away, disregarding his pleas.

Magnus kicked mud over his conquest and glanced at Leif. "They deserve nothing less my lad. If not them now bowing before us, then we at their feet will soon grovel."

Even as Leif wept, Magnus seemed pleased by his own brutality. But in all his cruelty he had failed to notice the blankness in Grit's eyes was vanishing. In them a fire—one likened to that in his mother's—had sparked. The more Magnus slugged away at Given, the larger the flame grew, until not even the Diamond Mind of Derog could control the boy. For though outwardly he resembled his father, in his chest pounded the Heart of a Gallant—full of grit —and no one was to abuse his Mot. He sprang from Leif's shoulders with the ferocity of a wolf, clutching Magnus's face and sinking his tiny fangs deeply into the King's cheek. Bellowing in agony, Magnus tried to push him away but could not overcome Grit's powerful bite.

The king's retribution came swiftly nonetheless as Cadoc clawed into Grit's back and neck, tearing the young warrior limp and dangling from Magnus, the King's cheek flesh yet in the boy's teeth. Much like he had done to Orson, Cadoc cast the boy aside as though he were a piece of trimmed fat. Grit's tiny form plopped in the muck. Screaming, Given went to her son's aid and lifted him from the mud, but there was nothing she could do—he was dead. Her hopes were mangled, lying lifeless in her arms.

Grit had not died in vain though. Indeed, he had done what was needed, for during all the commotion, one of Magnus's other guards had sneaked beside the king and now stood unhindered and unblocked. He was a guard who, because of his form, had gained a favorable position in the king's presence, hoping that one day he would have the opportunity to destroy his lord. But this guard was no fool. Reckoning that Cadoc's strength could not be overwhelmed, he waited for the right time—a moment of distraction—to strike. Now, his wait had ended. With grizzly claws he swiped, first knocking the crown from Magnus's head, then cutting into the King's throat. And though the king was surely to bleed out from the second blow, the great black beast, the shepherd of bears, possibly for no other reason than to avenge his son, severed Magnus's head with his bite.

The crown—the body of Derog—with all its might had been thrown down once again, but the small Gallant child's body was lifted high. All honor and love was bestowed on him in his mother's tears—in her kisses and embrace.

CHAPTER 27. A GREAT CHORUS

THE DEROHEED guards struggled to shake loose the chains that bound their minds while the Civitian soldiers, after seeing their king thrashed by the huge beast, fled. Now free, Aksel rushed to Given's aid, but Dane, for reasons he struggled to comprehend, went to the severed head of Magnus. The young prince who'd known mostly neglect and wrongdoing tore his clothes at the sight of his mangled step-father. Crumbling to his knees he cried, "Why didn't you listen? If you would have only turned, he would have forgiven you...Solas would have forgiven even you."

As Dane mourned, the heartbreaking cries of his brother reached his ear, and he looked up to see Seamus and York in the distance dragging Leif along as the boy struggled to free himself, fighting to return to his dead father. Dane ran to Leif and lifted the boy into his arms.

"There's nothing that can be done now," Dane cried. "He's gone."

"No, I need to see him," Leif screamed in protest. "I need to know."

But Dane held him tight. "We will gather his body for burial...you shall look upon him then, but not now. He is gone. He is gone."

Sobbing, Leif wilted in Dane's arms. York rested his hand on the boy's shoulder and wept as well. They had reason to mourn: Magnus, despite his vices, had been a good father to them both.

As they lamented, Aksel and Erlend, who'd witnessed the tumult with Vivid from the bottom of the hill, also came to their side. Though there was not much that could be done to ease the horror that plagued their hearts, the presence of Erlend was a small comfort to Leif and York at least, and Aksel did what he could to support Dane.

***

Near Magnus's corpse, Vivid knelt and tried her best to console Given who held Grit against her chest, praying there was a way to bring him back and wishing she could have stopped Cadoc before the fatal blow. Given glanced around and saw for the first time the crown knocked from Magnus's head, half-buried in the mud. A little closer was the king's headless body with hand still grasping the Heart, which for a moment she stared disdainfully at. After all the evil that'd been done on its account, how could she look any other way? In an instant her countenance changed as she recalled the time it somehow lifted Dane from the depths of infirmity while they traveled through Skeleton Wood. *Could its magic work again?* She wondered. *And if the Heart alone did so much good for Dane, how much more could all the relics do? Might they be able to rescue her son?*

After laying Grit gently beside Vivid, Given crawled over to pry the Heart free from the king's hand. Toward the crown she looked, but to her dismay it had been lifted by another. It seemed all of Magnus's men had fled Eurig's wrath after seeing him chew the king's head off, but one had crept back unnoticed. Magnus's foreign advisor, Baird, the one who'd schemed and plotted and delivered to the king the cunning to take control of the Deroheed, now stood wiping the mud from the circlet—Grits chance at salvation. Perhaps his hope all along was to steal the crown from Magnus and claim the power for himself, but evil would not triumph on this day.

Sometimes folk's strange actions have a way of making sense in the end. Though it only seemed like sentimentality at the time, there was a finer reason Vivid had kept the arrowhead spear even after its usefulness in catching fish in the Afon was gone. There was a reason she hadn't wasted it in battle though opportunities had arisen. Vivid didn't realize it even as she hurled it toward her target, but the arrowhead had been saved for its rightful owner. Baird, the very man who'd launched the arrow into Dane the night of his exile, was now being paid back in full. Vivid didn't miss; the spear struck Baird's chest, spiking him like a Rhun Gill as he held the prize to his head. He dropped the crown and fell forward with his eyes greedily fixed on the diamond at the center, The earth finished the work of driving the arrowhead through his heart. Vivid scooped the crown from before him and took it to her sister.

"Skeleton Wood," is all Given said as she took the circlet. There was no need for her to explain further, for Vivid already knew what had to be done. She had witnessed Dane's miracle as well.

With Given carrying the relics and Vivid holding the lifeless Grit —hobbled and drenched—they started for the cursed land, an ocean of death before them, the pouring rain helpless to wash the filth of battle from their minds. The sisters hadn't gotten far—not even to the bottom of the hill—before help came. Aderyn, still in bird form swooped down to them, and with her Cadoc. At first Given was frightened, but when she saw Aderyn's eyes she knew that her friend had been freed from Magnus's evil. No longer did they display sickening indifference; rather, there was now sorrow as deep as Coyote Lake and love as long as the Afon. Spreading her wings she bounced to Given, scooping her up in a downy warm embrace. She let Given down and looked sadly at Grit's body sagging in Vivid's arms.

"We must get to Skeleton Wood," said Given. "There he may find healing."

Without any understanding of how taking Grit to the cursed land could save him, Aderyn lowered herself so Vivid could climb on with him. Given would have to fly with Cadoc, the beast that had destroyed her friend and son, but she did not hesitate. His sins—which truly belonged to Magnus—had been forgiven. With her heart racing and filled with hope, she climbed upon the great winged beast, clinging once again to his thick mane now soaked by rain. Up they thrust with Aderyn leading into the blackened sky, the occasional bolt of lightning cutting through the darkness.

It was a fearful flight as rain pelted and thunder boomed, and Given prayed the whole time, never looking down, only out toward Vivid holding Grit, professing life in their direction. As they crossed the invisible border into Skeleton Wood the rain ceased; not a drop had fallen on the wasteland since Derog spoke the curse. When they'd landed, Given wasted no time digging a small hole and planting the Heart inside. She had Vivid lay Grit over the *seed*, and placed the crown onto his chest. They waited and watched, but nothing happened immediately—or for a while for that matter.

At length as her hope began to dwindle something happened. Though they couldn't see it, the barrier that blocked the waters from entering Skeleton Wood crashed, and it began to rain over the land. Hard drenching rain with acorn sized drops fell. The sisters alongside Aderyn and Cadoc, who'd taken human likeness once more, gazed in awe as greenery sprang from the black earth all around them. The winter had given itself up to spring. The curse in the land was lifted. Given could feel a burning—albeit pleasant—in her foot, and soon the pain from her broken ankle was gone. Surely Grit's healing would be next. But as minutes became hours still he did not stir. The magic that had ushered health to Dane and Given and life to that desolate place seemed powerless to help Grit.

Given in her despair removed the crown from atop Grit's chest and buried it beneath him as well. Nothing changed. After hours of waiting, realizing that no healing would come, she lifted the boy into her arms and began to sing Mot's song.

Leaning against Given, Vivid listened and wept, wishing she could vocalize the song that was in her heart. With little sign—only a slight tickle in Vivid's throat—the wretched grip of dumbness loosened, and she began singing along with Given. With the harmonious voice of Serenis herself, her voice resonated above the roaring rain and booming thunder. In a sudden, the lyrics changed, and from her lips came the song that had been caged in her mind since she was a small child.

> *All that's broken be made whole*
> *All destroyed be restored*
> *All that's torn shall be sewn*
> *Till all is healthy once more*
> *Till all is healthy once more*

To Given it was like a dream or distant memory coming to life before her. The song she so desperately tried to recall but couldn't was being sung by her speechless sister. But this was no time for her to enjoy the music or marvel at Vivid's new found ability. Laying her hand upon Grit, Given harmonized with Vivid, speaking life into the dead bones, while Aderyn and Cadoc joined from behind them. Beautifully, their song rang through Bella Floris over the sprouting grass and saplings.

As they sang, a breeze warm as breath blew, and it seemed that summer had arrived. Indeed, when they glanced up they could see a light, bright as the morning sun, beaming from the east. Their song continued as the light drew ever nearer, rolling back the blackened sky like a scroll. Soon they were encompassed not only by the light but by a throng that had come with it.

Around the four now stood a great company of warriors, most unrecognizable but some familiar. Given's eyes shone upon Torben and Eurig—no longer in bear form—their deep voices like great instruments echoed the healing song. To their left was Gar—kindness now his countenance—and to their right sang Erlend with a joy in his cheeks Given had never seen. Beside him stood Aksel, Given's shield. Dane knelt on one knee with Leif on the other, both serenading the tiny fallen hero. The chorus was a whirlwind blowing over Grit's body, lifting it from the grave, and as the song proceeded, Given began to feel the slight beating of his heart followed by the rising and falling of his chest. Soon, warmth covered him and his color returned. Smiling, he opened his eyes—yellow flames blazing for his Mot—and leaning forward he sprang into her arms. All present cheered or wept. Those who were in close fellowship joined the embrace. Dane's soul sang as he wrapped his arms around Given and Grit, and Aksel, discovering the beautiful Birdie among the rejoicers, tossed all restraint aside and kissed her with the passion of a man long bereft of a woman's touch. She objected not, and the entire assembly erupted in shouts and chants and song.

The light over the throng intensified and silence fell as the warriors began to separate and kneel, forming a pathway from the outer edge to the center where Given and company stood. Down the path treaded the mighty ram with horns that flashed like lightning, and upon him sat Solas, his clothes now gleaming white and eyes blazing with blue fire.

When the ram had reached the middle of the assembly, Solas dismounted and spoke, "Given the Gallant, everything asked of you, you have done. You have delighted me, and what's more, you have pleased my Father." He glanced around at Given's friends, "But you are not alone, for many here have labored, and it shall not go without reward."

A great shaft of light rose from the ram, and before every eye he was transformed, no longer standing on three legs but one. Given watched as the thing she'd reckoned from her dream was proven. Berthorn now stood where the ram had. They were one person indeed. But when Berthorn spoke a new revelation settled on the entire assembly—even Given—for his words were not those of a man or Deroheed but of a being limitless in power. Like a waterfall, blessings poured from his mouth, speaking life, purifying their minds. And with all authority he began to declare gifts to the listeners.

To Gar he said, "Dom, my child, bear much fruit." He smiled and repeated, "Bear much fruit." Gar flashed red, slightly embarrassed. He knew that which had been justly stripped away was now restored to him by the Creator's grace. No longer would he wear the shame of a eunuch.

When Berthorn gazed at Erlend, the Civitian captain cast his eyes toward the ground in shame. In the tomb of Auber Civitas Erlend had discounted Berthorn as a fool, not knowing at the time that he spoke with the wisdom of eternity. But Berthorn with joy said, "Lift your head in honor. With the master gone, you must care for his house until the heirs are of age…but be of new mind; your gates shall not shut." With that charge, Erlend would go on to govern Auber Civitas in justice until the sons of Magnus were old enough to rule; and in the spirit of Astrid he would see to it that all who entered the King's Gate were well-fed and housed.

To Aksel, who yet clung to Aderyn, he said, "The Civitian throne is rightfully yours, but I know your heart, your desire to live free. Though you would've been a worthy king, I will not force you into misery." He glanced from Aksel to Aderyn "You both have toiled long in loneliness, and without your work the cause would have been lost. May your reward be a lifetime together—one that far outlasts the span of man." Winking at Aksel he said, "It's time the bighorn had a captain with all his limbs." Bowing his head, Aksel accepted his new charge graciously.

With eyes full of love Berthorn turned to Vivid, "With your mother's voice, sing without ceasing songs of healing and comfort." As Solas had done before, Berthorn—without moving tongue or lips or making a sound—whispered to Vivid's thoughts, forcing tears down her cheeks. From that day, folk from all around began to seek out Vivid, allowing her sweet melodies to heal their bodies and minds. But in her heart she treasured a new song that only she knew. It was a song that she would someday sing in her Creator's presence for eternity.

At Dane Berthorn smiled, "You were fruit plucked from the tree and cast into the darkness, but forgiveness found its way into your heart, and you have become my son. Continue to shine in this wilderness. Bella Floris will be a city unmatched in beauty and love with you as its king."

On Given's cheek Berthorn placed his hand, "You were dealt a difficult task, but through many trials your hope remained. Teach your people this hope. Though many Gallant have fallen, others like you and your sister have been scattered. To you who have given much, I now give back. Gather your people, Given, Chief of the Gallant."

He lifted his voice so all could hear. "Do not mourn those lost in this fight. Their sacrifice was not in vain, and for their service they will sup with me as daughters and sons in a land never in want." Glancing into the crowd he caught the gaze of a woman perhaps only Given recognized and said, "Your work here is finished and the hour of rest has come. May the creatures of the waters do as you've taught them and your labors be passed to another." After speaking final blessings and words of encouragement he, Solas, and Nataurie were taken from sight in a blue-white flash.

Not a word was spoken for a long while as all present contemplated what had happened. The Creator had spoken to them, and though they knew their own unworthiness, he had made them feel loved and accepted. That such a power could care so deeply for them was beyond their comprehension.

As the assembly stood in amazement, five saplings sprang from the muck where Given had buried the relics. They grew rapidly, twisting together to form a single trunk that's top, in a short while, reached higher than the heads of the tall Civitian men. And as unexpectedly as anything that had happened, a noble hawk, red-tailed and freckle-bellied, sank from the heights, perched himself on the loftiest branch of the magnificent tree, and screeched hellos to his friends.

Nicholas Hoover writes with the hope his readers will be inspired to seek the One who created them and witness the life-changing effects of Jesus's love and the blessed Holy Spirit in their lives.

You can contact Nicholas at nickahoover@yahoo.com.

Made in the USA
Coppell, TX
24 October 2021